A FAMILY AT WAR

BOOK ONE IN THE FAMILY FEUD SAGA

ROSIE CLARKE

Boldwood

First published in 2008 as *The Lie*. This edition published in Great Britain in 2024 by Boldwood Books Ltd.

Copyright © Rosie Clarke, 2008

Cover Design by Colin Thomas

Cover Images: Colin Thomas

A CIP catalogue record for this book is available from the British Library.

Paperback ISBN 978-1-83518-140-9

Large Print ISBN 978-1-83518-141-6

Hardback ISBN 978-1-83518-139-3

Ebook ISBN 978-1-83518-142-3

Kindle ISBN 978-1-83518-143-0

Audio CD ISBN 978-1-83518-134-8

MP3 CD ISBN 978-1-83518-135-5

Digital audio download ISBN 978-1-83518-137-9

This book is printed on certified sustainable paper. Boldwood Books is dedicated to putting sustainability at the heart of our business. For more information please visit https://www.boldwoodbooks.com/about-us/sustainability/

Boldwood Books Ltd, 23 Bowerdean Street, London, SW6 3TN

www.boldwoodbooks.com

1

Emily stood for a moment at the top of the stairs listening to the music. Someone had put a Glenn Miller record on rather loudly, and the big band music reverberated throughout the house. It all felt so wrong, so very wrong with Daddy so recently dead. Oh, damn it, she didn't want to do this, she really didn't. For a moment her eyes filled with tears and she could feel the sense of loss strong and bitter inside her. Why did he have to die? He was still young, only in his early fifties.

She shook her head, her soft brown hair falling across her face. Emily was wearing her hair loose that afternoon because she was forced to put it up out of the way for work, though it suited her better down. But there was no time to think about your looks when you were manning the phones for the Fire Service. She had changed shifts with another girl to get this afternoon off, and now she wished she hadn't, but Frances had refused to let her get out of it.

'You've got to come to my party. You're my sister!'

'But I'm on duty...'

'You can change if you want to. You know you can.'

So of course she had given in. She sighed, knowing that she would have to go down soon or Frances would come and fetch her. It was her elder sister's twenty-first birthday and she was entitled to her party. Every last detail had been planned for months and the family had decided to go ahead despite being in mourning.

Except that it seemed to Emily that she and Connor were the only ones grieving for their father. Her younger brother was at school, and she had told him not to hurry home that evening because he wouldn't have liked to walk into this and would probably go out again at once. Daniel would be upset when he knew, of course, but he'd been injured at Dunkirk some weeks ago and they wouldn't let her see him at first. She had written to him about their father, of course, but there had been no reply.

She dreaded to think what Daniel would say if he knew about the party. She was sure he would never have agreed to it. Daniel would have thought it too soon, as Emily did herself.

She had five siblings: two brothers, Henry and Clay, were older than Daniel, both married and living in their own houses; then came Frances; Emily herself; and Connor. And then there was her father's wife, Margaret, a much younger woman he had married while Daniel was away. Dan had never met Margaret, though of course he had been told about the wedding, which had taken place after a whirlwind affair.

Emily's frown deepened as she thought about her step-mother. Margaret had agreed instantly to the party going ahead, though she might have been expected to reject the idea. Robert Searles was hardly in his grave and yet his widow's laughter could be heard echoing through the house. She clearly wasn't going to let her husband's death upset her for too long, Emily thought resentfully.

Oh, she must stop this. Her father was dead and she had to get over it. She had to move on, think about her own life.

She had never liked Margaret! Emily had tried hard to accept her father's second wife, but she had never really approved of her. In Emily's opinion, Margaret was too greedy, too calculating. She was attractive, with honey-blonde hair, green eyes that reminded Emily of a cat, and a wide mouth on which she wore far too much red lipstick.

Margaret had made Robert's life less lonely during his last few months – Emily was honest enough to admit that. For that reason she had struggled to keep the peace between them even when under severe provocation, but she could not feel warmth or affection towards her stepmother.

Sighing, Emily began to walk down the stairs. She was a pretty girl, just eighteen, slim, of medium height with softly waving brown hair that looked red in a certain light, and melting chocolate eyes. She didn't want to but knew she had to make an appearance at her sister's party. It wasn't just a birthday party, after all: Frances was going to announce her engagement to Marcus Danby – and perhaps a part of Emily's reluctance was that she had always liked Marcus herself.

She wasn't in love with him, of course. It was just that his dry sense of humour amused her. Marcus was serving in the air force, and his leave had happened to fall this weekend, which had worked out well for Frances. Lucky Frances! But then, she always seemed to fall on her feet. At least, it seemed that way to others. Emily wasn't exactly envious, but she wished that some of her sister's luck would rub off on her.

She paused to glance at herself in the large gilt-framed mirror at the bottom of the stairs, fluffing out her hair again. Rathmere was in the main street of Stretton Village and one of the best in the area. In fact, only Stretton Park was bigger and better, and that belonged to Mr Samuel Danby. Marcus was his eldest son, and everyone agreed that it was a perfect match between the families.

Emily caught a glimpse of her sister through the open door of the large front parlour. Frances certainly looked happy and beautiful. Emily felt a pang of envy, mixed liberally with warm affection and admiration. Her sister always got exactly what she wanted, and she had wanted Marcus since she was a schoolgirl in pigtails. Well, she had got it all now, and whether Emily approved of holding this party so soon after her father's death or not, there was little she could do about it.

'Ah, there you are, child,' Margaret said, coming out of the large front parlour into the hall. 'What on earth have you been doing?'

'Getting dressed.'

Margaret's eyes flicked over her stepdaughter disapprovingly. The dress Emily had chosen was grey with a white collar, elbow-length sleeves and white cuffs, perfect for a girl in mourning but hardly suitable for a party. Margaret herself was dressed in green silk, a pretty afternoon dress that would have graced any London drawing room. It was her colour and made her look younger than her thirty-five years.

'You could have chosen something smarter for this afternoon, Emily.' The disapproval was strong in her voice.

'It's what I felt like wearing.' Emily couldn't keep a note

of accusation out of her voice. 'After all, it is only a month since Daddy died, isn't it?'

Margaret's gaze narrowed. 'I hope you're not going to spread gloom. This is your sister's special day. Please don't spoil it for her.'

'I can go and change if you like.'

Before Margaret could reply, Frances came swooping down on them. Her face was glowing with happiness as she flashed her left hand under Emily's nose. She was dressed in a pretty blue outfit that suited her fair good looks down to the ground, and she looked beautiful.

'Isn't it wonderful? I'm just so lucky.'

The ring was a band of five large white diamonds set in platinum; expensive and just what Emily would have expected from the heir to Stretton Park.

'It's lovely, Frances,' she said. 'And yes, you are lucky.'

'I know,' Frances trilled. 'Marcus says we'll get married next time he's home on leave.'

'And when will that be?'

'In a couple of weeks. We'll have to do it by special licence, of course, but I've got my dress and there's no chance of a proper cake, anyway. We'll have a cardboard one as a decoration and make do with what we can scrounge for the tea...' She stopped and frowned as she saw Emily's face. 'What's wrong?'

'Do you think you should? Isn't it too soon after...' Emily swallowed hard. 'You know...'

'You mean because Dad is dead?' The light died in Frances's eyes. 'Don't be so mean, Emily. I was trying not to think about that today. Besides, I can't bring him back whatever I do.'

'You could wait for a while...'

'You don't know what you're asking. You've never been in love.' Frances screwed up her mouth. 'So many of them are getting shot down. It could be Marcus next...'

'Oh, Frances,' Emily said, looking contrite. 'I hadn't thought of that. I am so sorry.'

'Your trouble is that you never think before you speak,' Margaret said. 'You're just too selfish.'

'Don't say that to Emily.' Frances instinctively defended her sister. 'She wasn't being selfish. She's right about it being too soon after Dad's death – but we don't want to wait, and I'm sure he would say it was all right.'

'Yes, he would,' Emily agreed, and smiled as Frances put an arm about her waist. They were united in their dislike of Margaret, though neither would say anything bad about their stepmother openly. 'It's just me being silly.'

'Let's forget it for now. We'll talk later,' Frances said. 'Come and meet someone, Emily. Marcus has brought a friend along – he's rather nice.'

Emily arched her fine brows. Frances was always introducing her to Marcus's friends with just that phrase. She found most of the young men trotted out for her benefit either dull, priggish or just not her type. However, the latest in a long line of candidates was more interesting than most.

'This is Simon Vane,' Frances said. 'We've only just met this afternoon, but he flies with Marcus as his navigator – Simon, this is my sister, Emily.'

'Hello.' Simon grinned at her in a friendly way. 'Things are looking up suddenly. Here I was thinking the only pretty girl in the place was spoken for – and now you appear. It must be my lucky day.'

'Do you flatter all the girls like that?' Emily was smiling.

She was drawn to him immediately, liking his smile and his extreme good looks, but she didn't intend to fall at his feet.

'Certainly not! Cross my heart and hope to die.'

'Don't say that,' Frances said, and glanced at Marcus across the room. 'I'll leave you two to fight it out, I think. Bye for now...'

Emily watched her sister flit across the room to join her fiancé, turning to discover that Simon's eyes were on her. They were a deep blue, his hair a dark honey-blond, though his brows were darker, which made him very striking to look at. He had a lazy charm about him that Emily found attractive, though she noticed that his lips were quite thin.

What was it people said about thin lips? She couldn't recall for the moment...

'Do you have to stay here?' Simon asked, glancing around the crowded room, which was full of people he obviously didn't know. 'We could go for a spin in my car if you like...'

Emily glanced at her sister. Frances was laughing at something Marcus had said, obviously happy. Margaret seemed to be deep in conversation with Clay. They looked as if they might be arguing, though she had no idea why. Henry seemed not to have shown up, but he was probably busy on the farm, and he usually avoided anything like this if he could.

'I don't think anyone will notice,' Emily said, feeling reckless. 'Have you got enough petrol for pleasure jaunts?' Most people were suffering from shortages of all kinds because of the war, but she believed that there were ways of getting round the petrol rationing if you knew the right people.

'My father gets more than his share – privileged member of the Government's legal advisory service,' Simon whispered, and winked at her. 'He makes sure I have a full tank when I need it. For some unknown reason he is rather proud of me...'

'I expect he would be,' Emily replied. 'We're all proud of you. Let's go then. I've put in an appearance, and I didn't want to come at all.'

'Don't you like parties?' Simon asked as they escaped through a side door. He led the way to where his Morgan sports car was parked. 'Special present just before I joined up.'

Emily was suitably impressed. 'I haven't seen one of these before. It's beautiful – and yes, I do like parties, but not just at the moment.'

'Any particular reason why?' he asked with a lift of his brows.

'Hasn't anyone told you?'

Simon shook his head.

'My father died a month ago after a nasty illness. I haven't got over it yet.'

'I should think not!' He glanced back at the house, from which music and laughter could still be heard spilling out into the quiet village street. 'Bit soon for all that, isn't it?'

'Frances had been planning her twenty-first birthday party for months. Marcus sent her a telegram suggesting they get engaged. I suppose you can't blame them – the way things are...'

'No, it's a bit fraught at the moment. None of us know if the next mission will be our last.'

Emily slipped into the car as he held the door for her, carefully tucking her dress inside before shutting it. 'It must be terrifying. I'm sure I would never have the courage to go up in a plane, let alone go into battle.'

'Oh, you would if you had to,' Simon said, dismissing the subject with a shrug. 'One day I might take you up for a spin if you're game.'

'Are you allowed to do that?'

'Shouldn't think so for a minute,' Simon quipped. 'That never stops me if I want to do something enough. I might get a rocket from the CO but he won't ground me. Can't get enough of us as it is.'

He had started the engine. It roared to life as they shot down the High Street and round the tight corner by the church.

'Where shall we go?'

'I don't mind.' Emily laughed as he put his foot down. If he was trying to scare her, it wasn't working. 'You turn that way for Cambridge – the other will lead you to Ely.'

'Let's go there,' Simon said. 'We can walk by the river and then go to a tea shop and indulge ourselves. They had some rather good honey the last time I was there.'

'And when was that?'

'Yesterday. I am interested in the cathedral as a building. That's what I was training for before this lark started – classical architecture.'

'That sounds fascinating – and clever.'

'Fascinating, certainly; I can't vouch for clever. My father thinks it's just an excuse to get out of following him into the law. Now, you do have to be clever for that...'

'Have you designed anything yet – anything that has been built, I mean?'

'Nothing important. I was still studying, you see.'

'Will you go back to your studies after the war?'

'Probably, if I can. It's all I want to do. I'm not interested in being a barrister or sitting on the bench, as Father does.

Awfully proud of the old boy, of course – but each to his own. Wouldn't you agree?'

'Yes, I think so. My brothers have gone into farming, except for Daniel. He joined the Army at the start of the war, but I suppose he'll go back to the land when he comes home.'

'And what do you do?' Simon looked at her curiously. 'Anything interesting?'

'I left school at Christmas last year. My father wanted me to stay at home until I get married, but I would have liked to train as a teacher. I agreed to help out with volunteer work for the Fire Brigade, though. I'm on fire watch five afternoons a week in Cambridge. Two mornings a week I help out at the village school.'

'And is that enough for you, Emily?'

Emily liked the way he said her name, making it sound special. She liked the way he talked altogether. She considered for a moment before answering.

'Yes and no,' she said. 'At the moment the Fire Brigade needs girls like me to man the phones. They can't get enough of us, and it's a very important job. My shift is from one o'clock until seven at night, but I often don't get to my room until gone ten, sometimes much later. Most girls of my age are joining the services or becoming nurses. What I do is less glamorous but very necessary. Sometimes I have to take a mobile unit out if we're at full stretch. I had to take extra driving lessons and a special test for that. If there has been an explosion or a big fire in the gas mains it can be a bit scary.'

'Yes, I can imagine it might,' he agreed. 'And it is a necessary job – but what about when this is all over?'

'I'm not sure. I might go to college then. I haven't really thought that far ahead.'

'I expect you will get married and give up all thought of work.'

'Perhaps,' she agreed. 'But only if I find the right man.'

'So that means you haven't yet?'

'No, not yet.'

'I like the sound of that,' Simon said, and grinned at her. 'It means there's a chance for me...'

* * *

The pain in his arm was bloody, a constant reminder of the horrors he was trying hard to forget. Weeks of hellish agony proceeded by days of mental and physical exhaustion, and the terror of knowing they were stranded on that damned beach in France, with little hope of rescue. The fact that so many of them had survived Dunkirk was due in part to the courage of ordinary chaps. Men who had been put to sea in frail river craft to help out the big ships, often with nothing but luck and determination to see them through, sometimes succeeding where the larger navy craft failed. At times it seemed to Daniel that he could still smell the stink of oil from the ships that had been sunk during the rescue operation, hear the screams of men wounded or drowning, taste the blood in his mouth...

'May I sit there?' A young woman in a smart navy outfit was looking pointedly at the only spare seat in the carriage. Daniel realised his cap was in her way and mumbled an apology. 'Thank you.' She glanced at him as he winced. 'Oh, I am so sorry. Did I knock your arm?'

Daniel shook his head and turned away to look out of the

window as fields, trees and soot-ridden houses flashed by. She hadn't touched him. It was merely that every movement was an effort. It was July 1940 now and the memories were still as sharp, still as terrifying. If he'd had any sense he would have stayed in the military hospital for as long as they would have him. Already he was regretting his decision to make this journey, but Emily's letter had made him uneasy.

It was too late for him to attend his father's funeral, of course. Robert Searles had died a month previously, when Daniel was still marooned on that beach. He'd known nothing of it until his sister's letter had been given to him two days earlier. It had been opened, as all their mail was, and someone had decided to withhold it until he was considered strong enough to be told.

The shock, just when he'd begun to feel better and think fondly of a home visit, had been almost unbearable, especially as he had believed his father had come to him when he lay hovering between life and death. His eyelashes were moist as he thought about his father on that last day before Daniel had left for his first posting. Robert Searles had been so proud of his third son, the only one to volunteer to fight. Henry and Clay had both chosen to take exemption. They had claimed they were needed on the farm, and since the nation had to be fed, their claims had been accepted.

'I'm proud of you, son,' Robert had told Daniel, and he'd hugged him with visible emotion. 'I'll see you don't lose by it. When you come back you'll have land of your own – and that's a promise.'

'You don't have to reward me for doing my duty, Father.'

'You would see it that way,' Robert said. 'But I've been thinking of buying a nice little smallholding that's going begging, lad. I shall go ahead and put your name on it.'

Daniel had merely smiled and hugged his father one last time. The end of the war had seemed a long way away. He hadn't been sure he would survive, wasn't sure of it now. His arm was healing, his shoulder less painful than it had been. He'd been given three months' leave to recuperate, but after that they would want him back.

There had been no point in telling his father at that moment that he didn't want to follow his brothers on to the land. Robert wouldn't have understood. Farming was in his blood. He had done well, was a wealthy man, and his two elder sons had never considered doing anything else.

Daniel had an idea of what he wanted to do with his life, when and if he survived the war and returned in one piece. He closed his eyes, shutting out the waves of grief and pain that washed over him every time he thought of his father. It wasn't supposed to happen this way. His life was the one at risk, not his father's. It was difficult to understand how it could have happened, but apparently it had been an accident on the farm. Just a deep cut that had turned bad. Robert had refused to see a doctor until it was too late.

Anger slashed through Daniel. For God's sake, why hadn't anyone called the doctor sooner? Why hadn't someone noticed Father was ill? If he had been there... But he'd been stranded in France, expecting to die on that beach.

Regret tasted as bitter as gall in his mouth. Nothing could turn back time. His father was dead and there was no changing that.

He opened his eyes as he realised the train had stopped and it was time for him to get out. He had only one small case, the rest of his stuff having been lost in the disastrous landing at Dunkirk, but it didn't matter. He'd been given as much as he needed for the moment, and there were clothes at home, in his wardrobe, left there by the bright-eyed, eager young man who had thought war was a matter of honour.

He got out of the train, wincing as the pain started up again. No point in looking for anyone to give him a lift; he hadn't bothered to tell them he was coming home. It wasn't that far to Rathmere; he could walk it if he took it easy.

The road from the station became a hill as he approached the village outskirts, the beautiful old Norman church at the top rising out of a peaceful sunny afternoon, a cloud of pigeons fluttering around the tower. The sky was blue with just a sprinkling of fluffy white curls drifting in the distance, and from someone's garden came the scent of sweet-smelling flowers. He breathed deeply, glad to be free of the stink of the hospital at last.

Daniel stopped halfway up the hill to put his case down for a moment. Not much further now, but he was damned near exhausted. His strength wasn't back to normal yet, and the case seemed extraordinarily heavy, even though there wasn't much inside.

As he stopped to pick up the case once more, a young boy went whizzing by on a bicycle, then circled and came back to stare at him uncertainly. Daniel stared back, then started to grin as he recognised his younger brother.

'Is it Connor?' he asked. 'You've grown, lad!'

'Daniel?' Connor frowned as he noticed how pale and strained the soldier looked. It wasn't easy to recognise his brother, but some inner sense had made him circle back, seeing that the man was in difficulty. 'Is that case heavy? You can rest it on my bike if you want and I'll wheel it.'

Daniel hesitated, then lifted the case to rest over the seat and handlebars. 'Thanks. I could do with some help.'

'That's what made me come back,' Connor said. 'I

thought you might be in trouble. I'm glad you're home. Emily told me you'd been wounded. I thought that meant you were going to die.'

'Not this time,' Daniel said, his mouth set in a grim line. 'The bloody Germans had a good try, mind you.'

Connor laughed. 'You sound just like Dad when you swear.' His grin faded, his eyes becoming dark with grief. Daniel saw that he was struggling against tears. 'Did they tell you – about Dad?'

Daniel's throat tightened because he was hurting inside, just like Connor. 'Two days ago. Emily wrote but they didn't give me the letter because I was too ill for a while and they forgot it – damned idiots are always mislaying things. I came as soon as the doctors would release me.'

Connor blinked hard, his emotion turning to anger. 'It happened a month ago. It's been horrible since. I hate them all – except Emily. She's all right. She cares but the rest of them are glad.'

'Of course they aren't,' Daniel said. 'How could Henry or Clay – or Frances – be glad he's dead?'

'Clay and Henry can do what they like on the farm now. Frances is getting married soon – and she never cared anyway. She only married him for his money.'

'She? You mean Margaret...' Daniel frowned. He had not yet met his father's new wife... His widow now. 'Why don't you like her?'

'Emily doesn't, nor does Frances. She's all right to me, but she doesn't cry much. Emily cries all the time when she's alone – but she doesn't.'

'Not everyone behaves in the same way. I haven't cried yet. I was too shocked.'

'You will,' Connor said. 'I cried at the funeral. They said I was too young to go, but Emily took me. She hates it all as much as I do, but she's away in Cambridge for most of the week.'

'What do you hate?'

'Clay and Henry are always arguing. Margaret gets angry with them sometimes – and Frances is having a party today. That's why I came out on my bike. They were all laughing and dancing. It isn't fair. Not when Dad's dead.'

'I know it hurts,' Daniel said. 'It hurts like hell – but life doesn't stop because someone dies. We have to cope with our grief and carry on, at least outwardly.'

'But they don't care.' Connor pulled a face. 'When Peter Robinson's grandfather died, they all cried. No one cares about Dad except Emily and me – and you. You do care, don't you?'

'Yes, very much. I'm sure the others do underneath. Maybe they're just trying to hide it.'

'You'll find out,' Connor said darkly. 'How long are you home for? Have they given you a discharge?'

'I've got three months' leave, and then I've got to go back for a medical review. If my shoulder is better by then I expect they will find me a job. It might not be overseas, though. I could be given a desk job or something in administration.' He grinned at his brother. 'That's a big word for running errands to you and me.'

'Would you like that?'

'Not much. On the other hand, it wasn't much fun over there either. War is a rotten business.'

'You were at Dunkirk, weren't you?'

'Who told you that?'

'Emily. She said the telegram arrived telling us you had been wounded just after Dad died, and then a letter came from your commanding officer to say you were in hospital. Emily wanted to visit but they said only Dad could go – but he couldn't, because he was dead...'

Connor's face screwed up, but he held his tears back.

They had arrived at the house, which fronted quite a long space on the High Street, its six windows fitted with leaded bars and small panes of thick glass; the door oak and impressive with a black iron knocker. At the back, the garden sloped down the hill, giving magnificent views over the fens. Connor wheeled his bike around to the kitchen door and deposited Daniel's case on the step. He turned to look at his brother.

'I should sneak up the back stairs if I were you. You won't want to see them.' They could hear the music from where they stood; Vera Lynn was belting out one of the tunes she had made so popular.

'Are you coming in?'

Connor shook his head. 'I'm off to see Peter. His father has bought some new calves and I want to see them – talk to you later, then. I'll come to your room, if that's all right?'

'Of course it is. Have a good time with your friend.'

He stood on the back doorstep and watched his brother ride off. Then he opened the door and went in, feeling a wave of nostalgia wash over him as his eyes moved around the room. At least nothing much had changed here. There was still the huge painted dresser at one end, the long, scrubbed pine table and the elbow chairs by the range. The deep stone sinks looked to be overflowing with dirty plates, cups and glasses. A brandy decanter stood on the table with several glasses. Daniel walked over, his back to the door as he poured himself a generous measure.

'And what do you think you're doing?' a young woman's

voice demanded from behind him. 'Who are you – and who told you to help yourself?'

Daniel turned in surprise, looking at the girl with interest. She wasn't tall, probably only up to his shoulder, but she was pretty. Her hair was soft and fine, a light brown in colour, and she had what he thought of as hazel eyes. She was wearing a cheap dark blue dress over which she had tied a white apron, and since she was carrying a tray filled with the remains of party food, he imagined she was extra help brought in for the party.

'I was feeling exhausted and fancied a drink,' he said, keeping a straight face. 'I'm sure they won't mind.'

'Depends who you are,' the girl said, eyes narrowing. 'I suppose it's all right if you're one of the guests – but you should be through there, not here. You'll be in my way.'

'I'm sorry about that,' Daniel said. 'I'll try not to hinder you, though I can't offer to help. My arm doesn't work too well at the moment.'

'Been hurt, have you?' She looked at him intently. 'I've seen you before somewhere, a long time ago, though...'

'Perhaps,' he admitted. 'What's your name?'

'Alice Robinson. My father has a smallholding in the fen, but we live in the High Street now. Connor and Peter are friends.'

'And you've just got some new calves, I hear?'

'Who told you that?' Her eyes widened in surprise and then her cheeks turned pink as she understood. 'You're Daniel, aren't you? I remember seeing you at school, but you were a lot older than me, just about to leave when I was in my first year. I'm seventeen. I'm sorry I was rude just now – I didn't know it was you. No one said anything about you being expected home...'

'That's because I didn't tell them.'

'Oh...' She smiled at him suddenly, and he realised she was lovely; she had the kind of beauty that comes from inside. 'It's not a very good day for coming home – they've got a party on. Frances has just got engaged.'

'Good for her,' Daniel said. 'It's her birthday too – her twenty-first. I'm afraid I haven't bought her a present. Do you think she will forgive me?'

'I should think she will be glad to see you back.' Alice frowned as she saw that he really did look exhausted. 'Do you want to sit down? I could make you a cup of tea if you like?'

'I'll sit down if you don't mind. It was a long walk from the station, and I'm not as strong as I thought. The brandy will do me more good than tea, thanks all the same. Don't let me stop you working, Alice. Isn't there anyone else to help with all this?'

'Yes, there's Millie Salmons. She's clearing the table in the dining room and will be here in a minute.'

'Good grief, I thought she had retired before I joined up?'

'She had but she came back because all the young girls left when the war started. They all went off to join one of the services or become nurses. I shall have to soon – but I'm not quite old enough yet. So I help out here now and then, do a few jobs on the farm for Dad and help my mother at home the rest of the time.'

'She'll miss you when you go away.'

'They need us, either in the factories or the services. Dad doesn't want me to go into a factory, but I shall have to do something. I might drive people to hospital; they are asking for volunteers and I can drive anything. I started on the farm when I could hardly walk, on Dad's knee at first. I help out with driving the tractor when he's busy, and that's most of the time with the men away.'

'They have a lot of women drivers at the hospital,' Daniel said. 'One of them took me to the station, nice girl – but not pretty like you.'

'I'm not pretty,' Alice said, and blushed. 'Your sisters are lovely. I'm just ordinary.'

Daniel thought that Alice would look every bit as pretty as his sisters dressed the way they did in expensive clothes, with their hair done professionally. In fact he thought she was rather special altogether, whatever she wore.

'I don't think you're ordinary. I suppose you wouldn't come out with me one night – to the pictures in Ely? Not for a few days, though. I'll need to rest but then I'll be all right.'

Alice looked at him thoughtfully. He was probably six years older, but that didn't matter – it was the fact that the Searles were thought of as rich that bothered her.

'I'll think about it,' she said slowly.

'I don't bite and I'm quite nice really,' Daniel said. 'I'd like to know you better, Alice.'

'Maybe...'

Before she could finish what she was saying there was a cry of surprise from the doorway, and turning to look, Daniel saw Frances standing there.

'Daniel! You're home,' she said, looking thrilled. 'Why on earth didn't you let us know? Someone would have fetched you from the station.' She came towards him, her face bright with pleasure. 'It's so good to see you. We were all so worried about you, but they didn't want us to visit for a start and then...' Her smile dimmed. 'Emily said she would write. You do know about...?'

'Yes, I know about Father,' Daniel said. 'You're looking

lovely, Frances. I hear you and Marcus have taken the plunge?'

'Yes, Marcus got leave and we decided to do it today, as long as I was having the party.'

'I didn't manage to get you a present, love. I'll buy you something another day, when I go out – to Ely, probably.'

'Oh, that doesn't matter,' Frances said, looking uncertain as she approached him. 'Can I hug you – or will it hurt?'

'It will hurt,' Daniel said, 'but you can kiss me on the cheek. It's just my left arm and shoulder. They are still damned painful.'

'Was it awful, Dan?'

'Pretty bloody,' he said. 'We don't talk about it much. Tell me where you and Marcus intend to live when you get married – when is that, by the way?'

'He has been promised a week's leave in two weeks' time. We shall live at his parents' house for the present, I suppose. The wedding will be by special licence, of course, and a bit of a scrappy reception, but we don't care.'

'No, I imagine not,' he said, and he kissed his sister as she hung back nervously, afraid of hurting him. 'At least I should be able to get you a present for that – what would you like?'

'Anything,' Frances said. 'I've been collecting for ages so we've got most things anyway, and until we get our own house we don't need furniture. We shall wait until the end of the war for that.'

'I'll find something,' Daniel promised. 'Well, I think I'll go up to my room and have a rest.'

'Emily has been keeping it aired for you,' Frances told him. 'Have you seen her? I was looking for her, thought she might have come to hide in here, but obviously she hasn't.' She glanced around the kitchen as if expecting her sister to materialise out of thin air. 'I wonder if she went upstairs...'

'She went out with someone,' Alice told her, turning from the sink where she had been running hot water on to some of the dirty dishes. 'A young man with dark blond hair.'

'Thank you, Alice.' Frances nodded, looking pleased by the news. 'That will be Marcus's navigator, Simon Vane. Well, that's promising. She usually hates all the men I find for her, but Simon is rather dishy – and his father is seriously rich, too. Quite a catch I would say.'

'Don't let Marcus hear you say that,' Daniel warned with a smile.

Frances laughed, tossing her hair back confidently. 'Oh, he knows I wouldn't look at anyone else. He would love to see you, Dan. Won't you come and join us for a few minutes?'

'Sorry, not this time,' Daniel apologised. 'I'm worn out, Frances. If I don't lie down I shall probably pass out. I don't want to be the spectre at the feast.'

'Marcus will be disappointed; he'll be off soon – but you'll see him at the wedding, and that's not long.'

'No, it isn't,' Daniel said. It was too soon if anything, but he couldn't spoil his sister's happiness by telling her so.

He went out into the hall, using the back stairs to make good his escape. The last thing he needed was to bump into any of his old friends the way he felt at the moment. It would be better after he'd had time to adjust, time to get over the shock of coming home to a house that no longer contained Robert Searles.

Closing the door of his bedroom, he leaned against it, his eyes shut. His arm was throbbing and his shoulder felt numb. Sometimes he wondered if he would ever get the full use of his arm back, though the doctor had been hopeful.

The window of his room overlooked the High Street at the front of the house. He could hear voices as people left, calling their goodbyes and thanks, the doors of a couple of cars slamming. Some people still had petrol it seemed, despite all the shortages.

He made sure his door was locked before going across to the bed and sitting down. He sighed as he lay back, putting his feet up on the eiderdown without taking off his shoes and closing his eyes. He was so bloody tired he could sleep for a week.

2

'How was your sister's party?' Carole Mortimer asked when Emily arrived for work the following afternoon, which happened to be a Sunday. It was a warm summer's day, too good to be indoors really, and the office where they worked seemed stuffy and airless. 'Was it nice?'

'Yes, I suppose so,' Emily replied with a guilty flush. 'I was only there for a few minutes...'

'And what did you do then?' Carole was a bubbly, plump girl with bright blue eyes that sparked with laughter, and she was laughing now. 'You've got that look in your eyes, Emily. Who was he then?'

'What look?' Emily giggled as she saw her friend's expression, her guilt fleeing as suddenly as it had come. 'Frances introduced us at the party, and he asked if I wanted to go for a spin in his Morgan roadster...'

'So?' Carole demanded. 'What happened then?'

'We drove to Ely, walked by the river, had toast and honey for tea, and then he drove me home.'

'That's all?' Carole looked at her in disbelief. 'I don't believe you. Come on, now tell me the rest.'

Emily was saved from having to comply by the appearance of their supervisor, who sent them scurrying to their posts. She was glad of the intervention for she hadn't wanted to confess all of it to Carole. They were good friends, but this was something rather precious, something she wanted to keep to herself for the moment.

Simon had stopped the car in a quiet lane on their way home. For a moment or two he'd sat looking at her, then leaned forward to kiss her softly on the lips.

'I hope you don't mind? I've been wanting to do that all afternoon.'

'No, I don't mind. I liked it.'

'Then you won't mind if I do it again,' Simon said, taking her into his arms this time. His kiss had been passionate, demanding and yet tender, arousing feelings that Emily hadn't realised she could feel. When he let her go she sat looking at him, her eyes wide with wonder. 'You really are rather terrific, Emily.'

'Am I?' She felt faintly bemused, because she was way out of her depth. 'Thanks...'

'I'm not just saying it. I think I've fallen in love with you.'

'You can't... You don't know me yet.'

'How long does it take to know you're in love?'

'I don't know. Is that what this is – the shaky feeling inside and wanting to...? Oh, I don't know, but when you kissed me I wanted it to go on and on for ever.'

Simon laughed huskily. He gave her cheek a teasing flick with his fingers. 'Yes, that's it, Emily. I wanted to go on and on, and a lot more than kissing – but there's time for all that. I have to go back to my base tomorrow, but I get leave in two weeks. I shall come to the wedding, and then drive back to spend my leave at home. Would you come with me? Would your family let you?'

'My family...' Emily wondered who her family was now. She'd adored her father, and she was fond of her sister, but Frances wouldn't be there any more. It would be just Margaret and Connor at home in future. 'There's no one to stop me, Simon. I sleep at the hostel in Cambridge five nights a week. Margaret won't even know I'm not there.'

'Good.' He brushed a lock of hair back from her cheek. He seemed to be thinking deeply and his expression puzzled her. Just what was on his mind? 'I know my family will love you, and I think you will love them. Can you get time off from your job?'

'I shall just tell the school I'm needed – I only work as a volunteer there – and I'm due for some leave from the Fire Service so it shouldn't be a problem. I'll ask and tell you at the wedding.'

'That's a date then,' he said, and he kissed her again, gently this time. 'I do like you an awful lot, Emily. I think I might just have found the girl for me, the one I've been looking for.'

Now what did he mean by that? Surely he couldn't be talking about anything as serious as marriage this soon? And yet his words and the look in his eyes were making her heart beat faster.

Emily felt as if she were being swept away on a tidal wave. No one had ever kissed her like that, and they certainly hadn't looked at her the way Simon did, or said such exciting things. He had given her goosepimples all over and she half thought she was dreaming.

She'd woken from the dream very quickly when Simon

dropped her outside her door and went off without coming in to say goodbye to anyone else. Frances had pounced on her immediately, and her news had been so startling that she'd forgotten her magical interlude as she went upstairs to Daniel's room.

'Can I come in, Dan?' she'd asked, knocking softly. 'It's Emily...'

'Wait a moment...' The door had been unlocked a few seconds later and she'd been shocked at the change in her brother. Frances had told her he looked pale, but he was so thin and his face was grey with exhaustion. 'Sorry. I didn't want anyone coming in without warning.'

'Shall I go away and leave you to rest?'

'No, come in for a few minutes.' He smiled and leaned forward to kiss her cheek. 'Mind my left arm and shoulder. They're still a bit sore, and the journey tired me, but I'm all right.'

'You look as if you should still be in hospital.'

'I probably should, but I wanted to come home.'

'I ought not to have written, but I thought you would want to know.'

'Yes, of course. They only gave me your letter two days ago.'

'It's ages since I wrote.'

'Yes, I know. That's the Army for you. They lose everything – equipment, men, letters; nothing too small or too large for them to mislay.'

'Is it really that bad?'

'Sometimes it seems that way,' he said with a wry grin. 'It certainly felt that way on that damned beach. For a while we thought they were just going to leave us there, and we expected to die.'

'It must have been awful. We read about it in the papers and heard it on the radio, and I saw a newsreel at the cinema. I wanted to visit you but they said no, and then... I couldn't. It was so awful when Dad died. He was irritable for a couple of weeks or so before they finally took him to hospital, but we none of us knew anything was wrong. Margaret did try to tell him to go to the doctor's but he wouldn't, and then he got so bad that I rang the doctor myself. They sent him to hospital but he was in a coma by the time he got there and he just never came round. He had blood poisoning, they said... The wound had gone septic because he neglected it.'

'So it was his own fault then?'

'Yes, I don't know what had got into him. He was in a mood for some weeks, snapping at everyone, then he got much worse and I saw him hobbling. I asked him what was wrong and he shouted at me. None of us could talk to him.'

'He must have had something on his mind. You've no idea what was bothering him, of course?'

'I wondered if he might have quarrelled with Margaret, but I'm not sure. I don't know what else it could be – but Clay or Henry might. You know they wouldn't tell me anything important.'

'They still think you're a little girl, I expect, but you're not little Emmy any more.'

'No, I've grown up.'

'Working for the Fire Service, I hear?' Daniel smiled at her. 'I expect that keeps you busy.'

'There aren't many days without several callouts,' Emily said, and she gave him a wry smile. 'But we don't want to talk shop – how long are you home for?'

'Three months, I think,' he replied. 'I've got to see my own doctor next week and have regular check-ups, and then

I'll go back for a medical at the military hospital. After that I expect they will find me a job of some kind.'

'Then at least you will be here for a while – unless you want to stay with friends?'

'Most of my friends are here,' Daniel replied with a little frown. He didn't want to think about other friends, friends who had died – suddenly, some of them; others in slow agony, waiting on that beach. 'I can't do much on the farm or I would offer to help, but I'll give Henry a hand with the accounts if he wants.'

'Dad's lawyer wanted to talk to you when you were fit,' Emily said. 'I suppose it's to do with... Well, the land and things. I'm not sure how things have been left. Apparently, there's a small trust for me, but I didn't go to the reading so I don't know the rest. Henry probably knows.'

'Yes, I expect so,' Daniel said. 'I suppose I'd better come down now. It will be time for dinner soon and I could do with something, even if it's only a drink.' He frowned. 'I had better say hello to Margaret. We haven't met yet...'

* * *

'Stop dreaming, Miss Searles,' the sharp voice of her supervisor cut through Emily's thoughts. 'I've asked you twice to come into my office.'

'Yes, Miss Brown.' Emily came out of her reverie and got to her feet just as her phone started to ring. 'Shall I...?'

'Leave it to one of the other girls. I want to talk to you now.'

Now what had she done wrong? Emily knew that she had been lost in her thoughts when her supervisor called her, but she'd only answered three emergency calls that afternoon. For once they were having a quiet time of it, only a couple of small domestic fires and a potentially more serious one at the jam factory.

'I'm sorry if I wasn't listening, Miss Brown,' Emily said as she entered the office. 'My brother came home yesterday. He was wounded at Dunkirk and has been in hospital for weeks.'

'I'm sorry to hear that he was wounded, but having had experience of the reality of war yourself, Miss Searles, perhaps it will help you to understand why we need to transfer you.'

'Transfer me?' Emily stared at her in surprise. 'I don't understand – have I done something wrong?'

'Quite the opposite,' the supervisor said, and her sharp features relaxed into a smile. 'I think you are ready for more responsibility and more demanding work, Emily. They are crying out for girls like you in the big industrial cities, and I want to put you on my transfer list. You might be sent to Coventry or Liverpool, Southampton – or even London. How would you feel about that?'

'I'm not sure...' Emily was so surprised that she hardly knew how to answer. 'Yes, I suppose – if you think I could be of use?'

'Wonderful. I was sure you would agree, but some girls refuse to go because of circumstances at home.'

'No, I don't have that kind of a problem,' Emily said. Margaret wasn't going to object. They didn't really get on, and there was no one else to worry about her, though Connor might miss her. But he was usually out with his friends to all hours. 'My parents are dead, and my step-mother won't mind at all.'

'I'm sorry for your loss. I imagine the posting will come

through in about three weeks' time, and then you will get a few days' leave before you go.'

'Thank you. My sister's wedding will be two weeks yesterday, and I would like a few days off for that – after it, actually.'

'I'll make a note of that,' Miss Brown said. 'You will report back for work here after your leave and I expect we'll have news of your posting by then.'

Emily was feeling bemused when she went back to her desk, but news of a big fire at a local factory was breaking, and she didn't have time to think about herself or anything but coordinating the various fire crews.

It wasn't going well, and three firemen had been injured in a terrible explosion at the site. There were wild reports of it having been a bomb at first, but then it was established that it had been a gas main that caused the trouble. The news that three of their men were hurt cast a shadow over the girls. A few were in tears, because some of them had loved ones amongst the crews, and they all knew and cared about the brave men manning the engines and doing a very necessary job. They were used to fires and the danger, but when something bad happened it affected everyone.

The chaos and confusion caused by what was clearly a very bad fire kept the girls at their posts all night. No one thought of going home until it was all over, and so it was into the early hours before Carole and Emily walked back to the hostel together.

Carole was subdued because her fiancé's brother was one of the men hurt, and she would have to write and tell him about it.

'They lost their parents years ago,' she told Emily.

'There's only Terry and Jack now. If anything happens to Terry...'

'It may not,' Emily said, and squeezed her arm. 'Why don't you visit him in the morning, and then write your letter to Jack?'

'Yes, I suppose that would be a good idea. Would you come to the hospital with me?' Carole gave her a pleading look.

'Me?' Emily was surprised but didn't hesitate. 'Yes, all right, if you want. It's my morning for the school, but I'll telephone and let them know I'm not coming. I shall have to give it up soon anyway.'

'Why is that?' Carole looked at her curiously.

'They are transferring me somewhere – one of the ports or perhaps London.'

'Not you too,' Carole said, and pulled a face. 'They asked me but I said I couldn't go. My mother wouldn't put up with it. That's why I volunteered for this instead of joining the Wrens.'

'My father felt much the same,' Emily confessed. 'He wanted me to stay home until I got married, but let me join the Fire Service because I would have had to do something once the war started. He wouldn't have wanted me to go away, but it doesn't matter now.'

'You don't like your stepmother much, do you?'

Emily grimaced. 'No. It's awful of me, I know, but I shall be glad to get away from the house – though Daniel is home at the moment. I wouldn't have minded seeing more of him.'

'He can visit you wherever you are.' Carole looked thoughtful. 'I shall miss you. It makes me think I ought to have said yes. Do you think they would send us both to the same place?'

'I don't know. Why don't you see where they send me?'

'And then ask for a transfer?' Carole said, and nodded. 'Yes, I might do that. I can work on Mum in the meantime, tell her I have to go where they send me.'

They were both so tired when they got to the hostel that Carole didn't think to ask about Emily's day out again, and so she kept her secret to herself, thinking about it as she tumbled into bed to sleep for hours.

* * *

'What do you mean, Father was worried about the farm?' Daniel frowned at his eldest brother as they stood talking in the front parlour. 'What's the matter? I thought everything was going well.'

'It has done for years,' Henry replied grimly. 'But recently there have been so many new rules and regulations – you've no idea how demanding the Food Ministry can be, Dan. Everything has to be checked or rubberstamped, and we can't sell our own produce where or when we want; it's damned red tape all over the place. The profits were down the last year before the war because we had a poor harvest, and lately it has all gone from bad to worse.'

'That sounds serious.'

'Not really, not yet,' Henry said. 'It might be if things don't improve, but I'm trying to get on top of all the regulations. You know how much I love paperwork!'

Daniel smiled at his tall, lanky brother, the tallest of them all. Henry looked tired and more worried than he was letting on, his skin a bit sallow as if he might not be well.

'I know you are a good farmer, Henry, but Dad was

always the one who kept it all together. Neither you nor Clay was keen on school or maths, as I remember.'

'I can reckon what I need to in my head,' Henry said ruefully, 'but when it comes to putting it all down...' He growled low in his throat. 'It isn't my best job. Clay says the farm is too big for us. He wants to scale it down – go off on his own. Trouble is, Father left a bit of it to all of us – the girls, you, Connor and Margaret. The house is hers until she marries again, if she does – and then we have to pay her half what it's worth.'

'Sounds a bit complicated,' Daniel said. 'What about Margaret's shares in the farm?'

'She is willing to sell them now. At least, according to Clay, that's what she says.'

'Will that be difficult, in the present circumstances?'

'Depends how much she wants,' Henry admitted. 'Clay thinks she will be reasonable, but I've got an idea he's in for a shock.'

'I've only spoken to her a few times,' Daniel said, and looked thoughtful. 'She seems all right to me...'

'Oh, she's pleasant enough, but I think she is a schemer. She swept Father off his feet, got him to marry her before he knew where he was – and I think he regretted it.'

'What makes you say that?'

'Don't know,' Henry admitted. 'It's just a hunch. He was in a hell of a mood for weeks before he died. Part of it was the war and the regulations, of course, but there was more to it than that... I think he suspected her of having an affair.'

'Surely not? They hadn't been married five minutes.'

'I think Margaret expected more than she got,' Henry said shrewdly. 'They met when he was in London for some function, and it was a whirlwind affair. She saw the house and he spent some money on her, and she thought it was the good life, but then she realised that he didn't often go to London. She entertains as much as she can here, but it isn't the same as she was used to in town. I've seen some of her friends – rich and idle. She ought to have married one of them, but Dad was an easy mark. I think she will take as much as she can from us and clear off back where she came from.'

'That's a bit harsh,' Daniel said. 'You can't know any of this.'

'I saw her flirting with one of her men friends once. He's married and can't or won't get a divorce. I think she wanted him – that's why she took Dad on the rebound.'

'Well, you may be right,' Daniel said. 'I'll do what I can to help with the accounts while I'm home – but I can't manage anything too physical at the moment.'

'We can manage most of it. We've got a couple of Land Army girls now, and they do pretty well for amateurs. I'm going to try to get more soon. You'll have to take a look around when you feel up to it. Clay has made some improvements to the sheds and things, pulled down some of the older buildings and put up new. He argued with Dad over it for ages, but it's done now.'

'I'm sure you can sort him out,' Daniel said. 'Though if he wants to go on his own you might as well let him. It will only cause friction otherwise.'

'I said I'd ask you,' Henry said with a frown. 'It means deciding on his share. He wants a lot of the land in Chatteris Fen, because it's good potato and carrot land – but it's some of the best we own.'

'Couldn't we get it valued?'

'No land is worth much on paper at the moment, Dan. I

think he ought to be prepared to either take fewer acres or pay something – otherwise he's skimming the cream.'

'Well, perhaps we should all sit down with the solicitor and see exactly how things stand?'

'Yes, I think that is for the best,' Henry said. 'At least you'll be on my side, Dan. Clay has to realise there's the girls and Connor to think about as well as us three.'

'And Margaret,' Daniel reminded him. They lingered on the front doorstep for a moment as Henry remembered various bits and pieces, but at last he was ready to leave. 'I'll see you later then...'

Daniel waved as his brother went off in his battered old truck, its engine spluttering and banging all the way round the corner. He made a mental note to give it an overhaul once he was feeling better. At least he could do that while he was here, and perhaps it was a good thing he had come back when he did. It seemed that Emily had been right to be concerned. Things weren't as they should be, and it might be just as well that he had been given three months' leave.

As he turned back towards the house, he saw a girl walking towards him, her hips swaying enticingly, and he waited for her to come up to him. 'Hello, Alice Robinson,' he said, and grinned at her. She was wearing a pretty green dress and her softly, waving hair was swinging loose above her collar. 'And where are you off to this fine day?'

'I am going to catch the train into Cambridge,' Alice told him shyly. 'I've applied to be a Land Army girl and I've got to see someone there at two o'clock. My father says I'm better on the land than most of the girls he's seen that other farmers have taken on – and he thinks if they take me on as a land girl I can work for him.'

'I'm not sure it is as easy as that,' Daniel said. 'They might decide to send you somewhere else. Henry was telling me he has two at the moment and he's applying for more.'

'Maybe I'll work for him then,' Alice said brightly. She tipped her head to one side to look at him mischievously. 'Want to come to Cambridge with me?'

Daniel hesitated, then started to grin. 'Yes, why not? I haven't anything better to do.'

'Oh, if that's your attitude,' she chirped, but her eyes were dancing with laughter. 'I thought you might take me to tea after my interview – and there's a good film on in Cambridge.'

'You're on,' Daniel said, beginning to feel much better than he had for days. 'We'll have tea, go to the first house and then catch the last train home.'

'Mr Burgess is in the bed at the end,' the nurse said, looking at the two girls as they hesitated uncertainly. 'He is awake now, and lucky to be alive. The doctors thought he would die of smoke inhalation when they brought him in, but he's rallied, and has only a few small burns to his face and hands. You can stay for fifteen minutes, but that's all. He's still suffering from shock but I dare say two pretty girls will cheer him up.'

'Thank you,' Emily said. 'How are the other two firemen?'

'The news is not as good as far as they are concerned. Mr Harris died this morning, and Mr Jackson is badly burned, I'm afraid.'

'That's very sad,' Emily said. 'Ted Harris was married with two small children.' She felt tears sting her eyes as she left the nurse and followed Carole to the end of the ward. It was rotten for the woman whose husband had died, and by the sound of it another of the men was pretty badly burned.

The injured fireman they had come to see was lying in bed, his eyes closed. His hands were heavily bandaged, but she could see the red marks on his face, which had been greased but left open to the air. Clearly he had been luckier than the others. She swallowed hard, feeling sympathy for him and his comrades.

'Terry...' Carole said softly. Tears were trickling down her cheeks and Emily gave her hand a sympathetic squeeze. 'How are you, love?'

He opened his eyes and looked at her, then shut them again. 'Go away, Carole,' he said. 'I don't want a fuss.'

'But I wanted to help,' she said, glancing at Emily tearfully. 'We brought you some fruit...'

He opened his eyes again, looking at Emily this time. 'Have you seen enough? I'm not a bloody sideshow.'

She was shocked by his rudeness. She hadn't meant to stare at him. 'I didn't imagine you were. We came because Carole was anxious about you. All the girls are at the station.'

'Well, now you can tell them that I'm alive.'

'What the hell is the matter with you?' Emily asked. 'Two of your mates are in a lot worse shape than—'

'Do you think I don't bloody know that?' he growled, looking at her as if he hated her. 'I'd have been done for if Ted hadn't come back to get me out. It should have been me dead, not him. Now you can think what you bloody like!'

'Why should I think anything?' Emily asked. 'I don't know you and after this, I don't want to. I'll wait for you outside, Carole.'

She walked away, feeling hot and bothered. What a rude man! As if she'd gone there to gawp at him! She wouldn't have thought of coming to the hospital if Carole hadn't asked, and now she wished she hadn't bothered. Standing outside in the grounds, she looked at the cherry trees opposite. They must be a mass of beautiful blossom in the spring...

A girl's happy laughter caught her attention, and glancing across the road she saw her brother Daniel walking with a girl. They looked as if they were heading in the direction of a popular tea shop, which was just up the road from the hospital, and were clearly enjoying themselves.

Emily felt pleased to see that her brother was feeling better. The girl with him was Alice Robinson. She didn't know whether or not her father would have approved of the friendship. Frances probably wouldn't, but then, her sister was a bit of a snob. She thought the Searles and the Danbys were a cut above everyone else in the village, and money-wise she was probably right.

It didn't matter to Emily who her brother went out with as long as he was happy – besides, she liked Alice. She knew they hadn't seen her and she made no attempt to attract their attention as they crossed the road and disappeared into the tea shop.

Carole came up to her a few minutes later. 'I'm sorry Terry was so rude,' she said. 'He isn't usually like that. I think he regretted it after you left.'

Emily shrugged. 'It doesn't matter. What shall we do now? We've got an hour before we're on duty.'

'Shall we go to the Copper Kettle for tea?'

'No, not today,' Emily said. 'Let's walk into town and see if there are any decent dresses in that shop in Regent Street. I've just about got enough coupons for a new one...'

* * *

'Your Daniel's sweet on our Alice,' Peter Robinson said to Connor that weekend when they had returned from biking down the fens to count the bullocks on the washes for Peter's father. They had paused outside his house to chat for a few minutes before parting. 'She says he took her to tea at a posh place in Cambridge, and then they went to the flicks together – in the best seats, too.'

'What did they see? Was it a Western? I liked the one we saw at the fleapit in Ely that Saturday your sister took us in on the bus.'

'Yeah, Stagecoach, that's what it was called,' Peter said, and grinned at him. The cinema they called the fleapit always had films that had been to Ely before, but it was cheap for the kids to get in. 'I like John Wayne – but they didn't see anything like that. It was a soppy love film with Bette Davis – something daft if I know our Alice.'

'Your Alice is all right,' Connor said. 'I like her. She makes good cakes, especially that one with seeds in it.'

'I'm going to a party next week,' Peter said. 'The Harrisons down the lane are having a party for their daughter. Sheila is a bit daft but they have jelly and tinned fruit for tea.'

'Lucky you,' Connor said. 'I wish I was coming with you.'

'Your stepmother has lots of parties. I bet you get good food at them.'

'I never go,' Connor said with a grimace. 'It's bound to be cucumber sandwiches with the crusts cut off or something rotten like that. I hate her and I hate her stupid old parties.' He pulled a wry face. 'I wish she'd never married my dad.'

'You can come with me if you want,' Peter said. 'I'll tell Sheila to invite you. She does anything I want,' he ended boastfully.

'I bet she doesn't,' Connor said, and made a suggestive face. 'I bet she won't let you put your hand up her knickers.'

'She would,' Peter declared recklessly. 'I bet she'd even let me do it if I asked her.'

'Go on then, I dare you – ask her.'

'Nah,' Peter said. 'She's a nice girl. I might marry her one day.'

He wasn't going to admit that he had no idea how to do 'it' even to his best friend. He was ten going on eleven, just a year older than Connor, but he certainly wasn't ready for 'it' yet, even though most of the lads at school boasted all the time about what they'd seen or done.

'Me and Ken Briggs followed his brother John and Nora Roberts up on the banks last Sunday,' he said. 'I think they were doing it. He had his hand up her dress and he was lying on top of her and moving funny. You know...' He went through the motions and Connor laughed, his cheeks a bit red. 'We couldn't see much though, because we had to keep our heads low and Ken was laughing fit to pee himself. If his brother had caught us he would have given us a good hiding. He's a right nasty bugger, especially if he's had a drink or two.'

'Pity you couldn't see a bit more,' Connor said. 'I don't know how to do it yet – do you?'

'Nah,' Peter said, and he grinned, willing to admit it now that Connor had admitted he didn't know either. 'Alice says I'll know soon enough, when I'm ready.'

'Do you think she's done it?'

'With your Daniel?' Peter screwed up his face in thought. 'Nah, I shouldn't think so – not yet, anywise. She's looking all soppy and singing all over the place, but it's too soon. Alice isn't like that Nora Roberts. Ken said his brother says she's anyone's. She'll let any of them do it for the price of a drink up the pub.'

'I don't want a girl like that,' Connor said. 'I'm glad your Alice isn't that way – and I hope she marries our Daniel. If this flipping war was over he could come home and things would be better. They might take me to live with them, and you could come too.'

'Can't see my mum letting me go and live with them,' Peter said. 'She likes me around all the time. I do my delivery for Johnson's Groceries on the bike and then she wants me to stop at home with her while Dad goes to the pub. We sit and eat cheese on toast by the fire for a special treat if we've got any left – crumpets too sometimes, with her own jam or honey when we can get it.'

'Mother's boy!' Connor taunted, and yet he couldn't help envying his friend. It was a long time since he'd known what it was like to have a loving mother. Margaret certainly wasn't that, nor did he want her to be. He blamed her for his father's death, though he didn't have any real reason, but he was sure it was her fault in his own mind.

Peter grinned and aimed a punch at him. In another moment they were fighting on the ground, but not angrily, just in the way of friends, amusing themselves. Seeing them scrapping, a man passing called encouragement and laughed.

'That's it, give him one, Peter lad. Them Searles can do

with a bit of a lesson, stuck-up bastards. Heading for a fall, that's what they are.'

'Shut your face, pig brain,' Peter yelled after him, incensed at the insult to his friend, and then went back into the fight with renewed vigour. It ended as swiftly as it had begun when Mrs Robinson came to the door and called to them.

'Peter! Stop fighting with Connor at once! The two of you are more trouble than a pair of Bantam cocks, always scrapping. I want you to run an errand – and when you get back there will be a piece of cake for both of you, that's if Connor wants to stay for tea?'

'Yes, please!' both boys chorused together. It wasn't often there was cake for tea, though because their families had farms there were always some eggs and a bit of farm butter now and then. Peter gave Connor a hand up as they grinned at each other. It was good to be friends, good to be young, even if they did want answers to the burning question of how you did 'it'.

Peter took the shopping list and his mother's money and they raced off up the street, trying to beat each other to the shop on the corner, trying to be first. It was a constant competition between them, but it made their lives more rewarding.

* * *

Alice watched from the front window as the boys went racing up the street and smiled to herself. They were good boys, both of them, and she liked Connor. She had been polishing the front-room furniture with the window open and she'd heard what they were talking about as she worked.

Those rogues, the things they did and said! It had made her cheeks burn when they were discussing her and Daniel, but she was amused and had gone on listening, even though perhaps she ought not to have. She was glad Connor liked her, but sad that he hated his stepmother. She quite liked Margaret Searles herself, though she'd seen something one day at the house before Robert died, something she'd kept to herself.

It would make a fine old scandal if folk knew that she'd seen Margaret in her stepson's arms. Clay had been kissing her in a way that seemed to suggest that he at least wanted a lot more than a mere kiss.

Alice didn't know if there was anything more between them, and she didn't want to. She thought it was not very nice – not exactly incestuous because there was no blood tie, but Margaret had been married to Clay's father. And now Robert was dead. Had he known that his wife and son had been kissing? Had he guessed there was something going on between them?

He would have been terribly upset, because he was a good man, a decent man – one of the finest, Alice's father said. She hadn't dared to breathe a word of this at home, because her mother would have stopped her going to Rathmere, and she liked helping out there sometimes. She saw a lot of wealthy people when Margaret had her parties, and she admired the elegant clothes they wore and their jewellery. She wasn't envious of them, but she enjoyed seeing the things they had, and she wanted to keep visiting the house. Especially now that Daniel was home.

She liked Daniel very much. Her brother had been right about that. They had kissed the night he took her to the pictures, outside her house when he walked her home, but it was just a little peck on the lips. Not at all passionate or demanding, but then he was pretty done in by the time they said goodnight.

She had felt a bit guilty because he'd gone to Cambridge with her at her suggestion, and she'd apologised for making him do too much.

'Don't be sorry,' Daniel had told her. 'I enjoyed every minute and I want to do it again soon. When can I take you to Ely for the afternoon?'

'Perhaps next week,' she said. 'It depends what is happening – and how soon they tell me I'm officially a Land Army girl. I mostly help Dad with the pigs in the mornings, do a few chores in the house, and then I'm free in the afternoons unless Dad needs me on the tractor – or I come to your house.'

'Margaret isn't having a party next week as far as I know,' Daniel said. 'Let's say we'll go on Thursday if it's fine, shall we?'

'Yes, all right,' she agreed happily. 'I like market day and we can do some shopping for Mum if she wants it.'

Alice looked around her mother's small parlour. It all looked neat and tidy, the way she liked to see it, and smelled lovely of lavender polish. She had finished now for the day and thought she might go for a little walk up the street. After all, you never knew who you might see. She might even bump into Daniel if she was lucky.

It was nice that he wanted to see her again so soon, Alice thought. It was much too early to be thinking of marriage, though she did like him quite a lot.

3

Margaret smiled as she stepped into the steaming hot bath. The water was well above the government's recommended level, and perfumed with the expensive salts she liked. Robert had bought them for her when they met in London. They weren't easy to find these days, but then money could buy most things under the counter if one was enterprising enough. It was that she'd liked about Robert at the start. He had seemed rich, powerful and capable. She had wanted to make Michael jealous, but the whole thing had gone wrong somewhere along the line. She'd quarrelled with Michael, married Robert and ended up in this dump.

Not for much longer though, not if Clay came through for her. He had been hot for her from the beginning. She'd seen the lustful look in his eyes the first time they'd met, but she'd still had hopes of making it work with Robert then. However, he had proved more difficult to manage once they were married and his first lust had waned. He had wanted her desperately at the beginning, but she thought now that he'd never loved her. For Robert the land came first, and his children – particularly Emily, Daniel and Connor.

Robert hadn't trusted Clay, and he'd thought Henry a dull plodder. 'Henry's good on the farm but he's not a businessman. Clay is much the same, though he's sly and he's got his eye out for the main chance. Daniel is the one I'd put my money on. Maybe Connor when he's older.'

Daniel had been safely out of the way then. He was home now, but probably wouldn't interfere. Besides, Clay would do anything to get into her bed. She knew the brothers wouldn't consult Frances or Emily, and Connor was too young. So it was just Clay and Henry – and Daniel, of course.

Margaret wasn't sure how he would react when he was told how much she wanted for her share of the land, and the house if she could get them to buy. She had no intention of mouldering in this wretched village for the rest of her life. She had considered leaving Robert just before he became ill. He had begun to bore her, as most things did in this place, and she'd started to flirt with Clay a little. She hadn't intended Robert to see her, though.

Margaret frowned, feeling a pang of guilt. The foolish man! It wasn't her fault that he'd neglected the cut on his leg. She'd told him to go to the doctor's but he'd turned his back on her deliberately, ignoring her as he had since that incident with his son.

'It was your own fault!' she said out loud.

Robert's eyes haunted her sometimes. She had hidden his photographs in the drawer because she couldn't bear to look at him. His eyes seemed to accuse her, which was ridiculous because she hadn't done anything that terrible. A little flirtation, a few kisses were nothing, and she had no intention of taking it further. Even now, she was using Clay, stringing him along to get what she wanted. He thought she was waiting for a decent time to elapse, but as soon as she got her £20,000 she was off, back to London where there was a bit of life.

She had her eyes closed, enjoying the luxury of being alone in the house, and wasn't aware of the footsteps coming upstairs. When the bathroom door opened, she was brought out of her reverie with a start. At first she thought it must be Clay, and wished she had remembered to lock the door, and then, as she realised it was Daniel, she smiled. He looked so embarrassed, and yet he couldn't take his eyes off her.

'I'm sorry,' he muttered. 'I had no idea you were in here.'

'My fault,' Margaret said. 'I forgot to lock the door. I thought everyone was out.'

'I was. I came back.'

He seemed glued to the floor, unable to move. Margaret rose from the bath, her body soft, slender and glowing from the warm water.

'Would you hand me the towel?' She stood there unashamed, knowing it was probably the first time he'd seen a woman completely naked. He might still be a virgin, she thought, amused by his stunned expression. She took the towel from him, patting herself dry in a leisurely way before stepping out of the bath, then laughed softly. 'It's all right. You can look all you want – or you can use the water yourself. It's still warm.'

'I'm sorry. I should go.'

'Why? It's too late for my modesty. I don't mind you staying, as long as you behave.'

'I wouldn't...'

Margaret was laughing inside. The poor boy was so

embarrassed. He looked as if he might burst a blood vessel any minute!

'Don't be shy.' She reached for his hand, carried it to her right breast, placing it over the firm, full, warm flesh. 'Just so as you know what a real woman feels like.'

The spell was broken. She had gone too far. Margaret saw the horror in his eyes before he wrenched his hand back and turned away, slamming the door behind him as he left.

She frowned. She might just have made a mistake with Daniel. He was more like his father than she'd realised.

Daniel locked his bedroom door, leaning against it and breathing hard as he fought to control the surge of urgent need she had aroused in him. What the hell was the matter with him? It wasn't as if he didn't know how it was to have a woman that way; there had been a few, but most of them scrambled affairs in the back of a car or behind the shed on his father's farm, and none of them naked.

It was the shock of seeing her there like that – his father's wife – and the way she had just smiled instead of screaming at him or yelling at him to get out. And when she stood there, beads of water dripping off her, he had wanted to lick each pearl from her flesh with his tongue. Her body was so beautiful, soft and warm and very tempting. He had wanted her. The need had been urgent and powerful, and for a moment he had actually contemplated making love with her – his father's wife!

The feel of her breast had shocked him to sudden awareness of what he was doing, and in that moment he had been sickened and disgusted by her behaviour, and his own. He ought to have walked out the moment he realised she was in there, couldn't imagine why he hadn't done so. Yet his honesty forced him to admit that he had found her attractive from the first moment he'd seen her. Margaret was more than just attractive. She had that earthy sexuality that a lot of men found tantalizing, and he understood why his father, a widower for too many years, had fallen hard.

Daniel had been aware before this that he had pressing physical needs, which wouldn't be easy to satisfy here in the village. He could buy Nora Roberts a few drinks and then take her for a walk up the banks, of course, but he didn't fancy his chances with Alice much if he did – and he wasn't that desperate.

Alice was a decent girl, pretty, warm and exactly the sort of girl he would probably marry one day. Not that he had any thoughts of marriage yet. It wasn't right to marry while there was a war on; the girl might end up a widow before she'd hardly been a wife. Besides, Daniel had plans for his life, and he needed a few years after the war was over to get going.

Maybe it hadn't been fair to start seeing Alice in the circumstances. He ought to tell her he had plans for the future that didn't include marriage for a few years. Maybe he would speak to her after his sister's wedding this weekend, make sure she understood it was just a casual thing.

* * *

'You do look lovely,' Emily said admiringly as she looked at Frances in her expensive satin wedding gown. 'That dress is a dream. It's a good thing you bought it when you did, you would never have found anything like it now.'

'I know.' Frances did a little twirl in front of the mirror. She'd bought her dress two months before war was officially declared. On a shopping trip to Cambridge, she'd seen it displayed in the window of an expensive dress shop in Regent Street and, on impulse, tried it on. It was a simple design of satin, but heavily embroidered with beads on the hem and sleeves, and the lace overskirt was exquisite. She'd known as soon as she saw herself in the mirror that it was the one she wanted. Marcus hadn't even asked her to marry him then, but she'd bought it anyway, just in case. It had been covered with a sheet and hung in her wardrobe ever since, and now it was her wedding day. 'At least that part of it fits with the dream, Emily,' she went on, looking at her sister once more. 'I always thought we would have a fantastic reception, with Dad giving me away at the church – and then a honeymoon in Paris.'

'Well, at least you are marrying the man you want,' Emily said. 'And he has six days' leave to take you away somewhere. The reception might not be all you'd hoped for, but everyone has done their best.'

Friends and family had baked and scrounged, and there was a decent buffet tea and some good wine from the cellars at Stretton Park.

'Oh, I'm not complaining,' Frances said, her eyes shining. 'I'm happy just to be marrying Marcus.'

'It must be wonderful to know exactly what you want and get it,' Emily said. 'I've never felt about anyone the way you do about Marcus.'

'You will one day,' Frances said, and kissed her cheek. 'I thought you rather liked Simon Vane. You're going to stay with his family after the wedding, aren't you?'

'Yes, I am. He asked me and I said I would, but I'm not

sure now that it was a good thing. After all, I don't really know him.'

'You must have got on very well together that afternoon or he wouldn't have asked.'

'I suppose not.' Emily wasn't sure why she'd suddenly got cold feet – after all, she'd enjoyed her afternoon out with Simon, and he'd made her go tingly all over when he kissed her. 'It's just that things have changed. I'll be going away somewhere when I get back, and everything seems... not the same any more. You won't be living here and—'

'Nor will you,' Frances reminded her. 'I wonder if Daniel has thought about that. If he stays here it will be just him and Margaret – and Connor, of course.'

'I hadn't thought about that,' Emily said. 'That is a bit awkward for him, isn't it? After all, this is his home – but you know how people talk.'

'Well, I suppose they are both sensible adults,' Frances said, dismissing the subject. She picked up the blue lace garter her sister had given her and slipped it on. 'So, there's my luck – the veil was Mum's so I've got them all; something old, something borrowed, something new and something blue.'

'You don't need luck,' Emily told her, and she squeezed her waist affectionately. 'Marcus loves you, you love him – what more do you need?'

'I don't know...' Frances felt as if a cold wind had blown over her suddenly and her tummy lurched. 'Wish me luck all the same, Emmy.'

'Of course I do,' Emily said. 'All the luck in the world, dearest. We had better go now or you'll be late.'

'I've only got to walk over the road.'

'You still don't want to be late. I saw Henry arrive ages

ago. He's pacing about over there like a cat on hot bricks; that must mean Marcus and his family are already inside.'

'I wanted to ask Daniel to give me away,' Frances said. 'But Henry expected it so I couldn't say no...' She sighed but neither sister said what was on their minds. 'We'd better go then.'

Emily walked up the aisle behind her sister. She was wearing a pale green silk dress that she'd bought in Cambridge especially for her sister's wedding. It wasn't really a bridesmaid's gown, but a pretty afternoon frock that would be more practical afterwards. With all the regulations and shortages these days, she had been lucky to find something that would answer both purposes.

Simon Vane was Marcus's best man and Emily her sister's only attendant. They stood side by side, Simon giving her a smile of welcome as she joined him at the start of the ceremony. The sun was filtering through the stained-glass windows, making patterns on the worn stone floor. It was a beautiful old church, peaceful and familiar. Emily was glad her sister had chosen the church and not gone for a register office affair, as so many did because of the way things were at the moment. It wasn't as lavish a wedding as it might have been, but there were flowers in the church, and all their friends were dressed in their best finery; a happy occasion. Except that her father wasn't there to give the bride away.

Emily smothered a sigh. There was no point in wishing for the moon. Her father had gone and there was no way she could bring him back. She glanced to the side, thinking how smart Daniel looked in his uniform. At least he was home, and beginning to feel better if she was any judge. She noticed that he was sitting with Clay and his wife. She had thought Alice might be with him.

Alice had been at the house all morning, helping to prepare the food, but she'd said she was coming to church and would leave when the ceremony was over to get back to the house and help out at the reception. If Daniel was going out with her – why wasn't she sitting with the family?

* * *

Daniel could smell Margaret's perfume. It was distinctive and expensive, and powerful. He knew she was sitting just behind him, and the sense of her was playing havoc with his libido. He was annoyed with himself, but images of her naked body kept coming into his mind. He had woken from an erotic dream the previous night, only to realise that the woman he had dreamed of was his father's widow. Now, when his sister was being married, all he could think of was how enticing he found Margaret's perfume.

Damn her! He was suspicious of her, especially since Henry had told him how much she was asking for her share of the land and the house. Apparently, she couldn't bear to live there now that Robert was dead, and she wanted them to buy the house from her, but she wasn't going to let them off cheap.

Henry was against the idea. 'Put the damned place on the market,' he'd said when they met that morning just before the wedding. 'That's what I told Clay we should do. I wouldn't give in to her blackmail – but she seems to have him eating out of her hand...'

Daniel glanced at his second eldest brother. Clay was the nearest to him in age, being just two years older. He had married young, probably because his wife Dorothy had already been carrying their first child. They now had three, one for each year of their marriage. Dot had been a very pretty girl before they married, but she had put on weight and she always looked harassed and a bit untidy these days, as though life was all too much for her.

Was Clay faithful to her? Daniel knew that his brother had had quite a reputation when he was younger, and he doubted that a few words said in church would prevent Clay from straying. He wondered if Henry was right... If Clay had been caught in Margaret's pretty claws...

It wouldn't surprise him if his brother fancied her. Daniel could understand that only too well. He was doing his best to shut out the images of her naked body and the smile in her eyes, which had seemed to invite, but Clay was different. Given the chance, had it been offered to him, what would his brother have made of it? He wouldn't have gone rushing from the room like a green youth, that was for certain. Daniel was pretty sure that Margaret would be unwise to play with Clay the way she had with him.

Clay glanced at him sideways, an odd expression in his eyes. Suddenly, Daniel knew that he too was aware of Margaret's perfume, and that everything Henry had told him was true. Clay was caught – but what was he hoping for? Surely he couldn't be thinking of leaving his wife and children. What then? Did he just want to get Margaret into bed – or was she already sleeping with him?

Something was going on, he felt it instinctively. Maybe he would have a word with Clay later...

* * *

Alice thought Frances looked beautiful, and her dress was a dream – the kind of wedding gown that every girl wanted but few got. Frances was so lucky, but then the family was rich, or so everyone thought in the village. Alice's mother had warned her about getting her hopes up too high only that morning when she'd told her that she was just going to slip into church and sit at the back on her own.

'Don't let that Searles lad turn your head, love,' Mrs Robinson had said, sensing Alice's hurt that Daniel hadn't asked her to sit with him in church. 'I know he's asked you out a couple of times, but that doesn't mean much. His brother Clay had a name for going with the girls, and look at him now. I pity the lass he married, a baby every year, and him... Well, I'm not one for gossip, but I wouldn't want you to be in the same case, Alice.'

'Daniel isn't like that,' Alice told her. 'He's nice, Mum, honestly.'

'Then why hasn't he asked you to sit with him today?'

'I don't know – perhaps because he knows I'm going to leave as soon as they go into the vestry so that I can get back to the house and help when the guests start arriving.'

'Because that's the way he sees you? As one of the hired help?'

'I do help out there,' Alice said sensibly. 'It doesn't matter to Daniel or me. I know he likes me a lot.'

'But does he love you – does he respect you?' Her mother gave her a straight look. 'I can't see him asking you to marry him, Alice, and that's a fact.'

'Maybe he doesn't want to get serious yet, Mum. There's a war on – and I'm young. You and Dad would say I was too young if he asked me, wouldn't you?'

'Yes, we probably would,' her mother admitted, and she smiled. 'I've nothing against Daniel, love. I just don't want to see him break your heart.'

'He might hurt me,' Alice said. 'But I shan't let him break my heart – besides, he isn't like that.'

'Have it your own way then.'

Alice had dismissed her mother's warnings, but inside she couldn't help feeling a little hurt that Daniel hadn't asked her to sit with him in the church. He could easily have waited for her, walked her over from the house, but he hadn't mentioned it, even though he'd said they might go out one day next week.

Was he using her to pass the time away while he was home? Was he only going out with her because he was bored? She hadn't thought he was like that, but it was a bit disappointing that he seemed to have drawn back. She had thought he was really interested at first, but now...

Alice became aware that the bride and groom were going into the vestry to sign their names. That was her cue to slip out and get back to the house. Millie was coping on her own for the moment, but she couldn't do it all.

Emily took her place next to the bride and groom for the photographs. There was an official man from the photographer's studio in Ely who everyone used for occasions like this, and several amateur ones snapping away with their box cameras. The photographer was asking for a picture with the bride and all her brothers now so Emily moved away, standing next to Simon.

'At least they've got a good day for it,' he said, glancing at her. 'You look lovely, Emily. I like that dress.'

'Yes, I was lucky,' she said. 'I think it's pre-war actually. They got it out for me from a back room. Frances and I have shopped there a lot in the past so I expect we get special treatment.'

'Yes, I thought it looked better than most of what's in the shops now.' He raised his brows at her. 'You are coming with me later, aren't you?'

'Yes, of course,' Emily said. She was feeling better about it now that she'd seen him again. Simon was very nice and she had been silly to get cold feet earlier. She didn't understand why she had felt reluctant to meet his family, because usually she enjoyed visiting. Her father had always encouraged her to stay with friends and she was certain he would have approved of Simon, because he came from a good family; after all, it wasn't as if she was going off alone with him. 'I'm looking forward to it, Simon.'

'Good. So am I... Oh, it looks as if Marcus needs me. I'd better see what he wants. We shall have plenty of time to talk later.'

'Yes, we shall,' Emily said, and she experienced a feeling of pleasurable anticipation. It would be rather nice to meet Simon's family and have a little holiday before she started her new job. She went over to stand by Daniel after the photographer moved on to the groom's family. 'I thought Alice might be with you in church, Dan?'

'Oh, did you?' Daniel gave her an odd look. 'Why was that?'

'Aren't you going out with her? I saw you together in Cambridge one afternoon and thought you might be courting.'

'We're friends, of course,' Daniel said. 'We've been out a couple of times – but she had to get back to the house to help with the food and things. Margaret was relying on her. I thought it might be awkward if she had to walk the whole of the church to get out so I didn't mention it.'

'Oh...' Emily was surprised. 'I thought it might have been more than just casual when I saw you out together. She's a lovely girl, Daniel – don't hurt her, will you?'

'I know Alice is a nice girl. I have no intention of hurting her.'

Daniel's eyes strayed to where Margaret was standing. Clay was next to her, whispering something in her ear. It was obvious to him that he was very interested in her – and glancing at Dorothy, he saw that she had noticed too. He would have to speak to his brother, warn him not to get too involved – and the same went for Daniel himself. Margaret was trouble. If she wanted her money, the best thing would be to pay her and let her go before she caused mayhem.

'I know you wouldn't do it intentionally,' Emily said. 'But if you ask her out several times she may think—'

'Yes, well, I shan't,' Daniel said a touch sharply. 'Just forget it, Emily. I'm not a child and I'm not a womaniser either.'

'No, of course not. I didn't mean... Sorry.'

Frances was beckoning to her and she left Daniel to see what her sister wanted, feeling a bit hurt. She hadn't been preaching to him, but it had probably sounded that way. It was just that she liked Alice a lot and felt it must have hurt her to be shut out of an affair like this, treated as if she were just the hired help.

Frances wanted to tell her that they were ready to go across the road now. 'Is my dress all right at the back?' she asked. 'It keeps blowing about and I think it may have got dirty on the hem at the back.'

Emily had a quick look and reassured her. 'No, no, it's

fine, but I'll carry the train for you as we go over the road, shall I?'

'Yes, please, love,' Frances said, and smiled at her. 'I should hate it to spoil.'

They were ready to make the move now. Because the house was so close, everyone waited for Frances and Marcus to walk down the church path and cross the road, and then they all joined in the procession, holding up the traffic. As the only vehicle on the road was a horse and cart driven by an old man, he was happy to sit and wait, grinning and waving to people he knew as they trooped behind the bride and groom. It was quite an occasion in the village and he would have something to tell his wife when he got home.

Alice was waiting in the front hall to take hats and coats and hang them away in the cloakroom. Emily gave her a special smile, determined to slip into the kitchen and have a word with her before she left. But then everything started to happen at once, and she forgot about Alice as the speeches got under way.

Simon was very funny, teasing both bride and groom with wicked hints about the groom's reputation, and Henry made a short speech about Marcus being a lucky man. Marcus replied in kind. And then they were having the toasts, everyone tucking into the sandwiches, little pastry cases filled with chicken and a creamy sauce, and sausage rolls that made up the bulk of the buffet meal. It wasn't as lavish as Frances would have had in normal times, but they had managed very well. Someone had found some tinned fruit and jelly, and Emily noticed that Connor was helping himself for a second time, smiling to herself. If she knew anything, the extra portion was for his friend Peter. She went over to him and asked if he was enjoying himself.

'Yeah, it's all right,' he said. 'Frances looks pretty and so do you, Emily. I shall miss you when you go away.'

'I'll miss you too,' Emily said. 'But you'll be all right with Daniel and Margaret, won't you?'

'Dunno,' he said, and scowled. 'I could go and stay with Henry if I want, when Dan goes back to his unit, anyway. He told me that just now.'

'Well, I suppose you might,' Emily said, feeling a bit guilty. She hadn't considered Connor when she'd been asked if she would transfer somewhere else. 'It would mean you had a bit further to come to school, of course.'

'It's better than being with her on my own.'

Emily nodded, ruffled his hair and walked off to speak to Henry. He seemed to be having a bit of an argument with Clay, but they broke off as she approached and Clay went to join his wife, who had her eldest child on her lap and was feeding her a piece of cold chicken with her fingers.

'Connor was telling me you have asked him to stay with you?'

'Well, he may not be able to stay here much longer anyway. It depends on Margaret...'

'What do you mean?'

'The house is half hers if she wants to sell,' Henry said. 'And it seems she does, sooner than we can manage it. We may have to put it on the market.'

'Sell the house? But where shall we live?' Emily was stunned by his announcement. 'You can't, Henry. It's our home.'

'It was when Dad was around,' he said gruffly. 'Now it's just a house. I don't want it and nor does Clay – I couldn't afford it, not at her price anyway. Besides, you will be away most of the time, and you'll probably get married soon. You can stay with one of us if you need to, Emily. We'll manage somehow, I suppose.'

'Manage somehow?' Emily felt as if the ground had fallen away from beneath her feet. She hadn't expected this – to lose the home she'd known all her life. It made everything that much worse. 'Do we have to sell, Henry? What about Daniel and Connor? It's their home too. Surely we can keep it?'

'We're having a meeting soon,' Henry said. 'We'll know better then – but Connor will be all right with me. You and Daniel will find something, I expect.'

'Yes, if we have to,' she agreed, and walked away feeling pretty miserable. What was she going to do if there was no home to come back to? It had always been there, just as her father had been there for her, and now everything was different. She felt lost and lonely.

'Marcus says they are off in a few minutes,' Simon said. 'Your sister is going up to change out of her dress. We could leave as soon as they've gone – couldn't we?'

'Yes, why not?' Emily said. The mood she was in at the moment, she would be glad to get away. What she had expected to be a happy day had gone horribly wrong for her. 'Yes, all right. I'll go up to Frances now and say goodbye, and then we'll leave as soon as she's gone.'

She smiled at him, then ran up the stairs to her sister's room. Frances was struggling with her gown and turned to her sister with a look of relief. 'I was hoping you would come,' she said. 'Can you unhook me at the back, please?'

'Yes, of course,' Emily said, and started to unfasten the dress. She wanted to ask if Frances knew about the house, but decided not to cast a shadow over things. Frances would be back in Stretton in a week, and so would she. They could talk about it then. 'Has Marcus told you where you're going?'

'No, it's a surprise,' Frances told her. 'But I think it's down south somewhere – probably Devon I should think. I know Marcus likes it that way, and we had a holiday in Torquay with Dad once – do you remember?'

'Yes, of course,' Emily said. 'It was a couple of years after Mum died and we all went – Daniel and Connor too. Connor was just a toddler.'

'Marcus was there with his family. We all met up a couple of times. I think it was that summer I first knew I wanted to marry him.'

'Well, you have now,' Emily said. 'So be happy, love.'

'I intend to be,' Frances said, and hugged her. 'I shall be living with Marcus's family until we get a house of our own. Marcus has told me to keep an eye out and let him know if there's anything going that might be suitable.'

Emily hesitated and then decided to say nothing. It wasn't official yet. Besides, Rathmere might not be what Marcus was looking for.

When Frances was dressed in her outfit and going away hat, she kissed Emily again and then followed her downstairs. Frances threw her bouquet. She aimed it at Emily but she let it go by her and one of the other young girls stretched out and caught it.

Simon came to her as soon as her sister and Marcus had left, and she nodded, picked up her suitcase and let him usher her out of the house. She didn't bother to say goodbye to anyone. She had forgotten that she wanted to talk to Alice, and she wasn't in the mood to speak to the rest of her family. It wasn't fair that they had all known what was going on or that she had been left in the dark until now. It seemed that she was to have no say in the decision; they were going to present her with the results of their meeting and she had to accept whatever was decided.

'Cheer up, Emily,' Simon said as he heard her sigh. 'It won't be that bad, I promise. My family will love you.'

'Oh, it wasn't that,' she said, and looked at him apologetically. 'I've just discovered that my brothers and stepmother are probably going to sell the house.'

'Does that mean you'll be homeless?'

'I've been told I can stay with one of them when I need to, but it won't be the same.'

'Not a very bright prospect,' Simon agreed, and frowned. 'Never mind, Emily. You won't be there much in future. You can probably find somewhere to share with friends wherever they post you.'

'Yes, I expect so,' she said, and smiled. 'I'll face that when I have to – but I'm glad I'm coming with you today. I'm out of sorts with my family and that's the truth.'

'It's often like this when stepmothers or divorce comes into a family,' Simon said. 'My parents were divorced when I was young, but my stepmother is great. I get on well with her – all the family does.'

'I didn't know your parents were divorced. Do you see your mother at all?'

'Not often. It caused a terrible scandal at the time. She went off with an American millionaire. My father sued him for enticement and won; it cost the American a packet, but that was ages ago – and he could afford it.'

'It must have been upsetting at the time.'

'It was I suppose.' Simon shrugged. 'I remember feeling sorry for my father. He cried a lot and had a bit of a breakdown, I think. I blamed my mother. I still do, though she says that he was impossible to live with...'

'It's very sad,' Emily said, and looked at him curiously. 'Do you have any brothers or sisters?'

'No brothers, one sister; she is married now,' Simon told her. 'Vanessa's husband is something in the War Office – a fusty old devil but rich and clever. We don't see much of them. I don't particularly want to, personally. Her tongue is pretty sharp.'

'How old is your stepmother?'

'About the same age as yours I would think,' Simon replied with a slight frown. 'But a very different type. Amelia is horsey, not a bit flighty or sexy. I think Father wanted to make certain he didn't get a bolter this time.'

Emily nodded but made no comment. She knew what he meant about Margaret – there was something about her. She had suspected for ages that Clay was attracted, and she wasn't sure how Daniel felt. She had noticed him looking at Margaret a few times recently, but he wasn't as easy to read as Clay.

Emily was under no illusions about Clay. She knew that there was talk about him and various women, that Dorothy suspected him of having affairs, and she was pretty sure that he fancied his stepmother. And that was an awful thing to think! She shut her mind against it at once. Clay wouldn't do anything like that with his father's widow... Would he?

She wasn't going to think about any of them for the next few days, Emily decided. She was with Simon, who was very nice and whom she liked a lot. She was going to enjoy herself and let the future sort itself out.

* * *

'Did Emily say goodbye to you?' Margaret asked Daniel a little later that evening. 'I saw her go but she didn't even nod in my direction.'

'No, she didn't say goodbye to any of us,' Daniel replied. 'I think I upset her earlier.'

'Well, I think that is very rude of her,' Margaret said, and looked annoyed. 'I am going away for a few days myself and it's awkward, but there, if she can't be bothered to speak to me, she will have to fend for herself.'

'I shall be here,' Daniel said. 'When are you leaving?'

'Tomorrow. A friend of mine is picking me up, and we're going on to a party at the house of mutual friends.'

'I see – well, that takes care of a few questions I wanted to ask, but there are others. When should we expect you back?'

'Why?'

'I've been told you want to sell your share of the house, and we need to discuss it, Margaret. I'm afraid we can't pay what you want. You will probably have to accept less.'

'But it's worth every penny,' she said, and looked annoyed. 'I've had it valued so I know.'

'You may have had it valued, but try selling it at the moment,' Daniel said. 'It could take years to sell – but if you're prepared to wait, of course, you might get a better price.'

'What does Clay say about this?'

'Clay is only one. There are three of us – and Connor and the girls, of course. We have to think about them.'

'I shan't sell cheaply...' Her eyes glittered angrily.

'Think about it while you're away. I think we could manage half of what you've asked.'

'Three thousand – that's paltry!'

'Six thousand is about what we could get at this time,

and that's being generous. Twelve is out of the question. Even Stretton Park isn't worth that at the moment.'

'It's ridiculous,' Margaret said, and then hesitated. 'I'm sure Robert never intended that I should be made homeless.'

'No one is stopping you staying on here as long as you like,' Daniel said. 'But if you want to sell that's as much as we can manage. We can put the house on the market if you like, but it may take a few years. People aren't buying property much at the present, in case the Germans bomb it.'

'In this village?' She arched her brows mockingly.

'We have the aerodrome here, don't forget,' Daniel said. 'Maybe we've been lucky so far but we can't be sure it will last. The raids could start at any time. Hitler has only just got started. He will invade if he can and that means they'll bomb us, whenever and wherever they choose.'

'They might attack the aerodrome perhaps,' Margaret said. 'I know they had a couple of scares at the beginning, but it's been quiet since then.'

'The Germans have had Dunkirk to think about,' Daniel said. 'Give them time and you'll see what happens...'

'I'll think about what you've said,' Margaret agreed. 'What about my share of the land?'

'The same principle applies,' Daniel told her. 'We can't afford what you're asking, Margaret.'

'You could take a loan from the bank.'

'Henry says we already have. I'll know more after the meeting with the lawyers this week. I'll let you know then what our terms are.'

'Supposing I'm not satisfied?'

'You're only one shareholder,' Daniel reminded her. 'We must buy from you if you insist on selling but the value is low at the moment I'm afraid. If you want to sell you must understand that things are difficult just now.'

Margaret looked into his face and saw Robert's uncompromising stare. Daniel was very much like his father – and she had made a mistake that day in the bathroom.

'Excuse me,' Daniel said. 'I have to see someone.'

He turned his back on her, making his way to the kitchen. If he was lucky he would be in time to catch Alice before she left. He wanted to apologise to her. Emily had been right; he should have asked her to sit with him in church.

He'd been brooding on Margaret for a few days, but he was over it now. She might be the most sensual woman he'd ever met, but she was a scheming bitch and he was determined not to get caught by her as his fool of a brother so obviously was.

4

_____

Emily gasped as she saw the house for the first time. It was huge, a manor house of some kind, probably centuries old, she thought, and completely different from what she had been expecting. The grounds surrounding it were extensive and very beautiful, as was the house itself. The stone used in the building was a gorgeous Cotswold yellow and had faded to soft beige in parts over time. One wing of it overlooked a courtyard; another looked towards a lake; and the main section faced a landscaped park that seemed to stretch on into the distance for ever.

She turned to look at Simon in stunned disbelief. 'Is this really your home?'

'Yes. It's rather a shock, isn't it?' he said, grinning. 'I suppose I ought to have warned you, but some people are put off if I tell them it's a stately home.'

'It's the kind of thing you pay money to go and look at,' Emily said. 'I had no idea...'

'We don't do tours at the moment,' Simon replied with a wry smile. 'If Father goes mad and loses all the money we might have to one day. I know quite a few of his friends are thinking along that line for after the war.'

'Oh, I hope he won't,' Emily said. 'It's such a lovely place, Simon. I'm sure you would hate to have people gawping all the time.'

'I don't think I'd mind so much, but Father would hate it – and Amelia wouldn't like it either.' He smiled at her. 'Come in and meet them, Emily – and don't worry, they don't bite.'

'No, I'm sure they don't,' she said, but she was feeling a bit nervous as she got out of the car and walked with him to the door.

Inside, the hall was vast and echoing, but Simon hurried her through it to a small parlour at the back of the house. This was furnished in shades of green with pretty satinwood furniture and had French windows, and was much more welcoming than the echoing hall. The windows were open and she could see a lawn where chairs and tables had been set out, and a maid in a black dress and white apron and cap was serving Sunday afternoon tea.

As they approached, a woman got up and came to meet with them with a cry of delight. 'So here you are at last,' she said. 'We were beginning to wonder where you had got to, Simon.'

'Remember I told you it was Emily's sister's wedding yesterday? We came down by easy stages, having lunch at Winchester. Emily hasn't been down this way before and she wanted to stop and look at the view a couple of times.'

'And this is Emily?' The woman smiled and then leaned forward to kiss her cheek. 'How lovely you are. We were so pleased when Simon said he was bringing a friend, because he doesn't – if you see what I mean? I'm Amelia, of course, and my husband is just over here – Lord Vane, but just call him Vane, Emily. Everyone does.'

Another thing Simon had neglected to tell her. But it didn't matter what a person was called, of course, even if they were members of the aristocracy. It was the way they behaved, that's what her father had always said, and she crossed her fingers behind her back, hoping it was true. Her nerves had been calmed somewhat by Amelia's welcome, and by her appearance. She was certainly not beautiful, and she looked horsey, dressed as she was in jodhpurs and a worn tweed jacket, which smelled slightly of horses and leather.

Lord Vane was white-haired, and looked older than his wife by a good many years, his face lined and his eyes a rather tired blue, but when he smiled he looked younger.

'So here we are then,' he said, and he held his hand out to her, grasping hers firmly in a strong grip. 'We are very pleased to meet you, Emily. I had begun to think you had changed your mind, both of you – but never mind, you are here now.'

'We couldn't drive all the way last night, Father,' Simon said. 'We stayed at the hotel you always use when you break your journey to town. Separate rooms of course so you need not be shocked. Besides, everything is different these days. Women are doing men's jobs and they need to be more independent, don't they, darling?' He smiled at her. 'Emily was a bit anxious about what people might think at first but it was all very proper. They had a dinner dance at the hotel and we enjoyed it – didn't we, Emily? This is a holiday for her. We don't want to spend it all with you in this mouldering old ruin.'

'Oh, you mustn't say that,' Emily cried, shocked until she

saw that his father was amused. 'I see, you're only teasing. I think it's a beautiful house, sir. I'm very flattered to have been asked to stay. And it was all very respectable at the hotel...' She blushed, because perhaps she had been reckless; she hardly knew Simon but he had treated her almost like a sister, calming any fears she might have had.

'I am sure it was – and it's Vane to you, girl – and we're the ones who are honoured to have Simon's friend to stay. He doesn't bring many girls home, you know – says the sight of this place scares them all to death. They don't want to be forced into running it one day. Amelia says it's a job and a half, don't you, old girl?'

'It would be if I let it take me over,' Amelia said. 'But my horses keep me sane. What about you, Emily – do you ride?'

'I have done, just ponies and some of the farm horses,' Emily said, 'but nothing since I grew out of my pony. I was away at school for a while and then the war started. Father talked about getting me a horse but it didn't happen.'

'I'm sure I can mount you while you're here – if you would like that?'

'Yes, though I'm not sure how good I'll be.'

'Oh, I'll soon get you back into it,' Amelia told her with a satisfied look. 'Vane will try to monopolise you, of course, get you interested in his project – but don't let him.'

'For goodness' sake, we shall only be here a couple of days!' Simon told them. 'I want a little time with Emily myself. She has to get back to work by Friday afternoon, and my leave finishes on Saturday.'

'Well, we'll be glad to have you for as long as you can spare us,' Amelia said. 'The whole family is coming to dinner tonight, Simon. We thought we'd do things in style for once, as it's a special occasion.'

'It will be a wonder if Emily doesn't decide to cut and run,' Simon said, and looked at her apologetically. 'Sorry. I thought this was just an informal visit. I'm afraid you are going to get the royal treatment.'

Emily had bent down to pat one of the three spaniel dogs who had come nosing around her to see what was going on. She smiled, feeling very much at home, and not in the least put off at the thought of meeting his whole family. If they were all as pleasant as his father and stepmother she wouldn't mind staying here for much longer than a few days.

'I don't mind,' she said. 'You are lucky to have a family who go to so much trouble for your sake, Simon. I think it's all rather sweet.'

'Oh, well.' Simon flopped down in one of the basket chairs, making a fuss of the nearest dog. 'As long as you don't mind, bring on the troops. I dare say my aunts will bore you to death, and Vanessa will lecture us all, but we're used to it. You are the one who has to put up with it all.'

Emily laughed. She wondered why she had been nervous about coming here. It was exactly what she needed to soothe her bruised feelings. For the first time since her father's death, she was conscious of being at peace with herself and her surroundings.

'Daniel and I are in agreement on this,' Henry said, and stared at Clay angrily. 'She's asking far too much, and we just can't afford to pay it at the moment. Six thousand for her half of the house and another fourteen for her share of the land—'

'I'll buy the land in Chatteris Fen,' Clay said, surprising

him. 'If we get it valued it should almost cover what
Margaret is asking for her share of the land. I'll take my
share out and pay you the rest. You can borrow a bit if you
have to, surely? If you don't want to buy her out of the house
sell it to someone else. Sam Danby will probably buy it for
Marcus. He told me he was looking for something for him –
and it's the best house around. Danby has always had his eye
on it.'

'Where will you get the money to buy that land?' Henry
was staring at him in disbelief. 'It's a big chunk of cash, Clay.'

'So what?' Clay stared him down. 'I've got a bit put by
and I'll mortgage the rest. You can buy whatever else I've got
shares in off me if you like, take it off the money for the land
I want and make it up to her yourselves.'

'Are you saying you want out altogether?' Daniel looked
at him hard. 'How long has this been coming on?'

'A long time,' Henry muttered, clearly annoyed by Clay's
manner as much as his words. 'He argued with Dad for
months over every little thing – didn't agree with anything I
wanted to do on the land. Maybe it's best if he does cut and
run. We don't need him.'

'I thought you said that land in Chatteris Fen was the
best we own?'

'It is,' Henry said, 'but if he wants out, good riddance to
him!'

'I'll stick with you in the rest if you want,' Clay said. 'But I
want a farm and business of my own. If I don't buy the land
you'll have to sell anyway. You can't pay her without – can
you?'

'Not the way things are,' Henry said. 'But if we all stick
together we can force her to wait for a year or two.'

'No,' Daniel said. 'She's trouble for the family. Pay her

and let her go back where she came from, Henry. We're better off without her.'

'But...' Henry sighed. Without Daniel's support he couldn't hold out against Clay and he knew it. 'Clay is agreeing with her so that he can get the Chatteris land. We can't pay her unless we sell, and he wants it.'

'Of course,' Clay said, and grinned. 'She thinks I'm going along with her just to get into her knickers – the tart. I wouldn't mind having a bit of that if it's going, but it's the land I want. Well, what is your verdict? I spoke to the lawyer and he says she's entitled to her money if she wants it.'

Daniel looked at his brother with disgust. He could see that Henry was against the idea, but there was no point in trying to hang on to Clay if he wanted out. He would buy land on his own anyway, and there was no doubt that his money would see them out of a hole.

'I think we should let Clay have the land he wants,' he said. 'We'll pay Margaret nine thousand for the land and three for the house – that's twelve altogether. That way we keep the house in the family.'

'I'll want my share allowed against the land I'm buying,' Clay said. 'I won't push you for more at the moment. I can wait for anything I've got coming out of the other land.'

'If you're out, you're out,' Henry said. 'We'll get it all valued and borrow what we have to, settle it now and be done with it – are you in agreement, Dan?'

'If it's what you want,' Daniel said. 'Connor knows some-thing is up. He said he'll go along with anything I say – and the girls will do the same. They both have small trust funds. They will have to wait until we're making money again for anything else. Besides, Frances doesn't need it now she's married, and Emily won't complain.'

'I think we should sell the house to Samuel Danby,' Henry said. 'But if you want to keep it we'll hang on for as long as we can.'

'It's Connor's home and Emily's until she marries, and mine. I might buy the rest of you out when I come out of the Army – and I'll give Clay his share of the house now. So that needn't come into the land deal at all.'

'Well, if you want it that's different,' Henry said, looking relieved. 'I suppose we can manage to borrow a bit...'

'I'm sure we can,' Daniel said, and gave Clay a straight look. 'Be careful of her. You may think you're in control but she's trouble.'

Clay laughed and looked superior. 'You may find her too much to handle, but she's no bother to me, little brother. I intend to have my money's worth there before I'm done, don't you worry.'

'Don't forget who she is,' Henry said, and looked angry.

'She never cared a damn for the old man,' Clay said, and glared at his elder brother. 'I intend to make her pay for that – and a few other things. She thinks she's got me on a string, but she'll discover her mistake when I'm ready. If she'd behaved like a proper wife and looked after him, he might still be here.'

'Fat lot you care,' Henry muttered, and gave a shout of alarm as Clay lunged at him. 'Don't be bloody daft!'

'Leave it be,' Daniel said, catching hold of Clay's coat and dragging him back. His brothers were behaving like a pair of overgrown schoolboys. 'All we need is to quarrel between ourselves. We've got it sorted now, let's not make waves.'

'Dad went by the old ways,' Clay said fiercely. 'I wanted to break out and do something different – but that doesn't mean I didn't care. It doesn't mean I wanted him to die.'

'Of course you didn't,' Daniel said, and looked at Henry. 'Don't be daft, man. Clay didn't want him dead. Someone should have made him see the doctor sooner, but it's over now – we can't bring him back.'

'It just makes me sick... All of this,' Henry muttered. 'Why should that bitch have anything from us? She was only his wife for a few months. She gets away with a small fortune and we're left to pick up the pieces.'

'That isn't the point,' Daniel said. 'Dad made the will and we have to stick to it – she gets twelve thousand and not a penny more. Are we agreed?'

'Yes,' Clay said, agreeing instantly because it was to his advantage. 'I'll arrange the money for the land I want and get things moving there.'

'And I'll pay you your share of the house,' Daniel said. 'I'll get the money from the bank and you can sign a release over to me.'

'Well, I'm off then,' Clay said, clearly well satisfied with his day's work. 'I'll see you around...'

Henry sat staring moodily ahead of him as Clay went out, closing the door behind him with a snap. 'I'm glad you want the house, Dan,' he said. 'But he's got the best of it with that land, I'm telling you.'

'It was the best way out. He wanted the Chatteris land and nothing else would do. You know we couldn't sell very easily elsewhere, which would have meant borrowing all of it from the bank – and you said we couldn't do that at the moment.'

'We can't,' Henry said. 'We might have had to sell to pay her out if she forced us – but I wouldn't have sold that land if I could help it.'

'We can buy some more fen land when things get better.'

'Maybe,' Henry said, and stood up. 'They had us over a barrel between them, Dan. I wouldn't mind betting that Clay put her up to it in the first place. Told her to ask too much for a start, knowing we would have to negotiate.'

'Father bought me a couple of fields on the road to Ely,' Daniel said, and frowned. 'They've got a mortgage on them. I think it would be best if they were put down to grass while I'm away. You can use them for stock feed until I come home.'

'All right, it will save us hiring,' Henry said. 'You should have rent though...'

'It doesn't matter until I get home for good. I can just about pay the mortgage. I don't know what I want to do with them – I might sell after the war, but we'll hang on to them until then.' He smiled at his brother. 'Don't worry too much, Henry. Things will turn out all right, you'll see – this is just a temporary setback.'

'Well, it means we shan't have to borrow more than five or six thousand pounds,' Henry said. 'I suppose we have to be grateful for that.'

Daniel nodded, walking his brother to the door. He frowned as Henry went off in his battered old truck. With the best land sold off to Clay, and a loan of £6,000, Henry was going to have his work cut out to keep things going while Daniel was away. He wondered where all the money had gone. There had always been plenty when he was a lad, and he hadn't dreamed things had been steadily getting worse and worse.

A few more bad years and they could end up losing everything.

* * *

'I'm afraid that's the way it is, Alice. The farm is in worse shape than I imagined, though I'd rather you didn't say anything to anyone else.'

'Of course I shan't, Dan,' she said. 'But I'm not sure why you are telling me this?'

'Because I wanted you to understand why I can't think of getting married for years. I wouldn't anyway, not while there's a war going on...' Daniel saw the look of hurt in her eyes and almost wished the words unsaid. 'But the situation with the farm makes it worse. I shall need to work hard when I get home – put a bit of money by. I don't want to be stuck with a growing family and no money...' She flinched and turned away. 'No, Alice. I didn't mean it to sound like that... I really like you, and one day...' Her eyes met his and he smiled. 'If you haven't found someone you like better than me by then...'

'I don't think that will happen,' Alice said. 'Besides, I'm too young to get married yet...'

'Well, that's all right then,' he said and sighed with relief. 'As long as you understand...'

Emily thought the house was empty when she got back that Thursday evening. She invited Simon in for a drink, but although he hesitated, he shook his head, kissing her softly on the mouth.

'It's late, my darling,' he said, 'and the way I'm feeling right now I should probably end up seducing you. I want to wait – and I want you to promise to think about what I asked you. You will, won't you?'

'Yes, of course,' she said, and reached up to touch his

cheek. 'It was a lovely visit, Simon. I liked your family a lot, you know I did – and I feel something more than liking for you. It's just a bit soon for me.'

She had found everything a little overwhelming. Simon's family's friendliness had been fantastic, but there was no doubting it was a very different world. If she married Simon it would take a lot of getting used to, staying in a house like that sometimes, even though she had enjoyed every moment of her visit. It was lovely for a few days, but she wasn't sure about living in a house like that; the way his family lived was very different to what she was used to.

'Yes, I know I rushed you,' Simon said, and gave her an apologetic smile. 'But I'm sure you're the girl for me – and I wanted to tell you before someone else got in first.'

'Oh, Simon, that isn't likely to happen. Really, I don't go out with many men – just in a group sometimes. I've never had a serious boyfriend before you.'

'But you are serious about me – and you will think about getting married quite soon?'

'Yes, I shall think about it,' Emily said. 'I do like you an awful lot – I might even be in love with you – but I need a little more time.' His proposal had taken her breath away. He had come out with it casually as they were driving back from his father's house. She had laughed, thinking he was joking, but he'd stopped the car in a lay-by, turning to look at her.

'I wasn't joking, Emily. I want to marry you.'

'But you can't – you don't know me.'

'I know that you are beautiful, inside and out. I really care for you – and, as my father told you, I don't often take an interest in girls.' He reached out to touch her face. 'You are sweet and lovely and I should like you to be my wife.'

Emily had been so surprised she'd told him she would

think about it. She was still thinking about it, because it all seemed so sudden. She hardly knew him, but things were different somehow, because of the war or her father's death and her sister's marriage. The world she had known was changing and she needed something to hang onto in shifting sands. Before the war she probably wouldn't have gone to stay with Simon and his family and she wouldn't have dreamed of staying overnight in a hotel, even in separate rooms – but there was an urgency to life these days. She wasn't the only girl doing things that would once have shocked their families.

'I think we should write – get to know each other better,' she said, breaking her silence.

'That's all I can expect just yet,' Simon said. 'I'll write often and ring you when I can – once you let me know where you are. You will do that, won't you?'

'Just as soon as I can,' Emily promised. 'Are you sure you don't want to come in?'

'No, I think I'll get off,' Simon said, and kissed her once more. 'I have a call to make before I go back to my base. I'll expect your letter very soon, Emily – and don't forget me.'

'I shan't, believe me – and thank you for the holiday. It was lovely.'

Emily let herself in at the back door. There were no lights or music. Margaret always had the gramophone or the wireless on if she was here alone, so perhaps she was out somewhere. She was walking up the stairs, singing very softly to herself, when Daniel came out of his bedroom.

'You're home then,' he said, and smiled at her. 'Did you enjoy yourself?'

'Yes, thank you, very much. Daniel, I—'

'I want to apologise, Emmy,' he said before she could

finish. 'I was sharp with you at the wedding and I shouldn't have been. You were perfectly right about Alice sitting with me in church – but I've talked to her now and we've sorted things out.'

'What do you mean?'

'Let's go down and make a cup of tea,' Daniel said. 'I'll explain. There are quite a few things you need to know.'

'Yes, all right,' she said, and turned to follow him down. He filled the kettle himself and set it on the range to boil, so Emily fetched the tray and a jug of milk from the pantry, as well as a few biscuits. 'Go on then, tell me the worst.'

Daniel smiled at her wryly. 'I thought you'd know something was going on so I'll tell you everything. Margaret wants her share of the land and the house. We couldn't afford to buy her out at the moment, because there's no money in the bank. Actually, we're in debt, but that's not the point. Clay has offered to buy the land in Chatteris Fen, and we've accepted his offer. We can then buy Margaret out of the land, and the house – and still keep it. I'm going to pay Clay his share from the house and then I may buy it after the war. Henry isn't too pleased about sacrificing some of the land, but we can buy more when things recover.'

'So we can stay here?' Emily felt relief sweep over her. 'It's not that I shall be here much, but it's nice knowing it's here to come back to, Dan.'

'That's what I thought. But when Margaret goes we shall have to make some sort of arrangement for Connor. I thought we might let Frances and Marcus have it on a temporary lease, providing that it remains our family home and Connor stays on.'

'Yes, that sounds good. It would suit Frances, I know. She

doesn't really want to live with Marcus's family, but she didn't have much alternative.'

'None of us will get anything other than the trust funds, which don't amount to much, but until we get on our feet again things will be tight. I'm going to be honest with you and tell you that if Henry can't pull the business round we could lose everything.'

'Oh, Dan! Are things really so bad?'

'Yes. It came as a bit of a shock to me too. It means we're all going to have to be careful with money for a while. If Clay hadn't bought the land in Chatteris Fen the bank might have foreclosed, but we should weather the storm now – if we're careful.'

'I don't need anything,' Emily said. 'I'm going to be paid a bigger allowance from the Fire Service when I'm moved, and I have a little of Grandmother's legacy left so I'm fine.'

'I knew you wouldn't complain. We've got to watch the pennies, Emmy. Otherwise we could still go under.'

'I never knew the farm was in trouble. No wonder Dad looked so miserable those last few weeks.'

'I dare say he had a lot to worry about.' Daniel wasn't going to tell her about Clay. She didn't need to know and the less said the better. 'So that's that side of it – and now I'll tell you my side of things. I've already explained to Alice.' He tried not to remember the disappointment he'd seen in Alice's face when he'd told her he couldn't marry for a few years.

'What do you mean you explained?' Emily asked, breaking into his thoughts.

'I told her that I like her a lot – I might even feel more than that – but I can't marry for a few years. I wouldn't while there's a war on, because it wouldn't be fair to her, and afterwards I want to get on a bit, make some money. It's even more important now that we're in trouble with the land.'

Emily nodded, looking thoughtful. 'It isn't really my business, Daniel. I just thought you should be fair to Alice.'

'Well, she knows how I feel now, and she says she understands. We're going to see each other as close friends, but if she wants to see someone else while I'm away that's up to her. I don't want to work on the land when I come home, Emily.'

'Not work on the land?' Emily was surprised in a way, but in another she had sort of expected this. 'What do you want to do then?'

'I want to set up a garage for myself,' Daniel said. 'I've always been good with mechanical things. You know I helped Dad keep the traction engine running for the farm, and I'm good with trucks, cars – anything that has an engine. I've improved my skills since I've been in the Army, done a course with them as part of my training.'

'I suppose it's a good idea,' Emily said, a bit doubtfully, and he laughed.

'I don't intend to be a grease monkey all my life, Emily. I shall start out that way and then move into selling cars. If I can buy second-hand vehicles, do them up, respray and then sell them on, I'm sure I can make money.'

'You seem to have it all planned,' Emily said, and smiled at him affectionately. 'I hope it works out for you, Daniel. Will you sell your share of the land after the war?'

'Not unless Henry is in a position to buy,' he said. 'No, I'll keep my share of it and help out with the accounts. I'm better at that than Henry – but I shan't work on the land.'

'But you want this house?'

'If I can manage it,' Daniel said. 'If the worst comes to the worst we may have to sell, but not just yet.'

'I think Marcus's father might buy it,' Emily said. 'But I would rather you had it if you can manage to keep it, Dan.'

'Well, we'll see how things go. I've got a few pounds put by.'

Emily nodded as he made the tea and brought the pot to the table. Daniel was her favourite brother apart from Connor, and she knew he'd worked hard for what he had, and of course they had all been left a little money; the girls from their maternal grandmother, the boys from Grandfather Searles. Except Connor, who hadn't been born when his grandfather died. She'd always expected their father would put that right, but it seemed he'd waited too long. Connor was the only one who didn't have anything, except some shares in the land – land that was already mortgaged and might have to be sold if things didn't go well.

'What about Connor?' she asked. 'Does he know how things stand?'

'I've told him but he doesn't seem bothered,' Daniel said, and frowned. 'I've got a couple of fields along Ely Road, Emily. I've told Henry to put them down to grass while I'm away. There's a small mortgage on them, but if I can manage to hang on to them I'll probably give them to Connor when he leaves school.'

'That won't be for a while,' she said. 'I'll help you with the mortgage if I can. We'll do it together for Connor – if that's what you really want?'

'Leave it to me for the moment. I'll ask if I get stuck.' He smiled at her. 'And now – tell me about your visit. What were Mr Vane's parents like?'

'You'll never guess,' Emily said, and giggled. 'They live in a huge country house, more like a manor house except that the moat was grassed over long ago and banked with roses. And his father is Lord Vane – Vane to his friends, and me.'

Daniel's brows rose. 'Is the house falling down about their ears or are they rich?'

'Rich, actually,' Emily said, her cheeks pink. 'But very, very nice. They all made a fuss of me, because Simon doesn't take girlfriends home apparently – and he asked me to think about marrying him.'

'Good grief! You've only just met him, Emily. It's far too soon to think about getting married.' Daniel frowned at her. He hadn't objected to her going to stay with Simon's family, because the Vanes were respectable people, but now he wondered if he ought to have stopped her. It was just that with the war and everything he wouldn't be around much and Emily was old enough to choose how she wanted to spend her life.

'Yes, I know, that's what I told Simon, but he still wants me to think about it. He says we could get engaged on my birthday in October, and then marry at Christmas.'

'Is that what you want?'

'I don't know,' she said, and shook her head as his brows went up. 'I was very happy staying there, Daniel. They are such lovely people.'

'It's Simon you're marrying, not his family.'

'I know...' She sighed. 'I like him a lot and he makes me feel... sort of excited. You know what I mean?'

'Yes, I know exactly. I hope you haven't been carried away by all this excitement?'

Emily laughed. 'You don't need to become the heavy-handed brother, Dan. I'm not stupid, and I shan't get caught in that trap, I promise you. I might decide to get engaged on my birthday – after all, I shall be nineteen by then.'

'A great age,' Daniel said, and ate the last of the biscuits. 'But if you really want to get married I shan't try to stop you – not that I'm the one you have to persuade. I suppose Henry is your guardian now.' He sighed. 'I wish Father hadn't died. Everything seems to have fallen apart... The family, I mean.'

'Yes, I know. As for being my guardian, Henry would do whatever you say. You must know that,' Emily said. 'Not that you have to worry for the moment. I shan't do anything foolish.'

'I'm glad to hear it,' Daniel said. 'I'm going to the pub now – want to come?'

'Thanks, but I've got a few things I need to get ready. I report back for work tomorrow and then I shall be moving to my new posting.'

'Any idea where that will be yet?'

'It could be anywhere,' Emily said. 'I shall just have to wait and see when I report in tomorrow.'

'Good luck then. I shall miss seeing you when you go.'

'I shall miss you too. What are you going to do with yourself?'

'I thought I'd go through the farm accounts for Henry, and then I'll tinker about with some of the machinery. I saw a car for sale in the local paper the other day. I might buy that and start working on it. Henry says there's an empty barn I can use for anything I like at the farm.'

'Well, you won't have time to miss me by the sound of it,' Emily said. 'Good night then, have a nice time.'

'I'll see you before you leave,' Daniel said. 'Connor is at his friend's house for the night. So don't worry about him.'

Emily nodded, rising to swill the cups under the

remainder of the boiling water in the kettle as he went out of the back door.

She rinsed out a few clothes and hung them out on the line, then sorted out the things she wanted to take with her when she moved on. Her thoughts now were centred on the coming transfer, and her few days with Simon and his family seemed almost a dream.

Emily was surprised when they told her she was going to Liverpool. The city seemed far away and alien to her and she'd secretly hoped for London, which was only a couple of hours on the train from home. However, she couldn't pick and choose and she knew that the ports and industrial cities were likely to experience heavy bombing once things really got under way. At the moment the Luftwaffe seemed to be concentrating on shipping in the Channel and only a few raids had actually happened on British soil, but it was simply a matter of time, of course. People had been expecting the blitzkrieg to come since the previous September, but for some reason Hitler seemed to be holding back from attacking the big cities.

'Liverpool?' Carole stared at her disappointedly when Emily told her. 'Mum will never let me go up there – mucky, dirty place, all slums and dockers. I hoped they would send you to London.'

'So did I,' Emily admitted, and shrugged. 'But we go where we're sent. I suppose they need help. I don't really mind. Apparently, the lodgings I've been given are in Birkenhead, which is over the river and nicer, so Miss Brown says.

She knows the area well and she says some of it is lovely. You don't have to live in the slums, you know.'

'Well, I suppose not,' Carole said. 'I'll have to think about it.' She was silent for a moment, then, 'I promised I would ask so don't bite my head off – Terry Burgess would like you to visit him in hospital.'

'What on earth for?'

'I think he wants to apologise. I don't really know – but he was in a better mood last time I saw him.'

'I'm glad he's feeling better,' Emily replied. 'But there's no point in my going. I don't even know him.'

'Well, I promised to ask. You don't have to go.' Carole looked at her curiously. 'What was your sister's wedding like?'

'Oh... nice,' Emily said. 'Frances was happy. I had a tiff with my brother but we made it up later – and I went to stay with friends for a few days. They live somewhere near Winchester, in a lovely house right out in the country.'

'Lucky you,' Carole said. 'Nothing exciting ever happens to me. It's all because of this rotten war.'

'Yes, it has a lot to answer for.'

She turned away as the phones started to ring. It was the beginning of a busy afternoon and an even busier evening as one of the local factories sustained some damage in a small explosion. Fortunately, no one was hurt this time.

It made Emily think about the fireman who had been hurt though, and the next morning she decided she would visit him after all. Her first reaction had been to dismiss his request, but now that she'd had time to consider she realised that she wasn't angry. It wouldn't kill her to visit Terry Burgess, and she could leave if he was surly.

As it happened, he was sitting in the day room reading a

magazine when she arrived. He looked at her a little awkwardly and then launched into an apology.

'It was a foul thing to say to you, Miss Searles. I was feeling rotten and I took it out on you. Will you forgive me?'

'I should think I could manage that,' Emily said, and laughed. He still had a nasty blister on his cheek, but the heavy bandages on his hands had been replaced with thin cotton gloves. 'I might have felt as you did in your place. It isn't very pleasant to go through what you did, I should imagine.'

'Others have it worse. Look at some of the poor devils in those convoys. We've been lucky here so far, but it won't last.'

'No, I don't suppose so.' She was wearing the dark blue skirt, white blouse and navy cardigan she wore for work, her hair pulled back into a neat plait, but her skin had a peach bloom and she looked lovely. 'My brother says it's going to be a long war.'

'Is that the one who was wounded at Dunkirk?' He had obviously been asking questions about her, Emily realised.

'Yes. Daniel. He doesn't talk about it much, but I think it was pretty awful. He was lucky to get back.'

'It's a wonder they got as many away as they did.' Terry hesitated awkwardly. 'They're going to discharge me in a few days. Would you come to the pictures with me one day?'

'I'm sorry but I'm being transferred in a couple of days. They're sending me to Liverpool.'

'Just my luck,' he said ruefully. 'Would you have come otherwise?'

'Yes, I don't see why not.' Emily smiled at him. He was nice-looking in a rugged sort of way, and she quite liked him. 'I'll send you a postcard to the station house, let you know how I'm getting on if you like?'

'Thanks.' He grinned at her. 'I suppose that's the fortunes of war. It was decent of you to visit me again, Emily.'

'No trouble. I hope your hands will be better soon.'

'They're healing. I wasn't sure they would but I can move the fingers now. It hurts like hell, of course, but they tell me I'll be back to work in a few months.'

'I'm really glad,' Emily said. 'Well, I have to go now. I'm on duty again this evening, and then I get a couple of days off before I report to my new post.'

'Good luck, then. Take care of yourself up there.'

'I shall.' She smiled at him. 'Have a good war.'

'You too.' He grinned, watching her as she walked the length of the common room, her hips swaying enticingly. 'Just my bloody luck.'

5

Margaret looked around the bedroom, making a mental note of things she intended to pack when she left. Those silver items on the dressing table, not strictly hers but pretty and given to her to use when she married; and that Lalique glass vase on the window sill. She might as well take as much as she could; they'd screwed her down to the last penny for her share of Robert's assets. She was going to get as much as she could before she left.

She felt a lot better in herself now, the guilt almost gone. Robert was a grown man, responsible for his own health. Her few days away had refreshed her, making her see life differently. Her affair with Michael Knight wasn't exactly on again, but it probably would be once she'd settled back in London. He'd told her about a decent flat going in Belgravia, and she knew it wasn't too far from his office. He would be near enough to visit when he had a few hours to spare.

Michael's business was one of those considered vital to the war effort. She knew it had kept him out of conscription and gave him certain privileges, besides earning him a lot of money. She'd been a fool to quarrel with him, and an even bigger one to marry Robert. Michael and she understood one another and she would settle for what she could get in future...

Her thoughts were interrupted when she heard something outside her door. She turned, thinking it might be Emily or Daniel, but when the door opened suddenly, she stiffened, her nerves jangling as she saw who it was.

'What are you doing here?'

'I knew you were back. I wanted to see you.'

'You could have waited downstairs.'

'Oh, no, I've had enough of waiting,' Clay said, eyes narrowing. 'You've kept me dangling long enough. You got what you wanted, now it's my turn.'

'I don't know what you mean...' Alarm bells were ringing. There was something odd about him at that moment, a glitter in his eyes that unnerved her.

'Then perhaps I'd better show you.' Clay moved towards her purposefully. Margaret backed away, smothering a scream. 'Don't be shy. You've been asking for it for months. Now you're going to get it.'

'You're drunk!' She could smell the drink on his breath. She put up her hands defensively. 'Stay away from me...'

'I've had a couple, but don't worry. I can still give you what you want.' His eyes glittered. 'Thought I was your lap dog, didn't you? Well, now I'm going to teach you to sit up and beg.'

Margaret gasped. She knew there wasn't any point in pleading. She had met this sort before, though he'd kept his nature well hidden while his father was alive. But he wasn't going to get his way easily. She would fight to the last.

'Do this and you'll be sorry,' she said. 'If you know what's good for you, you'll get out now.'

'I know what's good for me, all right.' He struck her across the face, and she went for him with her nails, scoring his cheek and drawing blood. The next minute he lunged at her, grabbing her around the waist. He was shaking with excitement, beads of sweat on his face. She could taste the blood on her lips as he ground his mouth on hers, his teeth bruising her. She struggled, clawing at him where his flesh was exposed, tearing his skin. She brought her knee up sharply but he was ready for her and avoided the crippling action. He swung her round, forcing her arm up against her back. Then he thrust her forward so that she fell face down across the side of the bed.

Margaret screamed then. She screamed again and again as he used her in a way she had never thought to experience. And then it was suddenly over. She lay face down on the bed, weeping into the covers as she felt him move away from her.

'So now you know who you're dealing with,' Clay rasped. 'That's for my father, bitch. That's how we treat cheating whores around here. Take what you can and get out of this house and this village. Next time I might not go so easy on you.'

Margaret lay where she was, listening to him leaving, his boots clattering down the stairs, the front door slamming behind him. Shudders ran through her as she realised that he had gone. The shock and horror of what had happened to her kept her where she was for several minutes, unable to move. It had all been so quick, so sudden. She could hardly believe it had happened, except for the pain and the feeling of humiliation.

When at last she could move, she went into the bathroom and locked the door. She wretched over the toilet but though her mouth tasted vile nothing came out. Turning on the bath taps, she let the water run, pouring in the last of her precious bath salts. She didn't think she would ever feel clean again, but she had begun to gather her thoughts.

He wasn't going to get away with this. She would make him pay. Somehow, she would make him pay...

* * *

Daniel saw the light on in the sitting room as he came in from the kitchen. He had been to the pictures in Cambridge with Alice and afterwards had stopped for a cup of tea with her parents. The house had been full to bursting point, because the Robinsons had taken in a couple of lodgers – New Zealand airmen who were now fighting with the Royal Air Force and had been sent to work at the aerodrome. He wondered about the light; Connor was staying with Henry for the weekend so it must either be Emily or Margaret.

He hesitated on the threshold as he saw Margaret. She was pouring brandy from a decanter on the sideboard and as she turned, he saw the cut on her lip. It had swollen and she looked awful.

'What happened?'

'It's hardly your business.' Her tone was sharp, bitter.

'You're still family.' Daniel's gaze narrowed. 'Someone did this to you – who was it?'

'If you really want to know' – she laughed harshly – 'it was Clay. He walked into my bedroom two hours ago and raped me.'

'Raped...!' Daniel stared at her. He felt stunned, wanting

to dismiss it as a lie, and yet he knew it was true. 'My God! The stupid fool. I am so sorry, Margaret. Is there anything I can do – get the doctor for you or something?'

'You can ring the police if you like, have Clay arrested.'

'He deserves to be punished...' Daniel felt sick. He stood there staring at her as his stomach churned, imagining the scene, the horror of what his brother had done. 'I'll thrash him for this. I promise you he won't get away with it.'

'It isn't enough,' she said coldly. 'I want five thousand pounds or I go to the police.' She walked towards the telephone, her hand hovering over it. 'Shall I ring them or will you?'

'It would ruin him – us. I know he's a bastard. What he did is unforgivable, Margaret, but he has a wife and children.'

'He should have thought of that before he raped me. Five thousand pounds is my price for silence – take it or leave it.'

'Henry couldn't borrow any more from the bank and Clay has borrowed to buy the land. I doubt they could raise a thousand between them at the moment.'

'Then he'll go to prison. I've got bruises all over me to prove my case.'

Daniel thought it over. She would go to the police, he knew that. She might not succeed in court, but the damage would have been done. In a village like this the family would never live it down. Every one of them would be tarred with the same brush, even though they hadn't done anything. If it were just him, he'd take her to the police himself, but there was Emily and Connor to think of; his brother's wife and children. What would become of them?

'I could raise two thousand,' he said. 'It's my only offer, Margaret. Refuse and I'll ring the police myself.'

She looked at his set face, realizing there was no room for manoeuvre. Daniel was no fool. Robert had been right about that much. 'And you'll thrash him? You promise?'

'You can be sure of that,' Daniel said, his mouth drawing into a thin line. At that moment he wanted to kill his brother for the trouble he'd caused. Margaret might be a grasping woman, but she hadn't deserved this – no woman did. 'I'll have it out with him in the morning, and I'll give you the money in cash tomorrow afternoon.'

'You won't go back on your word?'

'No, I shan't do that. Once I've given it I stick by it.'

Yes, she believed that. It was why she'd chosen to target him rather than his brothers. A part of her wanted to see Clay punished and the rest of the family with him, but she knew she was going to take the offer. She couldn't wait to get out of this wretched place and she would never bother to come back. She had made a big mistake when she married and in future she would be more careful.

'Then I'll take your word.' She finished her drink. 'I'm going to pack my things. I shall be leaving as soon as I get my money.'

Daniel nodded. He didn't say anything as she left the room but he was sick and angry inside. Clay deserved much more than a beating. As to the money, it was all he had, his savings for the future, for the garage he wanted after the war. But he'd been left with no other choice. Margaret could – and would – have ruined them all. He had ensured the innocents were protected and that she would leave them in peace, but at the cost of his dreams.

He swore out loud. Clay could pay him back. He would give him a good thrashing in the morning, and he would make sure he got his money back from him somehow.

* * *

'You were a bloody fool to promise her so much,' Clay muttered, holding a stained rag to his nose. The fight between them had been long and hard, for they were evenly matched. Neither had really won, but Clay was sure his nose was broken. 'Stupid whore asked for it.'

'Stupid or not, she didn't deserve what you did,' Daniel told him. His lip was cut but he was in marginally better shape than his brother. 'She was Dad's wife – and no woman deserves to be treated like that. You behaved like an animal, Clay.'

'Bloody white knight,' Clay muttered, but he couldn't meet Daniel's eyes. 'You should've let her go to the police. It was her word against mine.'

'And how do you think Dorothy would have felt? Who would she have believed? She would've died of shame – and what about the rest of us? We have to live here. It's only because it would have shamed them that I stopped her going to the police.'

'Well, I've no money to pay her. I've borrowed up to the hilt on that land.'

'I'll pay her. You can give it back to me when the war is over.'

Clay muttered something and Daniel glared at him.

'Don't think you're getting away with it. I shall want that money when I come back, so don't forget it. You may think you've got away with this but you'll get your comeuppance one of these days.'

'All right, all right, damn you,' Clay said. 'I'll see what I can do. Things should be better by then.'

'I'll want it whatever, either in cash or land – suit yourself.' Daniel stared him down. 'You were a fool, Clay, and it's your debt, not mine. Think yourself lucky you're not sitting in a police cell with a prison sentence hanging over you.'

Clay pulled a face but said no more. He'd had a few drinks and the thought of Margaret alone in the house had got to him. He'd wanted to hurt and humiliate her, but he didn't want to lose everything. Dorothy would leave him if she knew, and things had been looking brighter now he had the land he wanted.

'I admit I was a bloody idiot. We'll sort it out when you get back – but I still think you were a fool to pay so much.'

'She wanted five thousand. If I'd had it I would probably have paid her. You deserve all you get, Clay.'

Daniel turned and walked away. His brother had shown no sign of remorse and it sickened him. What he knew and what he'd seen disgusted him. A part of him wished that he'd picked up that phone and let Clay take his punishment, and yet he could imagine how Dot and his sisters would feel if they knew Clay was a rapist.

Walking away, Daniel got into the old Ford he'd bought for a few shillings from someone's barn a couple of days earlier. He had managed to get it going and with the ban on the sale of new cars it should bring him in a few pounds once he'd smartened it up. It was going to take a long time to replace the money he'd promised Margaret, because he might never get Clay to pay up, but he would get that garage somehow. When the war was over.

He looked at his watch. Frances would be at the station very soon. Marcus was going straight back to his base following their honeymoon, and she'd asked Daniel to meet her.

He wouldn't be able to buy the house now. He would

have to tell Henry and Emily. Their best hope now was that Samuel Danby would buy it for his son and Frances.

* * *

'Do you mean it?' Frances looked at him excitedly. 'Can we really have Rathmere? I know Marcus will say yes. I'll phone him this evening but I'm sure of his answer already. He has always liked this house.'

'I'm glad you're pleased. I was going to try and keep it for the family but something else came up.'

'You and Emily and Connor are welcome to stay as often as you want,' Frances said. 'At least until we have a family.'

'I shall be looking for a place of my own after the war,' Daniel told her. 'Connor can stay with Henry or me after that – but until then he would be company for you.'

'Yes, of course. I shall be glad of him here while Marcus is away. Emily too when she wants to stay.'

'Let's hope Marcus agrees then.'

'I am sure he will.' Frances's face was glowing. There was no doubt that everything in her world was satisfactory, and for a moment Daniel envied her, her surety, her confidence in the future. 'But are you sure you don't want it, Dan?'

Daniel smiled and shook his head. Of course he wanted the house Grandfather Searles had so lovingly built; it was his home and he had formed his plans around it, but the situation was hopeless. He was going to need every penny he could save for his business. If the house had to be sold, it was best it went to Frances and Marcus.

* * *

Emily knew that something was wrong when Daniel told her he couldn't keep the house after all. He'd been so pleased that he was providing them all with a home, and now he was definitely brooding.

'What happened?' she asked. 'Was it something to do with Margaret?'

'Yes, in a way,' he said, and shook his head as her brows lifted. 'No, I'm not going to tell you. She has gone now and I don't think we shall see much of her in future. She doesn't like village life.'

'No, I know. She was bored here, wasn't she – with Father and all of it? It's a pity he married her.'

'Yes, it is,' Daniel agreed. His father's marriage had cost the family dear, one way and another. It wasn't just the money. She had been entitled to her share, but things had changed. Henry and Clay hardly ever spoke these days. Henry was still sore over losing their best land and would be a long time forgiving his brother. Daniel hadn't told him about the rape but Henry knew there had been a fight between him and Clay, and he suspected something was going on. 'It would have been better if she had never come here.'

'I tried to like her for Dad's sake,' Emily confided, 'but I never did. I'm glad she's gone.'

'I can't say I'm sorry.' Daniel frowned at her. 'So you're off to Liverpool tomorrow. Shall I come with you on the train and see you settled in?'

'Do you want to?' Emily felt pleased. She was a bit nervous about the whole thing. 'Yes, I should like that, Dan. Unless you have something more important to do?'

'No, nothing more important than seeing you're all right,'

he told her with a smile. 'I shall feel better about you if I know where you are. You're my little sister, you know, and it's a big bad world out there.'

Emily giggled because he was teasing her. She found herself telling him about the injured fireman she'd visited in the hospital.

'He did the right thing apologizing to you.'

'He didn't have to. I was annoyed at the time, but I didn't blame him, not really. It was awful for him. His friend had died and he didn't know if he would ever be able to work again.'

'He sounds a decent bloke.'

'Yes, I think so. He asked me out, but I told him I was being transferred.'

'Would you have gone out with him otherwise?'

'I might... Yes, I expect so. I like him.'

'You haven't made up your mind to marry Simon Vane then?'

'No, not yet,' Emily said. 'To be honest, we were so busy at the station that I haven't really thought about it much. Simon is going to ring me when he gets leave – or he will when I give him my number. I'll see what I feel like then.'

'That's a sensible girl,' Daniel said with a nod of approval. 'Give yourself time.'

It was worth every penny of the money he'd paid Margaret to keep quiet, Daniel thought as he said goodnight to his sister. Emily and Frances would have been so ashamed if Clay had been arrested. He'd done it for them. The money had gone now. He would just have to find a way of earning some more...

* * *

'Have you noticed how many Irish people there are here?' Emily asked as they explored Liverpool together. They had already deposited her suitcases at her new lodgings, and Daniel had declared himself satisfied both with the area and the landlady. Emily was going to be living in a private house, but with three other girls from the Fire Service who were already living there, one of whom was called Maura and was Irish. 'I love the way they talk, don't you?'

'It's easier on the ear than the Liverpudlian slang,' he said, and grinned at her. 'I couldn't understand one word in ten that old feller said when we asked him the way to the Albert Docks.'

'I think he was pulling your leg,' Emily said. 'When I explained that I was with the Fire Service and needed to get to know my way about the city he soon changed his tune.'

'Well, I dare say he knows they need girls like you, Emily. I'm proud of what you're doing, you know. You didn't have to come here. It isn't going to be as easy as it was in Cambridge.'

'I know that, Dan. I want to do my bit. I think it was when Terry Burgess and the others got hurt – and you being wounded at Dunkirk – that made me realise we've had it easy at home. It's time I learned what life is all about, and proved I'm not just a spoiled daddy's girl.'

'Well, if you get scared or miserable you can always go home. Frances says there will always be a room for you – until you get married, of course.'

'Yes, I know.' She pulled a face. 'It would have been better if you'd been able to keep it as our home until after the war, Dan.'

'I did my best, Emily. I'm sorry I let you down.'

'It wasn't you, I know it wasn't,' she said, sensing his

disappointment. 'Henry says he thinks Clay had something to do with it, but he doesn't know what.'

Daniel set his mouth hard. 'Just leave it, love. All right?'

Emily saw his grimace and knew that he wouldn't tell her about whatever had happened to change his plans. She hugged his arm, smiling up at him.

'Carole said Liverpool was all grime and slums, but I like what I've seen. There are some lovely old buildings down there by the Albert Docks, and Sir George's Hall is nice – the Anglican Cathedral too.'

'Of course it is,' Daniel said, glad the subject had been changed to something more comfortable. 'It has been a thriving port for a long time – since the river silted up at Chester I believe. Sadly, it played a big part in the slave trade, but it has also been a magnet for immigration over the years – that's why you hear so many Irish voices.'

'Yes, I suppose so,' Emily said. 'I liked Maura, which is just as well since we're going to be sharing a room – though not beds, thank goodness.'

'So you think you'll be all right here then?'

'Yes, of course I shall,' she said. 'There are theatres and shops and cinemas, and that reminds me – I'm starving. We passed a rather nice tea shop just back there. Shall we go and have something to eat?'

'Just the ticket,' Daniel said, and smiled at her. 'My treat – and then I shall have to think about catching a train. I might only get as far as London tonight, but I can stay there and go home when I'm ready. I might look up a couple of friends...'

* * *

Afterwards, Daniel thought it must be his fault that the Germans chose to make their first real attack on London that night; they must have known he was coming, and having missed him at Dunkirk, wanted their pound of flesh.

It was late when his train pulled into the station, and the bombs had already started. He was grabbed by a woman with a small child, her panic conveying itself to him as she told him she was going down to the Underground to sit it out. He went with her, partly to help carry the child, because he could see that she was terrified, and partly because he had no idea of what else to do. He could hardly go looking for lodgings during an air raid.

The Underground station was filled with people, all of whom looked bewildered and scared. They had been expecting this to happen for months, but now it had they hardly knew what to do with themselves. It was one thing when the bombs fell on the ports or shipping areas, but this was hitting houses, shops and offices, destroying great chunks of their city, and they looked at one another in disbelief, hardly crediting that this was happening to them.

Some people were sitting on the ground because they had rushed out so hurriedly that they hadn't had time to bring anything with them. It was the first time any of them had experienced this kind of thing and they looked at each other nervously. One or two had food and they offered it to the person sitting next to them. Gradually, the atmosphere of terror seemed to ease and a man started telling jokes. A few of the others glared at him, but most laughed. Then someone took out a mouth organ and started to play a tune. An old man dressed in ragged clothes got up and did a little jig to the music and a few people clapped. Most people were silent, mothers hugging their children, lovers sitting with their arms about each other.

Daniel felt lonely. In the army he'd had comrades to laugh and joke with, and there was always something to do. Here he felt isolated, useless. If he died in this place, would his family ever know? He saw a little boy sitting alone crying and felt in his pocket to find half a bar of chocolate. He offered it but the child shook his head and wiped his sleeve over his dirty face. Daniel sat with his back to the wall and tried to shut out his surroundings, concentrating on what he would do when he got out of here.

When the all-clear came at last, they filtered out into the early morning air, still feeling stunned and shattered by what had happened. A strange red glow hung over the city, but when morning came it was discovered that it was mostly the docks, airfields and power stations that had taken the worst of the attack. A few bombs had fallen on the city, but people began to breathe again as they realised it wasn't as bad as they had feared. Not yet anyway. But now the Germans had started, there was no telling what they would do next.

Daniel had been uncertain whether to go home or visit friends in town. Now he decided he would stay on and see friends, visit various places he'd always wanted to see, and just amuse himself. If he went back home it would feel as if he were running away. He found himself wishing that he was back with his unit. The bloody Germans! He wanted to get back to the front and do his bit – just like Emily.

* * *

Emily was glad Daniel had telephoned her that morning. The news about the bombing had been on the radio and she'd been worried in case he'd been caught up in it. He was worried about her, in case she'd been bombed where she was, but she was able to tell him that she hadn't seen or heard much, but she was due to start work that afternoon, and then she would probably be in the thick of it.

The Battle of Britain was now well and truly underway and twenty-one cities and towns were bombed that night. Emily's introduction to a war zone was bloody and shocking, and she was terrified by the reports coming in from all over the city. The fire engines and their crews were working flat out, and still the fires raged. Gas mains had erupted, explosions from them adding to the general carnage and chaos.

The airfields were getting their share of it according to the news over the next few days. Maura's fiancé was an airman and he telephoned her once at their lodgings but had to ring off abruptly as the siren went again.

'They have to get their planes in the air quickly, because the Germans will blow them to bits if they're stuck on the ground, but once they're up there our lads are a match for most of them,' Maura told her. 'Sure, if they don't go home with their tails between their legs sooner or later I'm a Dutchman.'

Emily wondered how Marcus and Simon were getting on. She had written to the address that Simon had given her but as yet he hadn't left a message for her. She knew he must be busy; all the pilots were stretched, because they were the thin blue line and all that was preventing Hitler from invading.

The days went by in a blur of rushed shifts at work, when the phone never stopped ringing, and the horror of seeing bombed houses and holes in the road as she went to and from the fire station. Emily was soon so tired that all she wanted to do was eat and fall into bed. Her eyes were gritty with tiredness, and she felt numbed, because that was the only way she could deal with her feelings.

When she came home in the early hours one morning to find Maura sitting on the stairs with a telegram in her hand, her shoulders shaking as the sobs wracked her body, Emily knew what must have happened.

'Has John been shot down?'

'Yes – he's in hospital, but...' Maura looked at her with tear-filled eyes. 'They say he's badly burned... Half his face and all down one side of him. His plane crashed in the Channel in flames.'

'I'm so sorry,' Emily said, torn with pity for her. 'Have they said you can visit him?'

'No, nothing like that. I'm going to get a letter from his commanding officer.' Maura looked at her. 'I'm not sure I want to see him like that. John was so handsome... It was why I was mad about him.'

'But he's still the man you love.'

'I don't know,' Maura said. She jumped to her feet and ran upstairs. 'I don't know if I can face it...'

Emily watched her go, feeling sympathy for her plight. It was an awful situation. How could she be sure she wouldn't react like that if it was someone she loved... Simon? Did she love Simon? She thought perhaps she did but sometimes it seemed like an impossible dream. Surely her visit to his home had been in another lifetime? This dreadful, dreadful time they were all going through now was so draining that she didn't have enough energy to think about anything but work.

It was hard to get through the days and nights, and she knew that in London the people were suffering even more, if that was possible. The Luftwaffe had been concentrating on the capital for a while now, as if the Germans thought the way to break the British spirit was through the Londoners.

'If they think that they're plain daft,' Daniel told her when he telephoned her one morning. 'You should see them in the Underground, Emily, laughing and cracking on as if it was a party. That first night they were shocked, but they've got the hang of it now; they bring their sandwiches and a bottle of tea; some of them sing and play with the kids. If Hitler thinks he's going to break us this way, he's mad. Mind you, I think he must be. Only a madman would have started all this.'

'You've stopped on in town then, Dan?'

'I couldn't go home; it would have been like running away. I've been helping with the Civil Defence. They give me jobs to do for them, though I can't do the rough work just yet, but I can drive people and I can hand round cups of tea. I'm making myself useful.'

'Good for you, Dan.'

'Have you heard from Simon recently?'

'No. I'm a bit worried. I expected him to ring ages ago. You don't think he's...?'

'I'm sure his family would have found a way to let you know,' Daniel said. 'Those fly-boys are doing a magnificent job, Emily love. Be patient and I'm sure he'll ring you when he can.'

'I wouldn't have time to see him at the moment anyway,' she said. 'When I get home all I want to do is sleep. I'm not sure I can take much more of it.'

'You'll take it,' Daniel told her. 'The same as we all will. It must be costing the Luftwaffe a lot of men and planes to keep this up, love. It will have to end soon.'

'I just hope you're right,' she said as he rang off. 'I just hope you're right.'

Saying a prayer now and then was all they could do for the moment, Emily thought, and added one for Simon. She was thinking about him more these days, perhaps because Maura had been so unhappy. Her fiancé had wanted her to marry him before he went back to his base the last time, and she'd wanted to wait for her big wedding and all the trimmings at Christmas.

'And now we'll probably never marry,' she said, tears trickling down her cheeks. 'They think he may not make it, Emily. I hate the bloody Germans! I wish they were all dead!'

It was a wish echoed by a good many women in similar situations all over the country.

Maura had ended up weeping in Emily's arms, and Emily had wept too for her friend and the man who had been so cruelly hurt. She understood how Maura felt. She had lost something precious and now all she could think about was what might have been. It made Emily think about Simon, wondering where he was and when she would see him again.

* * *

'Simon!' Emily stared at him in disbelief when she came off work that afternoon. He was standing outside the station waiting for her, and he looked so weary that her heart turned over and she knew that her feelings for him were much more than friendship. 'Oh, Simon. I've been so afraid... When you didn't phone—'

'I couldn't, Emily,' he told her, his eyes moving over her hungrily. 'I didn't get your letter for ages – some mix-up they said, but it happens too often, and then, well, we've been at it night and day. I've been ordered to take a rest along with the rest of my squadron. I've got seventy-six hours, Emily, and I wanted to spend it all with you. Can you get some time off?'

'I can ask a friend to cover for me,' she said. 'I'm off until tomorrow night anyway, and Maura will take my next shift if I ask her. Can you wait here while I just go and see what she thinks?'

'Don't be long then. I've been waiting for this too long already.'

She smiled and went back inside the station house, catching her friend before she went back on duty.

'Of course I'll cover for you – why wouldn't I?' Maura told her. 'And take my advice, Emily – do whatever he wants. You might regret it if you don't.'

Simon was leaning against the wall, his eyes closed when Emily returned and kissed his cheek. He opened them immediately, hugging her to him fiercely and kissing her in a way that made her melt into him. He had never kissed her like this before, and she hadn't felt this way before, either.

'I love you, Emily,' he told her. 'Will you marry me, darling? Please say you will, because thinking about you, hoping you had made up your mind to say yes, is all that has kept me sane until now.'

She reached up to touch his face, the feelings swirling inside her. He seemed so intense, at breaking point, and it made her want to hold him. She'd only known him a few months but she loved him, of course she did, and she would be a fool to deny this feeling inside her. It was still a bit too soon for marriage, but these were not ordinary times. Maura had insisted on waiting and she was suffering for it now. Emily would be a fool to throw away her chance. Simon needed her love and she wanted to give it. She wanted to comfort him for all he had suffered.

'Yes, of course I will, darling,' she said. 'I love you very much and I do want to marry you.'

'I've got a special licence in my pocket,' Simon said. 'I bought it weeks ago just in case – will you marry me now, Emily? This afternoon if we can find someone to do it – or tomorrow?'

'Marry you right now?' Emily was shocked. She hadn't expected it to be quite so soon. 'I'm not sure. I would need permission, Simon – I'm not twenty-one yet. I'll have to ask Henry – and everyone will want us to wait, at least until your next leave.'

'If we wait it might be too late,' Simon said. 'There are men in my squadron dying every day, Emily. I know it's selfish of me, but I want you to be my wife now.'

He looked so wretched, so desperate, that she couldn't resist his plea. Besides, whirlwind marriages were happening all the time because of the war. 'I suppose I could ring Henry, ask him if he will give us permission. We could take the train overnight to London and then...'

'I've got petrol. I can drive us down there,' Simon said. 'If we start now we can be in London by this evening. We could stay at a hotel overnight, and then finish our journey early in the morning. All we have to do is telephone your brother and ask him to make the arrangements at his end. We don't need a fancy reception, do we – just the wedding and a blessing, that's all.'

'Yes, of course,' Emily said, swallowing her disappointment. 'Maura will let my landlady know that I'm with you.

We can leave straight away and that will save a bit of time. And if Henry says no we shall still be together.'

'He won't say no,' Simon told her. 'I had a few words with him at your sister's wedding, and he said all he wanted for his sisters was that they should be happy. If you tell him we're in love he'll understand.'

'Yes, I hope so,' Emily said. Daniel wouldn't approve of this hasty marriage, but it was Henry they had to ask. 'I'll telephone him when we get to the hotel and let him know what we want.'

'I've got a better idea. We'll ring him together this very minute,' Simon said. 'There's a box up the road and I've plenty of change. From now on we'll do everything together, darling.'

Emily smiled and kissed him. He was rushing her but he was desperate and she loved him. It was impossible to say no so she didn't. She held her hand out, he grabbed it and they ran like children to where his car stood waiting.

* * *

Henry was delighted that his sister was marrying a man of whom he thoroughly approved. As far as he was concerned, the young men who were keeping the Luftwaffe at bay were heroes and nothing was too good for them.

'I'll not only give you my permission, I'll catch the train to London first thing in the morning, Emily,' he promised. 'I'll bring Frances and as many of the family as I can muster. We'll see you married in town and that will save you wasting precious hours on the road. Besides, there are more places to get married in London.'

'There – I knew he would come through for us,' Simon

said after they had finished the call. 'Actually, I know someone in London I can ring this evening. He could probably arrange for us to have a church service rather than a registry office. It will be plain and simple, but you won't mind that, will you?'

'No, of course not,' she said. 'But what do I wear? I can't get married in this...' She glanced down at her navy skirt and cardigan.

'It doesn't matter,' Simon said. 'I've got a few pretty things in the car as presents for you. I asked my stepmother to buy them for me – and I think she came up trumps.'

'That's another thing,' Emily said. 'Won't your father want to be at the wedding?'

'He won't care just as long as we're getting married. He likes you, Emily, and he knows you'll make me a good wife.'

There was something odd in his voice at that moment that made her look at him hard, but he was smiling at her and she thought that she might have imagined it.

'Oh, well...' She smothered her sigh. A part of her still wanted a wedding like her sister's, but at least she was marrying the man she loved. 'As long as you're sure your father won't be offended.'

'He will be delighted I've finally got married,' Simon said. 'Besides, he wouldn't blame you, Emily. He approves of you, believe me; he told me you were exactly right.'

Right for what? Emily wondered, but let it pass. All that mattered was that Simon loved her and they were going to be married.

* * *

'I've taken a couple of rooms for tonight,' Simon said when he joined her that evening in the reception lounge at the hotel in the West End of London. 'Shall we go up after dinner and get some sleep? It's late and you'll want to be fresh for the morning. We've got a big day ahead of us tomorrow.'

'Yes, we could,' she said, and hesitated. 'Simon... I know this sounds awfully forward of me – but why two rooms? We could have been together. You don't have much time and—'

'And you are wonderful, my darling Emily,' he said, touching a finger to her lips, 'but I want to wait until my ring is on your finger. I love you too much to take advantage. Supposing something happened and we didn't get married? Supposing you fell for a child – what then?'

'It isn't likely, is it? Frances had a week with Marcus before he left for his unit and she hasn't fallen yet. It doesn't always happen straight away. Most women I know were married for ages before they had their first baby.'

'But it could happen,' Simon insisted. 'I love you, Emily. I can wait for another few hours. We're together. I know you're going to be mine tomorrow and that's enough for me.'

Emily could only hug him. There were not many men who would have refused what she'd offered. She knew that Maura and her fiancé hadn't anticipated their wedding night, because Maura had told her she'd wanted to wait, but a lot of girls did. Maura wished now that she had taken her chances, that she had fallen with child, because at least then she would have had something to remember her lover by.

'I think you are rather wonderful, Simon,' Emily said, and she kissed him in the hotel lobby. A couple passing smiled at them indulgently, though an older woman sitting by herself frowned in disapproval, as if she thought such a public display of affection unnecessary. 'And I'm glad Henry agreed.'

Her doubts had gone. Any man who loved enough to sacrifice a night in the arms of his loved one to protect her had to be worth a small sacrifice in return. They had the rest of their lives in front of them.

'We shall have a couple of days,' Simon said, and grinned at her. 'I am sure we can make up for lost time.'

6

Simon's friend in London turned out to be a bishop, who just happened to be related by marriage to Amelia's brother. It seemed that the relationship meant strings could be pulled and Arthur, as he insisted Emily call him, really did them proud. The wedding was booked for the following afternoon in a church decked out with flowers. One of Arthur's friends performed the service, and he joined them at the reception afterwards, swelling the numbers.

The hotel manager had joined in with a will, providing an impromptu reception at short notice. Somehow they had champagne, smoked salmon and game pâté on toast, as well as chicken and salad with potatoes roasted in their skins, though no one had been able to come up with even a cardboard cake.

Henry had brought his wife, Mary, and Frances and Connor with him, and Daniel was there, of course, although Clay and Dorothy had stayed at home because their youngest child was unwell, they said.

Arthur had given them a silver coffee-pot as a wedding

gift, and Henry had bought them a set of crystal glasses. Two of Simon's friends had attended the church service, but they stayed at the reception only long enough to present Emily with a silver milk jug and sugar tongs and drink a glass of champagne before leaving.

So it was just Emily's brothers, Frances and the happy couple who sat down to the meal.

'Not quite what you wanted,' Frances said, squeezing her sister's hand, 'but at least you had a dress to wear.'

'Your dress,' Emily said. 'It was generous of you to let me borrow it, Frances.'

It hadn't quite fitted, being a little long and too loose on the waist. However, they had tacked the hem up a bit, and Frances had pinned it inside with safety pins. One of them had stuck into Emily's back all afternoon.

'Well, I couldn't let you get married without a dress,' Frances said, and kissed her cheek. 'It was a bit of a rush, Emily...' She hesitated.

'Yes, I know,' Emily interjected, 'but Simon only had a couple of days and a few hours – and it was what he wanted.'

'As long as it's what you want too...'

'Yes, of course it is,' Emily said, and smiled.

'Only Dan thought you weren't too sure...'

Of course she was sure. Frances had made her wonder for a moment if she had let herself be rushed, but she did love Simon. She had felt a surge of love when she saw him looking so weary and defeated. It had made her want to hold him, to comfort him.

Henry wanted to get off that evening so he and his wife left to catch the train just before nine. Frances and Connor went with him, and Daniel a few minutes later.

'You'll want a bit of time together,' he said as he hugged

her. 'Good luck, love. Simon's a decent bloke. You'll be all right with him.'

'Yes, I know. He's wonderful,' Emily replied, and smiled. 'Thank you for coming, Dan.'

'I didn't get a chance to bring you a proper present, but I'll buy you something nice and visit in Liverpool – perhaps next month.'

'Just come and see me.'

Daniel promised, then took his leave of Simon. When they were alone, Simon poured her another glass of champagne.

'We could go dancing,' he suggested, 'but I've ordered another bottle of bubbly in our room – well, yours actually. It was the better of the two so I thought...'

'Let's go up,' Emily said, leading him towards the lift. 'You have to go back tomorrow afternoon.'

'I shall have to leave about twelve actually, and I can't get you back to Liverpool.' He looked oddly guilty. 'I suppose we should have waited until Christmas.'

'No, I'm glad we didn't,' she said, reaching up to kiss him on the lips. 'Let's go up now. We don't have much time to be together.'

'You're a wonderful girl,' Simon said. 'The only one I could ever have married. I promise I'll be good to you, Emily. I'll make you happy.'

He seemed so anxious, so desperate to make her believe him, that it sent a shiver down Emily's spine. Why was he looking at her so strangely, almost as if he were guilty of some crime?

'I am happy, Simon. You love me – what more could I want?'

Simon hesitated for a moment, then he gave her that

smile, the one that made her toes tingle. 'I'm an idiot, aren't I? Making you uncomfortable when all I want is to be with you. I do love you, Emily – very much.'

Her doubts fled in that moment as they joined hands and walked into the lift. Simon drew her against him as the door closed and the lift began to whirr its way to the top floor. His kiss made her tingle from head to toe and neither of them moved at first when the door opened, until they became aware that someone was waiting to get in.

'Sorry...' Emily said, and she giggled as she looked at Simon. 'We just got married.'

'Congratulations,' the woman said, smiling now. 'I hope you will be very happy.'

Emily would have thanked her, but the door of the lift closed and Simon was urging her down the hall. Once inside their room, he shut the door and locked it, turning to take her in his arms again. They kissed again and again on their way to the bed, fumbling with buttons, buckles and zips as clothes were discarded on the floor, and tumbled to the bed in a flurry of laughter.

Emily was riding high. She didn't know whether the champagne had gone to her head or whether this feeling was simply love. Whatever, it seemed to be special and lovely and fun as Simon kissed and teased her. He made a kind of game of their lovemaking, chasing her, pretending to spank her, play fighting and acting about in a way that kept her laughing, so that when they finally came together it was swift, passionate, and completely wonderful as far as Emily was concerned.

The fact that the actual consummation took hardly any time at all didn't matter. Simon had been so considerate, so thoughtful of her that she was over the moon with happiness. Afterwards, they lay in bed smoking a cigarette between them and drinking more champagne. Emily wondered if they might make love again, but then she realised that he had fallen asleep.

Poor love, she thought as she kissed his brow and then switched off the bedside lamp. He must have been so tired, and that was hardly surprising considering what he had been through. She snuggled up against him, feeling warm and content. She had been so lucky to meet Simon, and her doubts had completely disappeared after that wonderful lovemaking. She hadn't expected it to be quite that way, and she was grateful to her considerate husband for taking care of her.

* * *

'I feel awful that I can't take you back to Liverpool,' Simon said. 'But I've had to garage the car and take a train myself, Emily. I didn't have as much petrol as I thought.'

'It doesn't matter,' she said, and kissed him softly on the lips. 'I wish you didn't have to leave so soon, but I knew that from the start. How long do you think it will be before you get more leave?'

'Not for a while,' he said, and touched her cheek lightly. 'I was lucky to get this. You're so lovely, darling. I don't want to leave you at all, but I have to.'

'Yes, I know.' She stood back as the guard warned that the train was about to leave the station. 'It doesn't matter, Simon. We have the rest of our lives to be happy.'

'Yes, of course,' he said, but his eyes didn't quite meet hers. She realised he was thinking that he might be killed at any time. 'I'll ring you as soon as I can – and you will telephone Amelia? I'm sure they would love you to visit when you can.'

'I shan't forget,' Emily said, and blew a kiss as the train moved off with a great bellow of steam and a shrill whistle. She watched as it clanked and chugged along the length of the platform, gathering speed as it left the station, and she went on watching until it disappeared from sight, before turning away to catch her own train.

Once seated inside the rather smoky carriage, she opened her newspaper. The headlines were shrieking about the latest bombing raids over various cities and towns, bringing back memories that she had been able to put aside for a few hours. A cold shiver went down Emily's spine as she read the numbers of dead and injured.

Most of her family were safe enough in a sleepy little village that might see an occasional bomb falling on the aerodrome, apart from Daniel who was spending his sick leave in London – and her husband.

Emily looked at the wedding ring on her finger. It hardly seemed to belong there, and she was beginning to feel as if she had woken from a dream. But no, it was true; she was Simon's wife. They had made love twice, once when she was so high on champagne and excitement that she hadn't been able to stop giggling, and once in the morning before they got up.

The second time had been very different. Oh, Simon had been as considerate as before, but this time he was silent, intense, as if driven by his passion. For Emily some of the sheer joy of their first time had been missing, but it was still good and she'd had no reason to complain.

Afterwards, Simon had gone into the adjoining bathroom and she'd heard the water running as he took a bath.

When he came out, he was smiling but he still didn't say much. It wasn't until they were about to part that he'd begun to talk. She supposed that he was anxious about returning to his base, tense about the possibility that this might be all the time they would have together. He must have faced it as she had – he could be killed the next time he went up in a plane.

No, she wouldn't think like that! If anything happened to Simon it would mean that Marcus might be killed too, and it couldn't happen. She and Frances couldn't both lose their husbands. It wasn't going to be that way.

* * *

Daniel read the telegram with a frown. He had been asked to report for his medical in seven days, a little sooner than he'd expected. It meant he ought to go home, see to a few things. His visit to London had lasted much longer than he'd intended and he wanted to finish working on the car he'd bought. He could use it to get himself to the military hospital. If he was going to be based here in England rather than abroad, he might as well keep it for a while.

He had sent Alice a few postcards while he was in town and now he decided he would buy her a present. He had bought a silver teapot for Emily, and a large tin of toffee for Connor – but he wanted something special for Alice.

What would she like? He didn't really know her well, though they'd had fun together and she'd taken what he had to say about not getting married for a while in good humour.

He supposed, in a way, that by saying what he had he'd more or less committed to marrying her one day, providing that he came through the rest of the war and she hadn't met anyone else she preferred. Well, he'd never met anyone else he liked half as much, though he wasn't sure about being in love. Daniel wasn't ready to be in love just yet.

That didn't stop him thinking of buying Alice something special, though, and when he saw the pretty antique gold heart on a fine chain he didn't hesitate to buy it.

Paying Margaret had taken his savings but he still had his service pay and he hadn't spent much of it for weeks. He got fed at the various halls and hostels where he helped out, and he still had enough left to get home and take Alice to the pictures a few times.

* * *

Alice nursed her excitement as she read Daniel's postcard for the tenth time that day. He would be home that evening and she was longing to see him. She had been lucky enough to be accepted as a land girl and at the moment she was splitting her time, working for her father three days a week and three for another local farmer, which meant she got either Saturday or Sunday off.

The next day was Saturday and she'd already decided to work on Sunday. That meant she and Daniel could go out somewhere if he wanted.

Alice had missed him while he was away, but she was a sensible girl and Daniel had been honest with her. He liked her a lot but wasn't planning to get married for a few years. Although she would've liked to be married or engaged, Alice didn't feel let down or miserable. She was very young. She enjoyed her life and she knew her parents wouldn't want her to marry for a long time. Her mother had always warned her to be careful men didn't take advantage of her, but Mrs Robinson wasn't ready to part with her daughter yet, still thinking of her as a girl rather than the woman she was.

Alice wasn't desperate about marriage just yet anyway. All that mattered was that Daniel cared enough to be straight in his dealings with her, and to send her postcards. She hoped the army would give him a nice safe job at home. At least then she might get to see him sometimes.

'Daydreaming again! Those cows won't muck themselves out, Alice!'

She glanced over her shoulder. 'Sorry, Jim,' she said. 'I got a postcard this morning. Daniel is coming back for a few days.'

'You'll want tomorrow off, then?'

'Yes, please. I'll work Sunday instead.'

'Nay, lass. Take a couple of days off. I can manage for once.'

Alice thanked him and wheeled her barrow into the cowshed, attacking the piles of dung and straw with a will. The smell in here was strong and not many girls would want a job like hers, but Alice had grown up around farm animals and she took no notice of it. She smiled and whistled tunelessly as she worked. Jim was a nice man and only in his early thirties. It was a terrible shame he'd lost his wife so young.

* * *

'You lucky thing!' Maura hugged Emily when she saw her rings. 'I wish I'd done the same when I had the chance.'

'Simon was so – so down,' Emily confided. 'I felt that if I didn't agree he might... Oh, I don't know. I wanted to give him something and I'm really happy we got married, but do you think they will send me home? You know what the services are like about married women.'

'If you were in the Wrens they would throw you out sure enough,' Maura said cheerfully. 'I think our lot are more reasonable; they have to be, because there aren't enough of us. Anyway, why tell them? I said you'd been called home urgently. You needn't wear your rings at work. Keep quiet and you'll have no trouble.'

'I suppose I could...' Emily hesitated. 'At least for a while...'

'If you have a babby you'll be asked to leave anyway – you aren't, are you?'

'Not to my knowledge,' Emily said, and blushed. 'I'll keep it to myself then, talk to Simon when he comes home next time.'

'Good for you,' Maura said, and then bit her bottom lip. 'They say I can visit John next Sunday. I'm not sure if I can do it, Emily.'

'You want to see him, don't you?'

'Yes... But I'm scared. I think I might start crying or lose my nerve at the last minute.' She pulled a face. 'Would you come with me?'

'Yes, of course,' Emily agreed without hesitation. 'Don't worry, Maura, it probably won't be half as bad as you think.'

It was a horrid position to be in, Emily thought, feeling sorry for her friend. Maura loved John but she couldn't face the idea of him being badly scarred. No one knew how they would cope in such a situation. Emily shivered and offered up a silent prayer that it wouldn't happen to Simon.

They were busy every night that week. The Germans seemed to be saying it was all or nothing, and that was probably due to the bravery and skill of Britain's fly-boys. They were doing a magnificent job of shooting down enemy bombers, but they couldn't prevent the raids taking place. The newspapers were filled with all kinds of stories, veering from gung-ho triumph to deepest gloom.

Sunday arrived at last and the girls caught their train, then a bus to the military hospital at Portsmouth. Maura didn't talk much on the way there, and outside the hospital she almost lost her nerve.

'I can't do it,' she said. 'Sure, I know I'm the world's worst coward, but me legs have gone to jelly, so they have.'

'I'll come with you,' Emily promised. 'I visited a fireman in Addenbrooks Hospital who had been burned and it wasn't too bad, really. Where is John, do you know?'

'Down here I think,' Maura said in a hoarse whisper. 'It's one of those small wards with only a couple of patients...'

Emily gave her a quick squeeze. 'Bear up, love, it will be all right.'

However, when they finally stood at the airman's bedside, Emily felt the vomit rise in her throat. Terry's burns had been superficial to his face and nothing like this. John's scars were horrendous, his eyelashes and eyebrows gone, lids puckered and swollen, mouth like a red gash in skin that was brownish purple in some places and blistered. He looked hideous and pitiful and Emily's heart was wrung with pain for his hurt.

She glanced at Maura, who had gone a pasty white, wanting to find words of comfort for her friend but knowing there were none in this case. John had opened one eye and was looking up at them. She knew that he was aware of Maura's revulsion.

'Hello,' she said softly, in an effort to ease the tension. 'We've been thinking about you all the time.'

'Go away!' The hissing whisper was directed at Maura. 'They shouldn't have let you come here.'

Maura stared at him for a moment, the horror evident in her eyes, and then she turned and ran from the ward. Emily lingered for a few seconds. Her heart was torn with pity for her friend but most of all for the poor man whose life had been so cruelly shattered.

'I'm so sorry,' she said, but his eyes were closed. She doubted that he knew she was there. 'So very sorry...'

'What are you doing here?' a nurse demanded as she hurried towards Emily. 'You aren't allowed in here without clearance.'

Emily looked at her blankly. 'I'm sorry, I came with a friend.' Had Maura known she had to have clearance? Surely she must have done, but she'd chosen to ignore it. 'I didn't know—'

'You'll have to leave,' the nurse said. 'Visiting is only for family and you aren't – are you? I haven't seen you here before.'

Emily didn't bother to explain. She ignored the nurse and walked out of the hospital. Maura was sitting on a wooden bench, staring out towards the sea but seeing nothing, her eyes glazed, her face blank. It was clear she was suffering from shock. Emily sat down beside her.

'It'll get better,' she said. 'They can do quite a lot for burns now.'

'He would be better off dead. I wish he would die. I wish I'd never seen him that way.'

'You don't mean that, love.'

'Yes, I do!' Maura rounded on her, eyes blazing. 'You don't know – you can't know how this feels.'

'I can imagine it's awful.'

'But you don't know,' Maura said bitterly. 'He was so lovely.'

'He's the same person.'

'No, never! I can't see him again. I don't want to.'

Emily looked at her helplessly. Maura sounded hard and uncaring but she wasn't. She was hurting so badly that she didn't know how to cope with her pain.

'Give it a while, love,' Emily suggested, but Maura simply shook her head. 'Shall we go home?'

'You go,' Maura said. 'I want time on my own.'

There was nothing she could do but watch as Maura walked away. Following would only make her angry. The time might come when Maura could talk. Until then, Emily could only wait and be there when she was needed. She shivered in the chill wind, watching the grey sea foaming about the shore for a moment before turning away. The sky was dark, the weather dismal, making things seem even worse than they were.

She was thoughtful as she caught the train back to Liverpool. Maura was on duty that night but Emily would stand in for her. The poor girl was in no condition to work for the moment. She had been unhappy since the news of John's horrific accident had first come, but something had changed in her when she saw his face. Emily had noticed the spark go out in her eyes, and, remembering now the shock of what they'd seen, her heart wrenched with pity again.

* * *

As Emily left the train in Liverpool, she thought she might as well go straight to work. She could have a cup of tea in the canteen before she started the late shift.

'Emily...' The voice made her jump. She turned, wondering who it could be, and was so surprised when the man laughed at her expression. 'You didn't expect to see me, did you?'

'Terry... Terry Burgess,' she cried, feeling pleased as she recognised him. The scar on his cheek had faded considerably and he looked well, his eyes bright. 'What are you doing here?'

'I've been transferred. I'm training new recruits. They won't let me back on an engine yet...' He flexed his hands and she saw that his movements were still stiff, the scars very much more noticeable here than on his face. One thumb looked as if it curved in too much towards his palm but was otherwise flexible. He saw the direction of her glance and nodded cheerfully. 'They're still a bit of a mess and I need more skin grafts, but I'll get there. In the meantime the fire service need experienced men to train recruits. We're getting all the rejects from the army; too old, too stupid – flat feet, they'll do for us.'

'Oh, Terry,' Emily said, and laughed because he was clearly joking. His smile was making her feel better, lifting the gloom that had hung over her since leaving Maura. 'So will you be here in Liverpool all the time now?'

'Three weeks, then I'm going down south for a while, but I shall be back.' He hesitated, looking at her uncertainly. 'You wouldn't consider going out with me tonight, I suppose?'

'I'm on duty tonight and most nights for a while.' She explained about Maura and he looked sympathetic. 'But you could come to the station social evening next week. I shall be there, because it's my night off.'

'If you're going I'll be there,' he said, and grinned at her.

'I'm glad I bumped into you like this. I've got to meet someone in a few minutes, but I'll see you around.'

'Yes, I expect so...'

It wasn't until he had disappeared into the crowds milling around the railway station entrance that Emily realised she was wearing gloves. He couldn't have seen her rings and she hadn't thought to tell him she was married. Why hadn't she told him? She wasn't sure but it hadn't occurred to her. She thought it was perhaps because she'd kept it a secret at work. Sometimes she hardly felt married at all.

Emily pulled herself up guiltily. She was married! And she ought not to have agreed to meet Terry. It was just that she had been so very pleased to see him. But she would set him straight the next time they met.

* * *

'Oh, it's so beautiful!' Alice cried as she saw the gold heart on its slender chain. 'Did you really mean me to have it?'

'Of course. Why not?' Daniel smiled, feeling pleased by her excitement. 'It's not new. I found it on a stall on the Portobello, Alice. The man said it's Victorian – a love heart, he called it. And that's a diamond in the centre.'

'You shouldn't have spent so much but I'm glad you did! I love it, I really do.'

She wanted to say that she loved him even more than the necklace but she didn't dare. Daniel hadn't said anything like that to her, and it would be wrong for her to be first. It might look as if she were putting pressure on him for further commitment or an engagement ring, and she'd promised herself that she wouldn't. Daniel would ask when he was ready and she knew she had to wait, to be patient. The fact that he had bought her this lovely present made it so much easier, because it showed that he thought something of her.

He was walking her home after a visit to the pictures in Ely. They stopped outside her gate and he hesitated before putting his arms around her, kissing her softly on the lips, and then releasing her.

'I'll be getting back to the house then. Frances is expecting me.'

'Yes, I suppose so...' Alice smothered a sigh. Just for a moment she wished that he would suggest a walk down the bank, and then, as the cold wind whistled about her ears, she laughed inside. They'd freeze to death! 'Shall I see you before you go to the hospital for your medical?'

'Probably not,' Daniel said. 'It's Emily's birthday soon and I promised to visit her in Liverpool. But I'll let you know what happens, and if I can get back we'll go out again.'

'Yes, well, good luck then.' Impulsively, she kissed him on the mouth, then turned and ran up the path to her house.

Her mother was at the sink washing the supper things. From the amount of plates and cups it was clear the New Zealanders had been enjoying a good supper before going off to work at the drome. Her mother put their lodgers before them all, going hungry herself and cutting her family's rations in order to feed the young men, who were risking their lives for them nightly in the big bombers they flew.

'Had a good time, love?'

'Yes, lovely.' Alice hesitated then held out the box that Daniel had given her. 'Look what he bought me...'

Mrs Robinson wiped her hands before taking the box and looking inside. She frowned over the beautiful necklace and then handed it back.

'That must be worth a bob or two.'

'Daniel says he bought it from a market in London – but it's good, Mum; it's gold and that's a diamond.'

'It's not a ring though.'

'No, it's not a ring. We're not thinking of anything like that yet.'

'No?' Mrs Robinson studied her in silence for a few seconds. 'That's a good thing. You're too young to get married. I shan't nag you, love. Just don't break your heart over him. Remember, he's a Searles and they think themselves too good for the rest of us.'

'Mum, that isn't fair. Daniel isn't a snob.'

'His sister Frances is though – and so was that stepmother of hers. Most people were glad to see the back of her. Since Frances married Marcus Danby she thinks she is royalty. She would think her brother too good for the likes of you.'

'I think you are being unfair, Mum. Frances speaks when she sees me and Emily was always friendly. Besides, Daniel is honest and nice. I know where I am with him.'

'It's up to you, but keep a cool head. You know what I mean.'

Alice blushed but before she could answer her father came into the kitchen. 'That boy's calling for a glass of water again, Mother. Why don't you take the bastard a pail full?'

'Oh, Dad!' Alice said, and laughed. She knew her father didn't mean anything by it. 'I'll take it to him.'

'He's probably hungry,' her mother said. 'I kept the cheese for the lads, and he had bread and scrape for his tea.'

Alice felt in her pocket. 'Daniel gave me a packet of toffee for him. I'll take it up with the water...'

* * *

Emily was pleased that her brother was coming to visit for her birthday. It was a few days early, actually, but that didn't matter. He was making a special journey to see her and that was the important thing. He would be here the night of the social at the church hall and it meant he would be with her. She had begun to feel very guilty for telling Terry that she would see him there, and for keeping her marriage a secret.

She had decided to speak to her supervisor. It took a bit of courage to ask to speak to Miss Anderson, who was a rather sour looking woman in her late forties, but after all, they could only sack her.

Miss Anderson looked grave as Emily explained, and she was sure it was the end. She would be asked to leave and that meant she might have to work in a factory or on the land, and she didn't think she would enjoy that.

'Well,' the supervisor said when she had finished, 'if things were different I should probably have to let you go – but you know how busy we are, Emily. The truth is I can't spare you. You're efficient, hard-working and bright. I think we'll just forget this conversation. If I knew you had got married without going through the proper procedure of informing us, I might have no choice. Of course, if you become pregnant you will have to leave. That is why we do not encourage married women in our ranks. It is a nuisance when they leave after all the training...'

'So you want me to carry on as I have been?' Emily was surprised but relieved.

'It saves any awkwardness,' Miss Anderson said. 'But thank you for telling me. If someone telephones for Mrs Vane I shall know it's you.'

'Simon wouldn't ring here. He has the number at my lodgings.'

Well, that was a wasted effort, Emily thought as she left the office, almost wishing she hadn't bothered. She'd screwed up her courage and now she was still in the same position – which made things awkward.

* * *

'Oh, Emily...' Daniel looked at her half-amused and half in condemnation when she explained her predicament. 'I thought you'd told your supervisor at the start?'

'There wasn't time.' Emily pulled a face. 'Some of the girls are married, but they were either married before the war, with husbands serving overseas, or they got permission – and we all have to leave if we have babies.'

'You're lucky they didn't throw you out.'

'She would have if she didn't need me,' Emily said, and laughed. 'I suppose I could always go and work in a factory.'

'But you like what you do, don't you?'

'Yes, very much. Still, if it happens it happens.' She shrugged her shoulders.

Daniel frowned at her. 'You aren't regretting getting married, are you?'

'No, I don't regret it.'

She wasn't sure how she felt if she was honest. When Simon was with her she knew that she cared for him deeply, but he hadn't phoned or written since they'd parted and she was feeling uneasy. Was he regretting their hasty marriage? He'd been so reserved the morning he left... But of course it was just that he had to go back to his duty, and like every other airman at the moment he never knew if it would be his turn to die next.

Emily blinked as her brother nudged her.

'Who's that chap over there?' Daniel asked. 'He's been looking at you for several minutes.'

Emily glanced in the direction he had indicated and blushed. 'That's Terry Burgess. He has been transferred to a training unit until his hands are healed. You remember I told you about the fireman I visited in hospital?'

'Yes, I remember. You'd better go and have a word with him, Emily. Does he know you're married?'

'No, I haven't had time to tell him yet.'

'Is that why you aren't wearing your rings?'

'Miss Anderson said it was best not to for the moment.' She wrinkled her brow. 'But I'm going to tell Terry this evening. It wouldn't be fair not to let him know.'

She was interrupted by the arrival of Maura, who lurched up to them a trifle unsteadily.

'You must be Daniel,' she said, and smiled at him. 'Emily told me you were gorgeous but she didn't say how gorgeous.'

Emily frowned. She thought Maura had had a bit too much to drink, but Daniel could cope; and besides, she needed to talk to Terry.

She walked towards him, seeing the smile leap into his dark eyes with a sinking heart. She felt a deep reluctance to tell him the truth, but it had to be done. It would be unfair to let him believe that there was a chance of a relationship between them.

* * *

Daniel looked at the Irish girl with slight apprehension. It was clear that she had been drinking and as a rule he disapproved of girls who took too much strong drink. However, as he looked into her face, he realised that she was desperately unhappy and he remembered Emily telling him about their visit to Maura's ex-boyfriend at the hospital.

'We've met before,' he said gently. 'Don't you remember – at your lodgings? I came with Emily that first day.'

'Can't remember anything,' Maura said, and swayed slightly towards him. He put out his hand to steady her, thinking she looked as if she might fall. 'I feel awful...'

'I'm not surprised. Would you like me to take you home? I can come back for Emily.'

'Yes, please,' Maura said. Her face had a greyish-green look. 'I may be sick.'

'Let's get our coats,' Daniel said hastily. 'Keep breathing hard, Maura. Don't be sick in here. Everyone will see.'

Maura's head went up. He could see she was fighting her nausea, but she managed to keep it down while they collected their coats from the cloakroom. Once outside, the air hit her and she reeled. Daniel steadied her until she jerked away and retched into the gutter.

'Here,' he said, giving her his handkerchief as she finally finished vomiting. 'You'll feel better in a few minutes.'

Maura took the handkerchief, which had his initials in the corner, wiped her mouth and shoved it in her coat pocket. 'Thanks. I'll give it to Emily when it's clean.'

'All right. Do you want a coffee somewhere or shall we walk for a while? The air should sober you up.'

'Could we have a cup of tea?' Maura gave him a pleading look. 'If I go home too early I'll start drinking again. It's the only way I can sleep.'

'Emily told me what you're going through. It must be very hard...'

'You think I'm a selfish pig, don't you?'

'No, of course not.' Daniel frowned. 'It's difficult for you.'

'Harder for him...' Suddenly Maura started to cry. 'I want to love him but I can't. I hate myself for not being able to face up to it but I just can't bear to see him that way.'

'It's not your fault he was burned.'

'If I'd married him perhaps I might have—' Maura gave a sob, looking up at Daniel. 'Could we go somewhere – a hotel? Would you stay with me tonight?'

'Do you think that's a good idea?'

'Please. If I have to be alone...' Her eyes met his and the wildness in them scared him. 'I shall probably cut my wrists. Please stay with me. You know what I mean – really be with me? I trust you. You're Emily's brother. If it isn't you I'll pick someone up or kill myself.'

Suddenly, they both heard a bang coming from the direction of the docks, and a flash of fire shot into the sky. It looked as if they were in for another raid. Daniel put his arm around the girl protectively.

'We'll find a hotel,' he said. 'I'll stay with you, Maura, but that's it. I won't sleep with you. You're in too much of a state to know what you want.'

'Just stay with me, then,' she said, and smiled. 'I like you, Emily's brother. Help me just this once. I shan't ask again.'

If he left her she might do something desperate, and on a night like this anything could happen. Daniel knew he wasn't going to desert her, despite the warning bells in his head. He would be a fool to get involved with this girl, even though she was rather attractive...

* * *

Daniel woke with a start, turning his head on the pillow to look at the girl lying beside him. He must have been mad – mad to come here, and even more stupid to respond to her pleading and get into bed with her. He'd had no intention of letting anything happen when he'd brought her here. But in the night, he'd woken to feel her naked body close to his, her mouth kissing him where he'd never been kissed before. Daniel's sexual experience had been limited to the back seat of a car or a hasty coupling in the pub yard. None of the village girls he'd been with would have dreamed of doing something like this. It had shocked and then excited him and he'd forgotten all his good intentions.

As if that wasn't bad enough, she had been a virgin! She hadn't behaved like one, her hot, eager mouth and hands seeming to speak of experience beyond anything he was used to in the girls he'd known. It was Maura who had aroused the needs he'd been unable to suppress; Maura who begged him to take her, but that didn't make him any less guilty. He was older, supposedly wiser, and he'd known how desperate she was.

But he hadn't known she was a virgin. Nothing would have persuaded him to make love to her if he had, but it was done and he felt awful. He stared at her as she slept. What was he going to do now?

Maura opened her eyes and smiled at him. 'You haven't gone off and left me, then? Most men would have. I'm sorry for what happened. Sure, it was all my fault.'

'I had a bit to do with it.'

'But it was me that started it.' She yawned and sat up, then smiled at him. 'I'm hungry.'

Daniel looked at her warily. He got out of bed, gathering his clothes. 'We'll have breakfast downstairs.'

'Don't worry,' Maura said. 'Sure, I won't pounce on you again. You saved my life last night and I meant what I said – I shan't ask you for anything more. You can leave now. I'll be all right.'

'You shouldn't be alone. Shall I ring Emily for you?'

'I'm fine now. Why wouldn't I be? My life isn't over. I'll get by now, Daniel, I promise – and I promise not to tell Emily about last night.'

Daniel hesitated. 'I paid for room and breakfast. Are you all right – for money, I mean?'

Maura trilled with laughter. 'Sure, 'tis me should be paying you, Dan. It's a fine Irish name you've got – and you're a fine man. You've done me a power of good, so you have.'

Daniel smiled. In this mood she was very attractive and he was tempted to linger, but he sensed she didn't want that. Goodness knows why she'd been so delighted to lose her virginity to him, but obviously she was very satisfied.

'I'll go then – if you're sure you're all right?'

'And why wouldn't I be?'

Daniel nodded. He took his clothes into the bathroom. When he left a few minutes later Maura appeared to be sleeping.

He wasn't there when she opened her eyes. Nor could he know what was in her mind.

Maura prayed that she was pregnant, but if it hadn't happened this time she would find someone else to give her a child. It was the only way she could face life. If she could convince herself that it was John's child.

7

Emily couldn't get the hurt look in Terry's eyes out of her mind. He'd taken the news of her marriage very well, making no recriminations, placing no blame, but she'd sensed his disappointment and seen the hurt. It had made her feel awful, which was silly really because she'd never led him on or made any promises. Except to say she would go out with him, of course.

She had spent several minutes with Terry and he'd told her they could still be friends, though she hadn't quite believed him. There was an attraction between them that meant meeting him could be dangerous. Too many affairs started because women were lonely, their husbands away at the war.

Afterwards, she'd looked for Daniel until one of the other girls told her he had left with Maura.

'I think she was ill or something,' Sheila said.

'He probably took her home. I think I'll follow them, just in case she needs help.'

Walking through the darkened streets, which were a

product of the blackout she had learned to deal with, Emily heard the siren just before the bombs started to explode over the dock area. She was quite a way from home and she hesitated, unsure of what to do until a woman grabbed her arm.

'Come on, love,' she said in a broad Liverpudlian accent. 'We're goin' down the church vaults. You'd best come with us. It looks as if the bloody Germans have got it in for us again tonight.'

'Yes, it looks like it. Thank you.'

Emily went with the little group of women gratefully. There was no sense in doing anything else. She jumped as another bomb exploded a few streets away, allowing her companions to hurry her into the church. It was a Catholic church but the priest wasn't asking for proof of faith. He ushered everyone down the dark, steep steps to a large vault. There was an oil heater burning and lamps had been lit, while on a board set on a wooden trestle jugs of water and paper cups had been put out ready. This obviously wasn't the first time the people of Liverpool had sought shelter here.

Emily settled down, sitting on one of the orange boxes that had been placed around the vault; there were mattresses too and some of the older people had stretched out, apparently not prepared to let Hitler disturb their rest. Women and children huddled in groups, the little ones clinging to their mothers, eyes wide and anxious.

Emily was relieved to have found a safe haven and wondered where her brother and Maura were, hoping they were safe...

It was very late when the all-clear sounded, and the wind was bitter as she emerged from the church. Emily decided she wouldn't bother returning to her lodgings. It was obvious from the damage in the streets, the stink of smoke and the red haze over the docks that it had been a bad night. She was much nearer the fire station than her landlady's house and she might be needed.

She could hear ambulance, fire and police sirens blaring as she hurried on her way. The sky was bright orange in places and she knew that there must be some big fires; her colleagues would be stretched to breaking point.

* * *

Emily got back to her lodgings at half past ten the following morning, having been on duty the whole of the previous night. She met Maura coming down the stairs.

'And where have you been all night?' Maura asked with a teasing look.

Emily explained about taking refuge in the church and then deciding to go straight to work. 'Someone said you were ill at the party. I was coming back to see if I could help but I couldn't ignore the raid – and then I thought I might as well go to work. They were busy so I did a longer shift and now I'm beat.'

'I had a bit too much to drink the other night but I'm fine now. I'm going in early. I expect a lot of the girls have been working extra shifts. It's time I did my share. You look done in, Emily.'

'I'm going to sleep while I can. I'll see you later.'

Maura was looking better than she had for days, Emily thought as she undressed and got into bed. Maybe she was beginning to get over the shock of seeing how badly burned John really was. She might even feel like talking about it soon.

Emily yawned as her eyes closed. She was so tired! She

thought about Terry for a moment. From the look in his eyes it was clear he'd been keen on her. She sighed, thinking how difficult things were sometimes, then she pushed the fireman to the back of her mind and thought about Simon. It was strange that he hadn't phoned her even once since their marriage. He hadn't written either. Perhaps he'd been too busy. She just hoped he was all right, but if something had happened to him surely someone would have let her know by now... Wouldn't they?

* * *

Daniel tried to put the memory of that night to the back of his mind, but it stuck there like a burr, pricking his conscience and making him feel guilty. He didn't like the idea that he'd slept with a virgin on a casual basis; it wasn't fair to the girl, even though it had been her idea – and he felt guilty about Alice.

He knew that Alice considered they were as good as engaged, even though she was prepared to wait for a few years. If she guessed that he'd slept with a girl he hardly knew she'd be heartbroken. He didn't want to hurt Alice. He supposed the feelings he had for her were most likely love. It was his natural caution that was holding him back from admitting it, because if he gave his feelings free rein he would probably end up getting married before he could afford it, and that might mean years of hardship and struggling for them all. Especially if children came along too soon!

Children... Oh, God, he hoped nothing like that had happened that night! The last thing he wanted was to father an illegitimate child.

He fought the rising sense of panic. If Maura had a child what would he do? He wasn't the sort to walk away from his responsibilities, but it would ruin all his plans. He cursed himself for a damned fool. What had he been thinking?

He tried to push the unwelcome thoughts to the back of his mind as he prepared for his medical. He knew that his shoulder was much better now, though he felt twinges of pain every so often, and he had recovered full mobility. They would pass him fit for work; there was a need for trained men and he'd be wanted somewhere. It was just a question of whether he was sent back to a fighting unit or shoved sideways into a desk job. On the whole, he thought he would rather be out there fighting with the others. It made him so angry when he saw the newspaper pictures of buildings and homes burning, read the stories of families being killed or injured as whole streets were destroyed in the raids.

This bloody war! Daniel cursed Hitler for plunging the world into this inferno. Yes, he hoped they would send him back to his unit. He would like to kill a few Germans!

* * *

'When's that boyfriend of yours coming down again?' Jim Wright asked as he came into the sheds where Alice was doing the evening milking.

'I don't know,' she said, and looked up with a smile. 'He had to go for a medical. If they pass him as fit he will be returning to his unit – though he's not sure whether they'll give him active service or a desk job.'

'Let's hope they give him something nice and safe,' Jim said, and grinned at her. 'Don't want a lovely looking lass like you going to waste, do we?'

'We're not engaged or anything...'

'Wants a kick up the pants, does he?' Jim joked. 'Shall I gee him up for you, Alice? Better still, find yourself a rich American airman to go out with. That'll make Daniel jealous if anything does.'

Alice pulled a face and laughed. 'No, thanks – I don't want to get myself talked about. You know what they say about girls who go with the Americans!'

'One Yank and they're down?' Jim roared with laughter. 'No, I can't see you falling for something like that, Alice. You're a decent lass – you'd be better off coming out with me.'

Alice smiled but didn't comment. Once or twice lately she'd seen Jim looking at her, a rather wistful expression in his eyes, and she'd realised he liked her. She liked him too, but not as boyfriend. He was too old for one thing, and another... The only one she wanted was Daniel. She would wait for him even if it meant no engagement or marriage until the war was over.

When the milking was finished and the pans washed, Jim told her to get off home. She was singing to herself as she cycled up the hill to the High Street, feeling happy. Daniel had said he would let her know what was happening, and her heart leaped for joy when she saw him waiting by her gate.

'Daniel!' She was off the bike and rushing at him. He caught her in his arms, kissing her passionately, more urgently than she remembered, as though he really loved her. Her eyes were dark and intense as she looked up at him. 'What did they say?'

'It's good news, I suppose,' he said. 'I'm going to be based down in the south of the country for a while. They have transferred me to a maintenance corps. I'll be helping to keep trucks and staff cars going for a couple of bases, Army and Air Force. It seems they're a bit short of men who can tinker with engines at the moment. I may be sent overseas with the unit at some future date, but I'll be a back-room boy, not up front.'

'Oh, but that's good – isn't it?' Alice looked at him, her smile fading. 'You're not pleased, are you?'

Daniel pulled a wry face. 'I suppose I am in a way. At least it will stand me in good stead for the future – I'd like to run my own garage after the war – but I feel as if I ought to be out there doing my bit with the others.'

'But you've already done that,' she said, and squeezed his arm. 'I'm glad you'll be here. Perhaps we can see each other sometimes?'

'Yes, there is that,' he admitted, and laughed. 'I want to eat my cake and keep it, Alice.' He touched her cheek. 'You've got a black mark here.'

'It's cow dung, I should think,' she said, and blushed. 'It doesn't make a very good perfume I'm afraid.'

'Doesn't bother me. I was brought up around a farm, remember.'

'Yes, but you're all polished up and I—'

'Why don't you go in and get ready?' he asked. 'I'll go home and change into civvies and then we'll go out somewhere.'

'Oh, yes,' she said, and her eyes sparkled at him. 'I shan't be long, I promise.'

'I don't mind waiting a bit,' he said. 'Besides, I've got something to say to you tonight.'

Alice's heart was pounding as she ran into the house. Was Daniel going to ask her to get engaged? There had been

something different about him, something more urgent and
demanding in his kiss, and it had given her new hope that
perhaps he wouldn't want to wait quite as long as she'd
thought.

It was towards the end of November 1940 that Liverpool saw
the worst night's bombing they had suffered so far. The city
was devastated, and fires raged night and day. Emily and her
colleagues were working flat out, doing extra shifts, some of
them hardly sleeping. They all looked haggard and red-eyed,
their nerves stretched to breaking point.

It wasn't just Liverpool that was getting it, though. Coventry's ancient centre had been devastated and London was a
raging inferno. How much more could they take of this? Sometimes, Emily felt the despair sweep over her, and one of the
most worrying things was that Simon still hadn't contacted her.

She was beginning to fear the worst. Something must
have happened or he would have called, written – anything!

She wondered if she ought to telephone his father – or
perhaps it might be better to write him a letter? If she hadn't
been so busy at work and so tired, she would have been to
visit them before now. She made up her mind to get in touch
as soon as she had the time.

However, when she went into her lodgings, she saw the
letters lying on the hall table. Her heart started to race wildly
as she looked at the writing and saw one was from Simon,
the other from Frances. She hurried up the stairs to her
room, wanting to read Simon's letter in private.

Maura was standing in front of the dressing table in her

petticoat, looking at her reflection in the mirror, a pleased smile playing on her lips. She had her hand on her stomach, but she took it away as she turned to Emily.

'I saw there was a letter for you,' she said. 'Is it from Simon?'

'Yes, it is,' Emily said. 'I've been waiting for ages, but I suppose he hasn't had time.'

Maura pulled on her skirt and blouse. 'Well, I'm off then. I'll leave you in peace.' She picked up her coat and went out humming a little tune.

Emily stared after her. Maura seemed in a much better frame of mind these days. She'd seen her leaving the station with one of the firemen a couple of times, and from the way she'd been laughing up at him it looked as if something was going on between them. Was she going out with someone else now?

It seemed too soon in a way, and yet Emily couldn't blame Maura for wanting some fun in her life. Everything was so horrible at the moment. You had to have something to look forward to or life was pretty wretched.

She opened her letter and gave a cry of pleasure. It was dated recently and contained an apology and an invitation. Simon was sorry he hadn't been in touch but he'd been working all hours and though he'd tried to phone her a couple of times he hadn't been able to reach her.

Emily frowned over that. Surely her landlady or one of the girls would have told her if they had taken a message? She knew Maura would and so would her landlady, but she could ask the others.

She read on. Simon had a week's leave coming up and he wanted her to meet him at his parents' home.

...we ought to just visit them. You haven't been to see them I gather, and Father is a bit hurt over that. We can stop there one night and then go off somewhere on our own. Hope you've missed me as much as I've missed you, darling.

See you very soon,

Love, Simon

Emily had mixed feelings when she finished reading the brief letter. She'd been busy too, but she'd written to him several times, and to her sister and brothers. It was true she hadn't written to his parents, but that wasn't so easy, because she hardly knew them, and they could have written to her just as easily. Yet Simon seemed to be chastising her, which didn't seem quite fair.

However, she was looking forward to seeing him, and the memory of Terry's hurt face had faded now. She hadn't seen him again since that night at the social, and perhaps that was a good thing. She was married to Simon and he was coming home on leave.

Tucking the envelope in her handbag, she opened the letter from her sister next and smiled as she saw there was some good news for a change. Marcus had been home on leave a month or so earlier, and Frances was pregnant and wildly excited. She wanted Emily to come home if she possibly could so that they could have a really good talk. Tacked on at the end of her letter was something else to make Emily smile.

Frances had heard that Daniel and Alice were getting engaged at Christmas if he could get leave.

*The date isn't certain. But I was talking to Mrs Robinson
and she mentioned it so it must be right – she doesn't
want them to get married just yet, because she thinks
Alice is too young. Daniel hasn't said anything, but then,
he probably wouldn't. You know what he's like.*

Emily smiled and laid the letter down on the chest
beside her bed. She yawned as she took her skirt and blouse
off, getting under the top covers in her petticoat. She was
very tired and she would have to be early this evening, especially if she wanted to speak to Miss Anderson about taking
a week's leave.

* * *

Maura was standing by the bed with a cup of tea in her hand
when Emily woke. 'Rise and shine,' she said. 'You must have
been very tired, love.'

'Yes, I was,' Emily said, and took the cup gratefully. 'I'm
glad you woke me because I want to be in early tonight. I
want to go on leave four days from now.'

'Simon got leave?' Maura asked. 'He's all right then?'

'Yes, he's fine,' Emily said, and smiled. 'It was all good
news. My sister is having a baby and I think Daniel is getting
engaged.'

'Has he got a steady girl then?' Maura's smile seemed a
bit fixed. 'Sure, I thought he was footloose and fancy free?'

'Well, in a way he was until now,' Emily said with a little
frown. 'He didn't say anything to me when he was here last
month. And I only had a postcard to tell me he was being
transferred to a maintenance unit down south somewhere.
He hasn't been in touch since then, so I suppose he's busy.'

'Everyone has been struggling to keep up,' Maura said, and yawned. Her eyes went to the letter on the chest beside Emily's bed. 'When is your brother getting engaged then?'

'Frances thinks it will be at Christmas, though she hasn't heard anything official yet. I thought he was going to wait until after the war – but then, Alice is still young. They may have a long engagement.'

'They shouldn't do that, not the way things are,' Maura said, and her eyes shadowed for a moment. 'If I were her I should persuade him to marry me sooner rather than later.'

'What about you?' Emily asked. 'You've seemed a bit better in yourself lately.'

'Oh, I'm fine,' Maura told her. 'I feel much better about things. I had a letter from John's mother yesterday. She says they're going to let him out of that side ward soon, and they are talking about skin grafts to his face in a few months.'

'That sounds promising?'

Maura shrugged. 'I hope it goes well for him, but I shan't be visiting him. He isn't the same any more. Besides, I have other friends I want to see.'

Emily looked at her uncertainly. Was Maura behaving oddly, or was she imagining things?

She put down her cup and got out of bed, leaving the bedroom to visit the toilet up the hall.

As soon as the door closed behind Emily, Maura picked up the letter from Frances and read it. She scanned it quickly and put it back as before, a thoughtful expression in her eyes. She was carrying a child and she was pretty certain it was Daniel's, even though she'd been with two other men since. She had promised she wouldn't ask anything more of Daniel after that night, and she wouldn't... At least, she wouldn't if things went her way with a man she'd met recently.

He was pretty keen, and she thought he might ask her to marry him. She wasn't in love with him – didn't want to be in love ever again, because it hurt too much – but she liked him and he would do. All she needed was a ring on her finger so that she could give her child a name and a home.

Daniel was quite safe unless she got into trouble, and then she might just pay him a little visit at his home.

* * *

Emily got off the train and looked about her. Last time she'd visited Simon's family he had driven her, and she wasn't quite sure how to get to their house. She imagined it might be quite a way to walk. Just as she was wondering whether she could find a taxi, she heard a horn blow loudly and saw Amelia Vane waving at her from the station yard.

She smiled and walked quickly towards her. 'I was just wondering what to do,' she said. 'It was good of you to come and meet me. How did you know which train I would be on?'

'Simon said you were coming and there are only two trains that stop here today,' Amelia told her with a smile. 'I decided to meet them both, but you're nice and early so I shan't have to come again.'

'I should have rung you,' Emily said. 'Simon did give me the number but I didn't like to.'

'Why on earth not?' Amelia had got out of the car to take her case and now she moved forward and kissed her on the cheek. 'Don't you know we're delighted to have you in the family, Emily? Simon is so odd at times. We none of us thought he would marry, and it was a wonderful surprise when he told us that he'd married you.'

'I thought we should have come down and told you first, but there wasn't time.'

'It didn't matter,' Amelia said. 'We are just pleased it happened.' Her eyes moved over Emily's slender figure, bringing a flush to the girl's cheeks. Had Amelia thought she might be pregnant already?

'Vane is thrilled that you're staying here for a short time. He wants to get you involved in his project.'

'Oh, yes.' Emily vaguely recalled that he was writing and researching a history of his family in medieval times. 'I don't think I would be much good at it, though, Amelia.'

'I shouldn't worry,' she replied with a laugh. 'He only wants to bore you with all he's discovered. He will talk for ages to anyone who will listen. But once you're living here, when you give up your job and come to us, then you'll want something to do, won't you?'

'I shan't be giving up for a long time,' Emily said, frowning slightly. 'I like what I do and they need me. If I didn't work for the fire service I should probably have to go in a factory or something.'

'Oh, not now you're married to Simon!' Amelia said. 'Vane wouldn't have that. Besides, once you have children...'

'Well, of course,' Emily said, and blushed again. 'I'll have to leave once I... once we have children.'

'Well, there you are then.' Amelia beamed at her. 'We had better get back. Simon should be here very soon.'

Emily got into the car, feeling as if she were being taken over. She wanted children one day, of course she did – but she wasn't in a hurry to start yet, and she didn't want to leave her job and live here. When Simon came out of the air force she had hoped they would find a nice little house of their own. It wasn't that she didn't like his family or the lovely house they lived in; no, it wasn't that at all, but she had thought they would have somewhere of their own for a few years at least.

* * *

Daniel read the letter from Alice, then slipped it into the pocket of his drill overalls. He was working on a lorry that was a perfect pain to get right; it had broken down too many times of late and he'd had it in the ear from his supervisor, though it wasn't his fault. It needed new parts but there weren't any going spare and he was patching it up as best he could yet again.

Alice's letter had brought some sunshine into a dull day, he thought. It surprised him how much he looked forward to them now, and he was glad that he'd asked her to get engaged next time he was on leave. He'd put in for leave at Christmas and he'd just heard that he was getting three days, Boxing Day and the two following. So he wouldn't be there on Christmas Day but Alice wouldn't mind. She would be pleased with the ring he had bought her, and the nylon stockings he'd managed to get from an American he'd met at one of the pubs down here. It was surprising what those Yanks got hold of, he thought with a smile, and it had pleased him that he'd been able to buy the stockings for Alice.

He imagined her wearing them. She had nice legs, and a good figure altogether. Daniel found himself thinking more often these days about how it would be for them once they were lovers. He grinned as a picture of Alice wearing nothing but the stockings and garters came into his head. Yes, that would keep the chill out on a cold winter's night all right! He had begun to count the days until his leave.

Glancing up, he saw one of the canteen girls on her way over, and he turned back to his work, concentrating hard. Daphne had made her interest plain and he wasn't falling for that one. It gave him cold shivers thinking about Maura and the night he'd slept with her. Thank goodness nothing had happened. It couldn't have done or she would have tried to get in touch. He wouldn't be taking any more risks like that. He'd been a stupid fool! Alice was the girl for him and he didn't intend to risk their relationship now. Something had changed the night he'd asked Alice to get engaged, and he'd known all at once how important she was to him.

When Daphne spoke to him, he glanced up, grunted something and got on with his work, ignoring her. He had no intention of becoming involved with anyone else. In a few weeks he would be slipping his ring on Alice's finger.

* * *

'I thought we were only spending one night here?' Emily said as Simon began to dress for dinner. 'I was looking forward to going somewhere on our own.'

'I can't go off too soon,' Simon said. 'You know how pleased Father was to see us, and with the news of the wedding – he just wants us to meet all his friends.'

'But what about our plans?' Emily said. She wasn't sure why she was pushing him, but for some reason she was out of sorts. Simon had made love to her twice the previous night, but this time he hadn't bothered to play games or tease her, and it hadn't been very satisfactory somehow. She felt as if his loving had been almost furtive, as if he were doing what was expected of him rather than for pleasure – his or hers. It hadn't been good for either of them. 'Your family seems to think we're going to live here after the war. We aren't – are we?'

'Of course we are – some of the time, anyway,' Simon said, his gaze narrowed and hard. 'You must have realised that this place needs a lot of looking after? Father told you and so did Amelia.'

'Yes, but that's their job, isn't it?'

'For the moment, yes, but I shall help when the war is over. I'm the heir and it's up to me to help keep the estate running, Emily. Surely you knew that? You must have understood.'

'Well, I didn't, not like that,' she said, and frowned. She wouldn't have minded so much if she'd been asked, but it all seemed cut and dried. She was expected to be the dutiful wife, give Simon a couple of sons and a daughter, and then settle down to mindless chores that would bore her to tears. She wasn't interested in tracing the family back to the Middle Ages or in playing lady of the manor. 'I knew it might happen one day, but I thought we might have our own house. I like to cook and do my own flowers and—'

'Well, you can arrange flowers for the church, and for the house too if Amelia doesn't mind,' Simon said. He looked at her and realised she was genuinely upset. He moved towards her, taking her into his arms. 'I know this is all a bit much for you at the moment, darling, but you'll get used to it. Once we have children you'll find plenty to do – and there's always charity work. I'm sure my father or Amelia would be glad to have you on their own boards or help you find something that interests you.'

Emily melted a little in his arms. He could always do that to her with a smile or a kiss, and she did love him. 'But we shall have some time on our own, shan't we?'

'Yes, of course. I shall keep my flat in town, and we'll go up for a few days now and then. You can visit the theatre or museums or simply shop if you would rather, Emily. That reminds me, Father wanted you to know that he has arranged an allowance for you. It will be paid into a bank he uses in your name and you can do what you please with it – he's always generous with money so you'll be able to shop as much as you like.'

'I don't need money. I have my pay from the fire service.'

'Ah, yes, I was coming to that,' Simon said, looking at her oddly. 'I think you should give notice, Emily. It is too dangerous for you in Liverpool. I would much rather you were here.'

'You are in danger every day,' she reminded him. 'Why should it be any different for me?'

'Don't be stubborn, darling.' Simon looked at her set face. 'Well, I suppose there is no real hurry just yet – but think about it, for me? I worry about you.'

'I worry about you. Especially when you don't ring me.'

'I tried telephoning. I told you.'

'I asked everyone and no one had taken a message.' Emily's tone and eyes were more accusing than she realised.

'Don't be ridiculous! That Irish girl was there once, and the last time no one answered. There just wasn't time to keep on phoning you. If you had been here I should have been sure of you at least getting my messages.'

Emily bit her lip. It wasn't beyond the bounds of possibility that Maura had forgotten to give her a message. She had been in a bit of a state for weeks, and even though she seemed better now, she could have forgotten.

Sighing, she realised that she had been a bit unfair to Simon. She had known that they would live at the house one day, vaguely at the back of her mind. It was just that the family seemed determined to take her over. They were all very kind and nice, but she felt since her marriage she had become a part of the property rather than a person in her own right. She knew they would like her to give up her job and come to live here, become a part of the family firm. She'd seen the way Amelia's eyes went over her, as if hoping for a sign that she was already with child, and that had rattled and embarrassed her. Who did they think she was – a woman with hopes and dreams of her own or just someone to produce an heir for the title?

She wanted Simon's children one day, but not yet if she were honest. And she wasn't going to give up her job with the fire crews without a fight.

'Maura must have forgotten,' she said, and she gave Simon an apologetic look as she went to put her arms around him. 'It's just that I kept wondering why you hadn't rung me – and if you were all right.'

'Yes, well, it was unfortunate,' Simon said, and kissed her nose. 'Tell you what, we'll leave in the morning, go up to my flat in town and enjoy ourselves. We can do some shopping if there's anything decent to buy, have a bit of fun – like we did that night?' His eyes teased her and Emily smiled, feeling better. Her wedding night had been fun, but so far this visit had been awkward. Sometimes she thought Simon was two different people – the man she'd fallen for and a stranger she didn't know. 'You know I adore you, darling. I'm a bit on edge myself. It's been pretty rough these last weeks.'

'Yes, I know,' she said, immediately contrite, because she knew how hard it must be never knowing if this was the day your plane would crash in flames, taking you with it. 'I'm sorry I threw a tantrum. I've been working hard myself – but I do love you, Simon.'

'Well, so I should hope,' he said, and laughed. 'I might be a bit miffed if I thought you were tired of me already.'

'No, of course I'm not,' she said, and she laughed as he swept her off her feet and sat her on the edge of the bed. 'What are you doing?'

'Something I fancy,' he said, and pushed her skirt up over her thighs. 'I've been thinking about this for weeks...'

Emily gasped as he lowered his head, his tongue flicking up the soft inner flesh of her thigh. 'Simon... Don't you think we ought to go down? Dinner will be ready...'

'Be damned to dinner, my appetite is for something else.'

The wicked light in his eyes made her laugh. She arched back as she felt the first flicker of pleasure as he invaded her with his tongue, moaning softly as the sweet torture went on and on for some minutes. And then she was lying beneath him on the covers, and he was thrusting into her eagerly, hastily. Almost too soon he withdrew and went into the bathroom, leaving her still vaguely unsatisfied. He had given her pleasure, yes, but in the end he had seemed as if he wanted it over with, as if he had been merely doing his duty.

Emily shook her head, determined not to let this vague dissatisfaction spoil things between them. Simon loved her, he wanted her, worried about her being in Liverpool – so why should she feel that this was all wrong? It was silly but she had the feeling that Simon was merely playing a game, that their lovemaking gave him little or no pleasure. He had done what he had simply to placate her, keep her in a good mood.

Oh, she was just being silly! Simon had loved her from the start. He was always saying it, and he'd bought her lovely gifts – but he didn't look at her the way Terry did...

Emily felt guilty as she recalled the hungry look in Terry's eyes, the real pain she had seen there when she'd told him she was married. She mustn't think about that, and she mustn't let doubts creep into her mind. Simon made love to her often. Maybe it was her imagination that he seemed to be going through the motions rather than driven by real desire? Perhaps he was the kind of man who couldn't show his feelings at such times?

And yet he was good with words, and when they laughed together they had fun. It was just that she couldn't get it out of her head that he was making love to her because it was expected. Just as she was expected to give him an heir to the estate.

8

Emily returned to work with mixed feelings at the end of her leave. A part of her was sorry to be parting from Simon, because the second half of their holiday had been much nicer. Simon had been different in London, more relaxed, and they'd gone out to the theatre and restaurants, and drunk a lot of champagne, which Simon always seemed able to find; perhaps because he was well known at the places they visited. She had decided that it was just being with his family that made him seem different, and this time he took her back to Liverpool on the train, taking a lingering farewell of her.

'I'm not sure if I can get leave at Christmas or New Year,' he told her. 'But I'll let you know as soon as I can.'

'If you can't, I shall go home to Frances,' Emily said. 'I know I've got two days for New Year so do your best, but send me a postcard or something this time, Simon. Please?'

'Yes, of course, I'm sorry,' he said, and touched her cheek. 'I don't mean to be careless or hurt you, darling. I want to make you happy, but I'm an odd creature; you ask my family.

I have always had moods, and things are so bloody at the moment.'

'Yes, of course. I understand.' Emily smiled and kissed him. 'I love you, Simon. I'll try to be patient this time.'

'Things have to get better soon,' Simon said, and for a moment the grin she loved was in place. 'You go now, Emily. I have to catch my train in a few minutes, and you're all right now, aren't you?'

'Yes, of course.' She gave him a big hug and walked away. When she glanced back he was still watching her, but he was no longer smiling.

* * *

Connor loved having tea with Peter's family. It wasn't that they had much food – nothing special at any rate, just bread and marge; the government was becoming stricter about farm produce and you couldn't keep much of what you produced these days. However, there was usually a fresh egg from the hens in the yard, a few jam tarts and a slice for each of them of the big seed cake Alice had baked the previous evening. The reason he liked being with them was that they were such a happy family, all talking and laughing as they ate and drank their tea, sometimes with their mouths full.

Frances invariably complained if he spoke with his mouth full. It wasn't much fun living with her these days. She only had one thing in her head, and that was the baby. She was always knitting things, grumbling at her brother if he made a mess in the house, and telling him to be quiet. He missed Emily desperately, and Daniel. He wished that this rotten war was over and his brother would come home. He was longing for him and Alice to get married, because Dan had said Connor could live with them once he'd fixed himself up with a house.

'You'd better get home, love,' Alice said to him when she had finished clearing the table, the washing up neatly done and put away. 'It's dark out and Frances will worry. Do you want me to walk home with you?'

'No, I'm all right thanks.' Connor smiled at her. He really liked Alice and he was glad she was going to marry his brother. 'I'll run all the way – don't worry, the gremlins won't get me.'

Alice laughed and he called goodbye to his friend and Mrs Robinson and then went out sharpish. He had to force himself to leave the warmth and comfort of their big family kitchen, where he felt so at home. The trouble was, he didn't have a home any longer. The house belonged to Frances and Marcus now, and she was always making changes. It felt all wrong, as if his world kept shifting.

He wished his father were still alive. He hardly remembered his mother at all, but he hadn't noticed so much while his father was around. Now he felt lost and alone, and the only time he was really happy was when he was at Peter's house.

He kicked at a bottle lying discarded on the path, sending it into the gutter, and then picked up stones and threw them at it, trying to break the glass. Frances would be playing the gramophone while she knitted baby coats. She would tell him to kiss her and then send him to bed. He didn't really want to go home, but it was cold out and there was nowhere else he could go at this time of night. He might ask Henry if he could stop there for a while when school broke up.

He saw the girl get off the bus and hesitate as she walked

towards him. She was quite a pretty girl with dark hair, and when she spoke she had a funny accent, a bit like the tinkers who had come with the fair one summer, but softer and nicer. She smiled at him.

'Hello,' she said. 'Do you live in this village?'

'Yeah – just up the road, why?'

'I wondered if you could tell me where Daniel Searles lives?'

'Why do you want to know?' His eyes narrowed in suspicion.

'I have something to tell him,' the girl said. 'Is he at home?'

'Nah, he's working down south somewhere,' Connor said. 'I could tell him when I see him, if you like?'

'Is he still at that base near Southampton?'

'Yeah, I reckon.' Connor gave her a hard look. How did she know that? He made up his mind that he didn't like her, even though she was being friendly. 'He might have been moved up to Scotland, though. I heard someone say he was going overseas soon.'

'Oh.' The girl nodded, as if that settled something in her mind. 'You're sure he isn't here?'

'That's his house up there.' Connor pointed at his home. 'Go and ask if you don't believe me. I'm his brother so I should know.'

'You are Daniel's brother?'

'Yeah.' Connor gave her a defiant look. 'So what?'

'Give him this then,' she said, and took a small packet from her pocket. 'And if you see him tell him the lady who gave it to you is getting married at Christmas – will you do that for me? My name is Maura. You will tell him you saw me?'

'Yeah, if you like.' Connor shoved the handkerchief into his pocket. 'The bus is leaving any minute if you want to catch it, miss. There won't be another one tonight and there's nowhere to stay here.'

'Thank you.' She turned and ran towards it, scrambling on board and waving to him from the window as the bus moved off.

Connor shuffled his feet. He'd told her a lot of lies, but it didn't matter. Something about her had made him wary, and he had felt she might cause trouble for Daniel.

He fingered the packet in his pocket. It felt soft and he was curious about what it contained. Opening it, he saw that it was one of Daniel's handkerchiefs; it had his initials in the corner and there were others like it in the chest of drawers in his brother's bedroom.

Why had the girl come especially to bring the handkerchief? It seemed a waste of time to Connor. She could have sent it through the post, couldn't she? He shoved it back in his pocket, deciding he would put it with the others in Dan's chest and say nothing to him about the girl at all.

Emily was surprised when Maura told her she was getting married at Christmas. She had just returned from a short leave to visit family, and she had dropped her bombshell when they were alone.

'But...' Emily looked at her helplessly. 'I've seen you with someone – Steve Jacobs I think his name is – but you've only known him a short time, haven't you?'

'Long enough,' Maura said. 'Anyway, I don't have a lot of

choice. I'm having a baby and I want to get married. My father would have a fit if I didn't.'

Maura never talked about her family. She had a sister living in Ireland but she'd never mentioned her father before.

'Oh, well, that's lovely,' Emily said, and moved to kiss her cheek. 'I'm glad for you – if it's what you want?'

'I wanted a baby,' Maura said, and for a moment her eyes were bleak. 'Steve is all right. He says he loves me so I suppose we shall get on.'

The expression in her eyes was saying all the things she wasn't. Emily realised that behind her cheerful manner she was still very unhappy.

'Why don't you go and see John again?'

'No!' Maura recoiled, the grief twisting her face. 'I can't, Emily. I've thought about it again and again, but I just can't. I've got the baby and Steve will look after me. The past is over. I have to forget.'

Emily thought it was easy to say, but not so easy to walk away from memories.

'I hope you'll be happy,' she said softly.

'You'll come to my wedding, won't you?'

'Yes, if I can manage it,' Emily replied. 'Simon won't be getting leave until the end of January it seems, so I'm going home for a few days – but that isn't until the New Year. I want to see Frances. She's having a baby too, and she's very excited about it.'

'You aren't yet, are you? Do you mind?'

Emily shook her head. 'No, not for the moment. I thought I might be but it hasn't happened, and in a way I'm glad. I should have to leave the service then and go to live with Simon's family.'

'Don't you want to? You said they were nice, and that it was a lovely place to live.'

'Yes, it is, and I do enjoy being there. The first time I went I fell in love with the house and gardens. It's just...' She struggled to find the words. 'Now that we're married, they seem... Oh, I don't know! It's hard to explain, because they were nice to me, but I think they want me to give up my job and fit in with the family.'

Maura laughed. 'It's always like that with in-laws. You'll have to get used to it, love. Sure, it's one of the things we all have to contend with – the mother-in-law.'

'No, it isn't like that exactly. Amelia is lovely and so is Vane, but...' How could she explain that it was the effect his family seemed to have on Simon? Away from his family he was a different man. 'I'm probably being very silly. I expect when I get used to the idea I shall be happy enough.'

'Well, I don't care what Steve's family is like,' Maura told her. 'I'll go my own way, so I will, and the devil take it!'

It was nice to see Maura looking happier again, Emily thought. She would miss her when she left, but once Maura told their supervisor that she was having a child, she would be asked to leave anyway.

Emily wasn't particularly worried that she hadn't conceived yet herself. After all, there was plenty of time.

* * *

Emily came out of the pictures having enjoyed the big film *Rebecca*, Hitchcock's thrilling masterpiece of deception and betrayal. She had been to an early showing and emerged just as the sirens went, looking at her companion in dismay.

'Shall we try to get home or find a shelter?'

'Let's follow them.' Mary Jones, a friend of Emily's from work, pointed in the direction of a small crowd of people who seemed to know where they were going.

Emily didn't argue. Anything was better than being caught on the streets in a raid. They joined several women and children taking shelter in a church, but within twenty minutes the all-clear went and they realised it had been a false alarm. As they emerged into the cold of a December night, they could smell the enticing odour of coffee coming from a café further up the road and made a beeline for it.

Mary found them a table near the window, while Emily joined the queue for coffee and the plain biscuits, which was all that was on offer apart from some greasy looking Spam and chips. She carried her tray back to where Mary sat waiting.

'I don't know how some of these places make a living these days,' she told her friend. 'They can't get very rich out of tea and biscuits, can they?'

'Oh, they manage,' Mary said. 'I came here for pie and chips the other day. It was all right, though I'm not sure what was in the pie... It might have been chicken but I'm not sure.'

'They haven't got much scope at their prices,' Emily said. But cafés like these were only allowed to serve meals under two shillings, and they didn't often contain meat. 'I sometimes wonder how they think we can live on what—' She broke off as someone approached their table. She glanced up at the man carrying a tray with a plate of Spam and chips, some bread spread with yellow margarine and a cup of tea.

'Do you mind if I sit with you?' he asked. 'There aren't many seats left and I only got in a few minutes ago. The train was late because they wouldn't let us through at the last signal.'

'Terry...' Emily breathed hard as she saw him. 'Yes, of course you can. We're only having a cup of coffee. There was a false alarm a little while ago. I expect that's why they halted your train, just in case it was a genuine raid.'

'Yes, I expect so,' he said. 'I haven't eaten since this morning. Excuse me if I eat, won't you?'

'Yes, of course.' Emily turned to her companion. 'Mary, this is Terry Burgess. He's a fireman but he's training recruits now.'

'Nice to meet you,' Mary said, and she got up. 'I'd better get home, Emily. My parents will worry...'

'I'll come with you, if you like?'

'No, you stop and talk to your friend. I'm going to catch a bus round the corner anyway.'

Emily was silent after her friend had left. 'Mary is one of the few of us living at home. She's lucky really.'

'How are you, Emily?' Terry's eyes were on her as she sipped her coffee.

'I'm fine,' she said. 'I went to the pictures with Mary earlier. We saw *Rebecca* – it was good.'

'I haven't seen it,' Terry admitted. 'I took a friend's children to see *Snow White*, though. We all enjoyed that.'

Emily laughed. It seemed odd to think of the large, strong fireman enjoying a film meant for youngsters, and yet it was nice that he had taken his friend's children to see it.

'Are you still with the training unit?'

'I've been having a bit of treatment on my hands,' Terry said. 'I might get back to work properly next year, so they tell me.'

'I'm glad.' Impulsively, she reached across the table and took the worst affected of his hands in hers, stroking it gently. 'I hope this will be back to normal soon.'

'Emily...' His fingers tightened about her hand and she realised his grip was stronger than she had imagined. 'You know I care about you, don't you? I have no right but it doesn't stop what I feel inside. If ever you need anything...' He released her hand and sat back, pulling a wry face. 'And that was bloody daft when you're happily married, wasn't it?'

'No, not at all,' she said. 'I hope we are friends, Terry, and, if things were different...'

She left the words unsaid, knowing that she was treading on dangerous ground.

'He does make you happy?'

Terry's eyes were on her face, and she had the oddest feeling. For a second she wanted to tell him that she was afraid that she had made a terrible mistake, but she clamped down on her words. How ridiculous was that? She was in love with Simon. These doubts she'd been having would all vanish when Simon came home.

'Yes, of course,' she said, not meeting Terry's eyes. She stood up, knowing she had to leave quickly. 'I must get back now. I'm on duty early tomorrow and I need to sleep.'

'All right, but I hope I shall see something of you while I'm here.'

Emily smiled but made no comment. It would be Maura's wedding that weekend, and then came Christmas. It was just as well that she was going home for a few days soon. Terry was a friend, but it would be foolish to let it develop into anything else. She wasn't one of those women who had affairs just because they were lonely – and that was all that was wrong with her. She was missing Simon.

* * *

Alice looked at the beautiful ruby and diamond cluster ring on her finger. It was so beautiful, and she hadn't expected anything as expensive as this.

'You don't mind that it was my mother's?' Daniel asked as he saw her studying it again. 'I could have bought you something but it wouldn't have been as good as this. Father divided the jewellery between us a few years ago, and I kept this because I liked it.'

'It's lovely,' Alice said, her eyes shining. 'And I like it even more because it was your mother's – that makes it special and we shall always keep it in our family, pass it down to our son one day.'

'As long as you like it,' Daniel said, and kissed her. They hadn't had an engagement party as such, because they couldn't really plan very far ahead. Daniel hadn't been sure when he could get back until the last minute, and Alice had sworn she didn't mind. He had taken her out for a meal at a proper restaurant, not one of those places where you only paid a shilling or so, and they'd had a bottle of champagne, which had gone to Alice's head a little. Now they were sitting in the front room of his home, because Frances had gone to stay with her in-laws over Christmas, and Connor was staying with Henry. 'I do love you, Alice, and I never want to do anything to hurt you.'

Daniel drew her into his arms, kissing her hungrily. It was strange how he'd suddenly become impatient to make love to her. He'd thought he could wait until they were married, but recently he'd found himself dreaming of being with her that way, of feeling the softness of her skin next to his, of loving her.

'Oh, Dan,' Alice breathed close to his ear. 'It's lovely to be with you like this. It's the first time we've been here alone...'

'Yes.' His voice was husky, his breath rasping against her ear as he felt the sweeping desire. 'The very first time we've had the house to ourselves.'

'I do love you,' she said, snuggling up to him. 'I know it's ages before we can get married but if we were careful...'

Daniel sat back and looked at her. 'You don't mean...? You wouldn't, would you, Alice? I know we ought to wait...'

'But we both want to, don't we?' She smiled up at him, eyes wide and innocent. 'And we're engaged now.'

It was obvious that Alice thought it didn't matter now they were engaged; she trusted him to keep faith with her if anything happened, and of course he would. If they did have to get married sooner than he'd planned it wouldn't matter so much. He had some land of his own and he could find a house for them, even if he had to rent for a year or two – and surely things would be better for them soon? Henry was managing well enough, and he didn't have much more than Daniel.

His resolve was weakening. He wanted Alice so much, and it would erase that other memory. It still haunted him at times, made him feel disloyal to Alice, and if they made love it would wipe that night out, wouldn't it? She would feel the bond between them, and he wanted to marry her as soon as he could manage it anyway.

'Are you sure?' he whispered, though his heart was racing and he knew he would have found it hard to hold back now if she changed her mind. 'If you're really sure, Alice, I do love you so much.'

'Of course I'm sure,' she said, and smiled up at him. 'Shall we stay here by the fire or go upstairs?'

The bedroom would be too much like that other time, and it was cold. Here before the fire it was warm and romantic. Daniel threw some cushions on the mat, and then kissed her again. He began to unbutton her blouse, caressing her breasts, touching her further down as he slid her skirt over her hips, and she helped him to take off her stockings and the pretty camiknickers she was wearing.

In the firelight her skin was a pearly pink, and just as he'd expected she was rounded in all the right places, beautiful, warm and desirable. He couldn't have held back then to save his life, and his clothes joined hers on the floor. Then they were lying together before the fire, touching, kissing, whispering and finally loving. It was sweet and precious, and better than anything Daniel had ever known, and he realised how much he loved her and how precious she was.

He'd been a damned fool! What did the garage matter compared with this? He loved Alice and she was more important than anything else. He made up his mind as he held her close after the tumult of passion that he would marry her just as soon as he could get a decent leave.

'I love you,' he whispered, as he felt desire rising once more. 'Oh, Alice, I didn't know. I just didn't know how much...'

* * *

Alice lay in bed that night feeling the happiness seep into her very bones. She still tingled where Daniel had touched and loved her, and her lips felt swollen from his passionate, hungry kisses. She was his now, and they would be together for the rest of their lives. She was sure now that Daniel wouldn't desert her. Her lips curved in the darkness as she thought of how he'd hung back when she'd known how much he wanted her. And she had wanted him too, wanted to be a part of him, to know what loving was all about.

It had been wonderful, much better than she'd imagined. Some of the girls she knew said it was overrated, but Alice didn't think so. She had thought it got better and better, and they'd done it three times before Daniel had insisted he ought to get her home.

She giggled as she remembered that she had wanted to stay there in front of the fire all night, but Daniel had said Mrs Robinson would have his guts for garters if he didn't get her home. He had been right, too. Her mother had given her an old-fashioned look when she got in at quarter past twelve.

'And what time do you call this, miss?'

'It is our engagement night, Mum.'

'That's as may be,' her mother said, and fixed her with a sharp look. 'You're not married yet and there's many a slip betwixt cup and lip. Just because you're engaged doesn't mean you can do as you like. While you're under my roof you'll behave decently.'

'Yes, Mum, of course I will.'

Alice was too happy to let her mother's words bother her. She had everything she wanted from life now. Daniel loved her and he'd promised they would marry sooner than she'd expected, although he hadn't said anything for definite yet. But she could wait now that they were engaged. He wouldn't go off with anyone else, because he loved her.

* * *

Daniel was reluctant to leave the next day, but his pass had been for just forty-eight hours and he had to get back. He wasn't sure when he would get leave again, because they were so rushed at the depot. Trucks and lorries had a habit of breaking down when they were most needed, and some of the men had been posted to other bases. He knew he was lucky to be working in England so that he could see Alice, and hopefully make arrangements for their wedding soon.

When he got to his base and reported for work, he was surprised to be asked to see his commanding officer immediately.

'Ah, there you are, Searles,' Major Andrews greeted him cheerfully. 'Had a good leave, did you?'

'Yes, sir. I got engaged to my girlfriend.'

'Glad to hear you made the most of it. We may manage to give you another short break before we leave, but it's on the cards we shall have to go off at short notice, so don't count on it.'

Daniel felt a sinking sensation inside. 'Where are we off to, sir?'

'You know I can't tell you that, Corporal... But it's probably a lot warmer out there than it is here, as you'll see when you get your kit.'

Corporal? When had that happened? Daniel stared as Andrews smiled at him. 'What was that, sir?'

'You've been promoted. Bit tardy really if you ask me, you should have had it before now – but it's come before we push off so that's a good thing.' He frowned as Daniel hesitated. 'You're fit to see active service, aren't you? Not that you'll be in the firing line much. Too valuable. We need our engineers. Carry on, Corporal.'

Daniel saluted and knew himself dismissed. It had come as a bit of a shock to learn that he was being sent abroad. Warmer than it was here? He shivered in the icy wind. Anywhere would be warmer than here!

As he returned to his mates, they were whispering about where they were headed. Most of them seemed to think it might be Egypt.

'I reckon they're going to need a lot more of us out there,' one of the men said, and several others agreed with him.

'It might be Gibraltar or Malta,' someone else said. 'It don't have to be the desert.'

'Bloody Malaya or somewhere,' one of the others grumbled. 'I bloody 'ate them foreign places, can't stand the heat, me.'

Daniel frowned as he got on with his work. It didn't matter much where they sent him; it would amount to the same thing. He wouldn't be able to see Alice for a long time. He remembered their lovemaking, how good it had been, and wished he'd somehow arranged for them to be married before he came back. There was a chance that he might get a few hours' leave before he was sent overseas; the powers that be usually did that if they could, and he could only hope.

He would write Alice a letter, tell her that he was being posted and ask her if they could get married with a special licence if he managed to get back. All of a sudden, he couldn't wait to be married to the girl he loved, to know that she was his and would be waiting for him when he finally came home again.

* * *

'It's lovely to see you,' Frances said, and kissed Emily on the cheek as she met her at the station. She was driving a little Austin car, which Marcus had bought her when he was on leave before Christmas, because he said he didn't want her walking everywhere now she was having a child. 'You've just missed Dan, you know. He was here for a day and a half – spent all his time with Alice, of course. I imagine they will get married as soon as they can now.'

'Yes, I expect so,' Emily said, and looked at her sister intently. 'How are you, love? Are you feeling all right?'

'Never felt better,' Frances said, and laughed. 'I had a bit of morning sickness but it didn't last long. I'm just so excited I can't tell you – and it's good to have you home for a while. It seems ages since we were at home together.'

'It's not really my home now,' Emily said, smothering a sigh. 'I expect we shall live with Simon's family after the war, at least some of the time anyway.'

'That will be nice,' Frances said. 'They have a lovely house, I believe. Marcus has been there and he says Simon's people make his look like paupers.'

'That isn't true,' Emily said. 'I know they have money but so does Marcus's father.'

'Yes, but you know what I mean.' Frances looked a bit smug. 'We've both done well for ourselves. Whatever happens with the farm, we shall be all right.'

'What do you mean?' Emily looked at her in alarm. 'Has something happened?'

'No – but Margaret drained the kitty dry, didn't she? Henry was struggling to keep things afloat before that, and things aren't getting any better. It's quite possible that they may have to sell at least some of the land in a couple of years – that's what Marcus's father thinks. He is in a much better position, of course, because he has other interests. They own a lot of property in London, you know. It may not be worth so much at the moment, but it will be one day – and they have the packing factory as well, of course.'

'I know your father-in-law has money,' Emily said,

feeling a bit annoyed with Frances for being smug. 'But it's our family I'm worried about. Has Henry been saying something to you – is the problem imminent?'

'Oh, no, I shouldn't think so. It's just that Henry isn't good with figures. He shouldn't be running the farm on his own. It wasn't a good idea to cut Clay out altogether, especially since Dan can't help much.'

'But I could do some bookwork if Henry wants,' Emily said, 'just while I'm here. I'll telephone him in a few minutes and see what he says.'

'Oh, don't get involved in all that,' Frances said, and pulled a face. 'I want you to be with me while you're here. You've only got a few days.'

'We shall have plenty of time to talk and shop,' Emily said. 'If Henry is struggling I want to help.'

'I wish I hadn't told you now.'

'Well, you have,' Emily said, and then laughed. 'Don't look so miserable, love. You would hate it if the family went bankrupt, you know you would.'

Frances shuddered. 'Don't! I can't bear to think about it, all the sniggering and the whispers. You know, there's plenty of people who would like to see the family take a tumble.'

'All the more reason I should help Henry with the books while I'm here,' Emily said, and she smiled at her sister as they got out of the car. 'And now you can show me the nursery...'

* * *

Henry gave her a sheaf of papers, pulling a wry face as she started to leaf through them. 'I don't know what half these new regulations mean,' he told her. 'At least, I know what I've got to do and what I can't do – but it's all the forms to fill in and the returns for tax. I can't get my head around it, Emily. Dan did some of it for me in the summer, but I've sort of left it since then.'

'Give me a few hours and I'll know what I'm doing,' she told him with a smile. 'Don't look so worried, Henry; it can't be so bad, surely?'

However, when she started to work her way through the pile she discovered that he had let things slide badly. Amongst all the stuff from the ministry that needed to be filled in was a form that said he would have to pay a fine of £3,000 because of persistent lateness with the tax returns. It seemed that they had owed money for the past three years, which meant it wasn't just Henry who had neglected the books. She was surprised that Dan hadn't picked it up when he was home, but when she asked Henry he told her he hadn't given Dan everything.

'He couldn't have paid it,' Henry said, looking ashamed. 'I thought I could do it myself when things picked up...'

Emily could hardly believe her father would be so careless until she started to look through the accounts, and then she discovered that they had been losing money for a long time. At least if she got these latest figures to their accountant, they might escape paying the huge tax penalty that was being demanded.

How could her father and brother have been so foolish as to ignore this for so long? If Dan had known, he wouldn't have agreed to give Margaret so much as her share because it meant the estate was worth that much less. Surely Henry must realise that the longer they left things like this the worse it would get?

She filled in all the ministry forms and put them to one

side for posting, and then made a start on getting the bills and invoices into some kind of order. When she had finished she felt rather pleased with herself until she opened the current bank statement and discovered how deeply in debt they were as a family. And what made it worse was that Henry hadn't been paying the interest on their loan. He was just going to have to find the money from somewhere, otherwise they might end up losing everything.

Emily sighed as she put the statements back into the envelopes. She would have to persuade Henry to sell something – even if it did mean parting with some of their land. He wouldn't like it, but only the sale of a few acres would sort this mess out.

9

Daniel couldn't believe his luck when he was told he was getting a forty-eight-hour pass. He had already bought the special marriage licence and he sent Alice a telegram telling her to expect him home the next day. If they were lucky they could get married and spend the night together before he was posted.

Alice had replied to his earlier letter, telling him that her father had agreed to the wedding after some persuasion, though her mother wasn't pleased, because she still felt Alice was too young – and because it was all such a rush. Daniel didn't mind whether Mrs Robinson was pleased or not. All he wanted was to make sure they were married before he had to leave. It had given him nightmares wondering if Alice was pregnant. He would have felt so awful if he'd had to leave her and then discovered she was in trouble, but now everything was working out just as he'd hoped.

He had written to Henry too, asking him to look around for a house or cottage they could rent. Alice could go on living with her family for a while if she had to, of course, but she would like a place of her own. It would give her something to do while he was away. She could still work as a land girl, of course – but not if she had a child.

He'd been an idiot wasting so much time. They could have been married before this if he hadn't taken so long to make up his mind. Suddenly, everything had become crystal clear to him: he wanted Alice to be his wife, and nothing else mattered.

* * *

'Well, I'm sure I expected something different when you got married,' Mrs Robinson sniffed. Her eyes were red because she'd cried for most of the night. 'My only girl and you're getting wed in this havey-cavey style as if you were in trouble.' She blew her nose on her handkerchief. 'That's what everyone will say, Alice. It's not that I don't like him, just that it is not how it should be.'

'They can say what they like, Mum,' Alice said, determined not to let her mother spoil this day. 'I'm not and they can count up the months as much as they like.'

'But why couldn't he have got leave properly earlier? We could have had a nice wedding with a pretty dress and all the trimmings.'

'I've got a nice dress,' Alice said. 'Your dress, Mum. What more could I want?'

Her mother's wedding dress had needed some extensive renovation, but Alice was good with her needle and what she'd achieved in a few hours was little short of remarkable.

'You look lovely,' Mrs Robinson said, realising that she was being unfair to her daughter. She gave her a watery smile and then hugged her. 'I'm sorry to moan at you, Alice, but it has all been such a rush.'

'It was just the same for Emily,' Alice said, and hugged her back. 'And for lots of other girls, Mum. I couldn't let Daniel go overseas without getting married, could I? Supposing...' Alice swallowed hard. 'You know what I mean, Mum.'

Mrs Robinson knew only too well. It was a part of the reason she had been against the wedding. Alice could be a widow before she was even a wife, and if she fell for a child... But there had been no telling her. She was desperate to marry him and her father had stuck up for her.

'If it's what the lass wants,' he'd said, 'she's going to have it, Mother. We've no right to deny her.'

It didn't help much that Mrs Robinson suspected her husband had made a huge sacrifice in letting his beloved daughter have her way. Alice was the light of her father's life and he would feel it when she was no longer there to brighten his day. At least she was going to stay with them for a while, just until Henry Searles sorted out a house for them. Apparently, there was one down the fen they could have, though that was another bone of contention for Alice's mother. However could her girl bear the thought of living in a place like that?

* * *

Alice would have gone to live in Timbuktu if it meant she could marry Daniel before he went back to the war. She didn't care whether Henry found her a house or not; all she knew was that she was going to be married and have one more night with the man she loved.

Her father had seen the vicar and arranged for them to

marry at the church with the special licence. There was quite a crowd waiting outside when she arrived with her father in the car he'd hired specially, even though they wouldn't have had to walk all that far. 'My daughter's going to church in the best her old dad can hire,' Mr Robinson had told her proudly. 'Maybe we can't give you a fancy reception like your mother wants, but you'll have the car and there will be a nice little nest egg for you when you're ready to set up home.'

'Oh, Dad, I do love you,' Alice said as she hugged him.

And then she was walking down the aisle on his arm, and Daniel was waiting for her, looking smart in his best uniform and turning around to watch as she took her place at his side. He smiled at her then and the look of love in his eyes made her heart turn over. He was so handsome and so lovely, and she was the luckiest girl in the world to be marrying him.

Henry was standing with him, and he produced the gold wedding ring at the right moment. Daniel had bought the ring new this time, and it fitted her finger just as it ought. She was bursting with happiness when the vicar told them they were man and wife and Daniel lifted her veil to kiss her on the lips.

As they went into the vestry to sign their names, the sun suddenly came out, sending a burst of colour through ancient stained-glass windows on to the flagstones. It was surely a good omen: the day had been cold and dark when they left home and now as they came out of church with the bells ringing, the sun was shining.

Alice was covered with rice, rose petals and silver confetti as she and Daniel ran for the car. They were spending the night at a hotel in Ely, but Alice's mother had put on a small tea for them at her house.

Only a few guests had been invited, though friends and neighbours had been bringing plates round from first thing that morning, all with some little treat they had baked for Alice's wedding. She was a popular girl and everyone wanted to do their bit for her. Her father had killed a cockerel and her mother had slow roasted it in the oven the previous night so that it was cold for cutting when they returned from church.

It wasn't a lavish meal and there was no chance of any kind of cake, but Alice didn't care. Frances was in church, looking smart if slightly disapproving. Mrs Robinson had said she wouldn't come but Alice knew she wouldn't miss her brother's wedding, even if she didn't quite approve. All three of Daniel's brothers had turned up, and they gave her some money between them, because there had been no time to buy presents, but Emily hadn't been able to come. She had, however, sent a telegram of congratulations and wished them happiness.

Alice was already floating on cloud nine. She had thought she might have to wait for years to marry the man she loved, but now she was Mrs Daniel Searles, and she glanced continually at the ring on her finger as if she could hardly believe it. She had a lovely warm feeling inside her because Daniel kept touching her arm, and the look in his eyes told her that he was feeling much as she did.

'I'll see you tomorrow sometime,' her mother said, holding back the tears as she hugged her before they left in Daniel's car. 'Be happy, Alice.'

'I am,' Alice assured her, and she turned to her father, who hugged her tight but didn't say a word. 'I'll be at home for a while. You'll hardly know I'm married.'

'Off you go then, lass,' Mr Robinson said finally. 'Make the most of your time together.'

'We shall,' Emily said. 'Thanks, Dad. Thanks for today and everything.'

There were tears in his eyes as he gave her a little push towards her husband. They made a good pair, and he was glad his girl was getting what she wanted, even if it meant he had to let her go.

* * *

The hotel had given them the best room they had, and there was a bottle of champagne in an ice bucket waiting for them. Alice's father had only been able to get a couple of bottles of sherry, but Daniel, it seemed, had been luckier. He grinned mysteriously when she asked how he'd managed that, and he popped the cork.

Alice giggled when the bubbles went up her nose. She thought champagne had a funny taste and she liked her father's sweet sherry better, but she didn't tell Daniel that. Besides, it wouldn't have mattered what she was drinking. Alice couldn't care less about the dainty little sandwiches the hotel had supplied, or the fruit trifle, which wasn't a patch on her mother's, when she could get the necessary ingredients. All that mattered was that she was here with Daniel and they were married.

He asked her if she would like to go to the pictures, but she shook her head. She could go to the pictures any night she cared to, but Daniel was going away and what she wanted was to be with him, to love him and touch him, absorb every taste and smell into her memory.

So they just went to bed and stayed there until it was

time for Daniel to leave the next day. He had bought her a box of special chocolates as one of his wedding gifts, and they lay in bed eating chocolates and drinking champagne in between making love.

'Mum would think this very decadent,' Alice said, and giggled as she popped a lovely soft coffee cream into her mouth. The champagne had gone to her head a bit, and she felt as light as a feather. She had a feeling that most of the things she'd been doing would shock her mother, because Daniel seemed to do lots of things she'd never even thought about doing, but every one of them was lovely. 'Chocolate in bed – Mum would call that wicked.'

'You'll remember what we did,' Daniel said, and kissed her neck, his hand gently stroking her breast. He had such wonderful hands, Alice thought, and they sent shivers right down to her toes. 'When you think about this night you will laugh, and you'll remember me.'

'I shan't forget you,' Alice said. 'You needn't worry about that, Dan. You won't be getting one of those dreadful "Dear John" letters, I promise you.'

'No, of course not,' he said, and held her to him, stroking her back with firm hands that made her wriggle even closer. He hadn't even considered that, but there was always a chance that he might not come back. 'Never forget how much I love you. I know I talked a lot of daft stuff at the start about how it was better to wait, but I couldn't, darling Alice. I wanted to know you were mine so that I can think of you here, waiting for me to come home.'

'I'll wait for you for ever,' Alice whispered back. She loved him so much. She couldn't think about what might happen, because it wouldn't – mustn't! 'I love you so much!'

Daniel rolled her over on to her back, holding her

hands above her head as he began to kiss her. First her lips, then her throat and her breasts, his tongue teasing and stabbing at her as he worked his way down her naval to the moist hair covering her private parts, as she'd always modestly thought of them. Only now they weren't private any more, and what Daniel was doing to her had her wriggling and gasping as she writhed beneath him.

Afterwards, they lay quiet for a while. They had slept in fits and starts, waking to love again, to whisper and touch, make promises for the future but not think of what they both dreaded.

Dawn crept up on them, and it was Alice who gave Daniel a little nudge and told him he'd better go to the bathroom first and get ready. He glanced at his watch, his expression suddenly grim as he realised there wasn't much time left.

'I'll say goodbye here, Alice,' he told her, putting his arms about her for one last time. 'Then I'll drive myself to the station. Henry promised to fetch the car back so if you ring him he'll take you home.'

'I'll go on the bus,' she said. 'I might as well do a bit of shopping after you leave.'

'All right.' He kissed her but not as he'd kissed her earlier; this was a farewell, heavy with regret, the feeling between them tense with the misery of their parting. 'I love you, Alice. There's never been anyone else I loved, I promise you.'

'I know,' she said, and she kissed him one last time, then pushed him away. 'Go on, get up, love. You've got a train to catch.'

Daniel took an envelope from his pocket and put it on

the table beside the bed. 'Open it later,' he said. 'It's just things you might need to know.'

She nodded but didn't answer. She watched him pick up his things and go towards the door, waiting until he closed the door behind him, and then she buried her head in the pillow to muffle the sound of her sobs.

Emily was feeling tired as she came off shift that night, even though it had been a quiet night really compared to others they'd experienced of late – no bombs, just an industrial and a couple of house fires.

As she left the station to walk home, she felt the icy wind whistle about her ears and pulled her scarf tighter. The winter had seemed long and bitter, and she couldn't wait for spring to cheer them all up. She wondered if there would be a message from Simon waiting for her. It was almost the end of January 1941 and all she'd had were a couple of postcards to say he was fine and hoped she was managing. Sometimes it amazed her when she realised that seven months ago she hadn't even known Simon. She had met and married him in the space of a few months. It was no wonder that sometimes it all seemed like a dream. She didn't really know him at all.

The explosion just a couple of streets away made her jump, but she knew almost at once that it wasn't a bomb. Bombs had a special sound all of their own, and this was different – more like a gas leak. It happened too often. Pipes were disturbed in the bombing, and sometimes the cold weather affected them, but for some reason they showed no sign of damage for days afterwards, and then, all of a sudden, something happened and there was an explosion.

Emily ran around the corner. She could see that it was as she'd thought. The explosion had happened in a row of terrace houses, one of which had a gaping space where the front of it should have been, and two more were affected. She could see flames coming from the house where the explosion had happened.

Someone was already in the phone box on the corner and she could see from the frantic way the woman was gesticulating that she was ringing the fire brigade. Hearing children screaming, Emily instinctively went towards the damaged houses. She saw that a child was banging at an upstairs window, and the fire was already licking through from the back of the house to the front, but at the moment the stairs were clear. A woman had brought two children down but she was pointing at the house and screaming.

Emily went straight into the house and up the stairs. The child's screaming led her towards the right room but when she tried to open the door she discovered that it was locked. She tugged uselessly at the door but the handle wouldn't turn, and there was no sign of a key. She looked around for something to break down the door, seeing nothing but a chair, which she lifted and crashed against the door in a futile attempt to break it down.

Then, all at once, a man was beside her. 'Get out of here,' he barked at her. 'It will reach the stairs any moment.'

She recognised him at the precise moment he knew her, and gasped. 'Terry – the door is locked.'

'I know, her mother told me her father locked the boy in for disobedience and took the key off to the pub. Don't worry, I'll have him out. Get away from here, Emily. I can't look after you too!'

He ran at the door, putting his shoulder against it with

a great thud. Emily heard the wood splinter and realised
he knew what he was doing. Fortunately, the lock was a
cheap one and no match for the skill of an experienced
fireman.

The smell of smoke was choking now, and as she reached
the top of the stairs and looked down she could see that
flames had reached the front hall and were beginning to lick
at the foot of the staircase. She took her coat off and held it
over her head as she ran down the stairs, but the smoke was
so thick, she was choking and coughing by the time she
reached the bottom.

Emerging into the cold night air, she breathed deeply.
Her chest hurt but she was all right, she'd got out soon
enough. Moments later, she heard the siren and knew that
help was on the way. She could see the flames were shooting
up inside the house now and heard a woman screaming that
her son was going to die.

'No, he'll be all right,' Emily said, as much to comfort
herself as the distraught mother. 'Terry will get him out...'

But would he be able to open the door in time? She
watched in dread as the fire gained ground, terrified that
Terry would not manage it, and knowing that he would keep
trying even if his own life was at risk. And then someone
started cheering, and though a haze of tears, she saw Terry
coming out of the house. He was carrying a boy of no more
than five in his arms, and he'd wrapped the child's face and
head in his own coat.

The boy's mother rushed towards them just as help
arrived. Emily saw the firemen and ambulance people
surround Terry, the boy and his family. She couldn't move
for the first few moments, but then she was pushing her way
towards them through the crowd. She watched as Terry was

helped into the ambulance along with the child he had saved.

'What do you want, miss?' one of the ambulance men asked. 'There's no more room inside.'

'Is Terry all right?' she asked, and then caught a glimpse of him sitting on one of the stretchers inside.

He saw her and raised a hand as if to tell her that he'd seen her, just before the door was closed and she had to step back out of the way. She watched as the ambulance was driven away, not realising that tears were streaming down her face until a woman took hold of her arm.

'Are you all right, love?' she asked, looking at Emily. 'They might 'ave taken you to hospital too. You went in there first and all.'

'No, I'm all right,' Emily assured her, wiping the back of her hand across her face, not realising that it was smeared with smoke. 'I was just concerned for Terry.'

'Know him, do you, love?' the woman said with a smile. 'Your boyfriend, is he?'

'No... Just a friend.'

'Well, he's a right brave man whoever he is,' the woman said, 'and you can tell 'im Sadie Burrows said so an' all.'

Emily smiled, thanked her and said she agreed. Terry was extremely brave, especially after his previous experience, when he'd suffered terrible burns and tragedy. It showed terrific courage to go into that house without his colleagues or the equipment he needed.

'I shall when I see him,' she said. 'You wouldn't happen to know where they've taken him, I suppose?'

A man standing behind them said, 'They'll take him to the treatment centre up the 'ospital, I shouldn't wonder. He weren't 'urt bad nor were the kid, thanks to 'im, so they won't keep him in long. They've got too many what need beds more than he does.'

'Thank you.'

Emily turned away. She'd had a bit of a shock and she was feeling shaky inside now that it was all over. To see Terry in action like that, to know he might be overcome by smoke or fire, had made her realise how much she liked him – and that was something she ought not to be thinking.

* * *

Emily had her breakfast early. She had decided that she would go to the hospital and ask if Terry had been brought in, but just as she was finishing her tea, her landlady came into the dining parlour to tell her that she had a visitor. Putting down her cup, Emily went into the hall, wondering who had called. She felt a start of surprise and pleasure as she saw Terry standing there.

'Oh, Terry, how are you?' she cried, going towards him with her hands outstretched. A great surge of relief and pleasure went through her. He had been so brave and she'd been afraid he might suffer for it. Thank God he was all right!

When Terry caught her in his arms and kissed her, she clung to him for a moment before moving away and giving him an embarrassed look. She hadn't meant that to happen!

'Sorry, I got carried away...'

'Doesn't matter.'

She smiled. 'I was so worried about you but they wouldn't let me come with you in the ambulance, and then I felt a bit shaky. I was going up to the hospital this morning to see if you were there.'

'I thought you might worry,' he said, and smiled at her.

'And I was worried about you, Emily. You had inhaled smoke too. They ought to have taken you in for observation, same as the rest of us.'

'No, it didn't matter. I was all right,' she said. 'I think they are stretched to the limit as it is.'

'But you could have been overcome by smoke.' He looked at her in concern, clearly upset by the thought. 'You might have died...'

'Yes, if you hadn't been there,' she agreed. 'I was trying to find a way of breaking that door down. Does your shoulder hurt?'

He rubbed it ruefully and admitted that it was very sore. 'I missed my axe,' he said, 'but I've seen cheap doors like that before and knew I could break it with my own force. And I didn't want you risking your life in there...' His voice had gone a bit croaky. 'You know I care about you, Emily.'

'Yes, of course,' she said, very conscious that her landlady wasn't far away. 'Wait just a minute while I get my coat. We'll go somewhere and have a coffee if you have time?'

'I'll make time.'

Emily nodded and ran upstairs, grabbing her coat, scarf and bag, then went down to join him in the hall. It was cold out but brighter, the damp mist that had hung over the city for a while having cleared.

Terry looked at her but neither of them spoke for a few moments.

'You were wonderful,' Emily said after a short silence. 'People were saying how brave you were last night after you'd gone in the ambulance.'

'It's my job,' he said. 'I wasn't sure I would ever be able to do it again, and what happened last night was as much for me as anyone else. I had something to prove to myself. I'm going to ask them to put me back on regular service as soon as my treatment is finished.'

'If that's what you want, then I'm glad for you.' She understood that the incident that had killed his friend had lingered in his mind, and also that the rescue of the child had somehow helped him.

'Let's go in here,' Terry said, choosing a quiet hotel rather than a busy café. 'I know this place. There's a comfortable lounge where we can sit and have coffee and biscuits. We can talk there – and we do need to talk, don't we, Emily?'

She hesitated, looking into his eyes for a moment before saying, 'Yes, we should talk, Terry.'

They went inside the old-fashioned, discreet hotel. The lounge was panelled in mellowed oak with soft carpets, comfortable if shabby armchairs and little tables, and there were only two tables occupied. Terry led her to a secluded corner, ordering their coffee from a maid in a black dress and white apron.

'It's stuck in the Edwardian era, but it's decent,' he told Emily with a grin. 'At least we shan't be overheard here and we don't need to shout at each other.'

'It's comfortable and quiet,' she replied. 'You said we should talk and I agree, but nothing has changed. We're friends, good friends – but I'm married.'

'But you're not happy, are you?'

Emily thought about her marriage. She had gone into it hastily, mainly because Simon had been so desperate. It was true that she wasn't happy. She had been feeling uneasy about things for a while, though she hadn't acknowledged it to herself. Simon's behaviour on his last leave had aroused small doubts she'd suppressed, but sitting here with Terry she was forced to admit they were there at the back of her mind. She had a suspicion that she might have made a mistake, yet even if that were true, there was nothing she could do about it.

'No, not really,' she admitted after a moment or two. 'I care about Simon, but I... I'm not sure he really loves me.'

Terry nodded. 'I knew something was wrong. I could sense it.'

'It may just be the war,' Emily said. 'I don't honestly know. Simon has moods. Sometimes we're good together and then... Well, he hasn't written to me properly since the last time we were together. I've had a couple of brief post-cards. I thought he was going to get leave before this, but he hasn't written to tell me anything.'

'A lot of men aren't good at writing letters. It can't just be that, Emily?'

'No, it isn't.' She shook her head over her own thoughts. 'It sounds so stupid when you say it out loud...'

'Nothing you could say would sound stupid to me.'

'I think...' She hesitated again, then went on as he smiled at her. 'I think Simon married me because his father wants an heir for his estate.'

Terry stared at her in silence for a moment, then nodded. 'It's the way of people like that, to marry for the sake of a son to carry on the name. But what gave you that idea, Emily? Why do you think Simon doesn't love you?'

'He says he does, but somehow I have started to doubt it.' She wrinkled her brow as she tried to express her thoughts clearly. She couldn't tell him the intimate details of her life – that Simon only seemed to be able to make love to her if he made a game of it, the feeling she had that he didn't really want her – that he was doing his duty as a husband. 'I can't explain, but things aren't right... between us in that way...' She bit her lip, her soft hair falling across her face.

'I see...' Terry looked thoughtful. 'He must be an idiot if he doesn't know how lucky he is.'

Emily laughed. There was no doubting that Terry thought she was special and the look in his eyes made her feel much better.

'It isn't just that, it's other things – like not bothering to write or phone. Little things I can't explain. I don't even know why I feel this way myself. Frances told me that Marcus rings her all the time, and he comes home more often. I don't understand why Simon can't, unless he doesn't want to.' She shook her head, brushing her hair back from her face. 'Or am I being selfish? Asking too much? Perhaps it is me... I've let him down...'

'I don't think so.' Terry reached for her hand and held it. 'I don't believe it is your fault.'

'I hadn't realised how I truly felt until this moment. Talking to you...' She shook her head. 'I shouldn't even be doing it... But you are right, I am not happy.'

'So what are you going to do about it, Emily?'

'What can I do?' She read the answer in his eyes and withdrew her hand. 'No, I couldn't. It would be too awful of me. I don't have any real reasons for a divorce, Terry. I shouldn't have married Simon in such a rush. I know that now. If I'd waited for a while, until we knew each other better, it might have been different.' In normal times she would probably never have married him. She admitted it to herself for the first time.

'Why not – if he doesn't love you?'

Emily looked down at her hands. She wasn't wearing her rings. She seldom wore them these days, because she hardly felt married at all. Her relationship with Simon wasn't a normal one, and she couldn't deny that to Terry. She couldn't deny the strong attraction between them, the feeling that he might have been the one for her if she had waited and not given in to Simon's persuasion. She shut the thought out at once, but it wouldn't stay shut out. Terry was brave and strong and she really liked him. Perhaps she might have found happiness if she'd married him – only she hadn't and she was stuck with the consequences.

'I'm married, Terry. People I know don't get divorced very often. I would have to have a very good reason to ask Simon to let me go.'

'You know I love you. I think you love me.'

'I think I could,' Emily said, not wanting to admit that she was already halfway there, 'but that isn't a reason to break my marriage vows. You know it isn't. You can't just walk off and leave someone because you decide you're not satisfied.'

'So you're going to carry on knowing that you don't love him and he doesn't love you? One of these times you'll fall for a child and then you will be really trapped. Wake up, Emily. You should make the break now while you can!'

She stared at him helplessly as he leaned towards her, kissing her softly on the lips just as their waitress returned with the tray of coffee. The woman didn't turn a hair as she deposited the tray, turned, and left them to serve themselves.

'I have to think about it,' Emily said, tears hovering. 'I'm not sure. It might just be me being selfish.'

'I don't think you could ever be that. Listen to me, Emily. It isn't just for my sake that I'm telling you to face the facts,' Terry said. 'I want to marry you, but I'm not asking you to leave him and marry me just like that. I think you will be very unhappy one day if you don't, that's all.'

'Yes, I think you may be right,' she agreed. 'I wish I'd listened to Daniel. He told me to wait... And yet he went and did the same thing himself just before he was posted. He and Alice were married by special licence just as we were.'

'Perhaps it was right for them. It often is. If you are in love it's natural to want to be together.'

'I thought I loved Simon. When I'm with him...' Emily sighed. 'Don't push me on this, Terry. I can't just walk away like that. I have to see Simon again, talk to him.'

Terry nodded and picked up the coffee pot, poured them each a cup. She watched his hands, imagining them on her body, touching her. She wasn't wrong about Simon feeling it was his duty to make love to her. He had never once looked at her in the hot, hungry way Terry did! She felt the regret wash over her – regret for what might have been.

'I will talk to Simon,' she said, 'but I'm making no promises.'

'I haven't asked for any.'

'No,' she said. 'You haven't...'

* * *

After she'd left Terry, Emily went window shopping in town, then bought herself a much-needed pair of shoes for work. She'd been saving her coupons for them but as she caught the bus that would take her back to her lodgings, the pleasure of the purchase was marred by the conversation with Terry. Was she right to blame Simon for her dissatisfaction with their marriage – or was she making something out of nothing? Perhaps it was her who was wrong? Perhaps it was because she was attracted to Terry?

Emily didn't like that thought. It gave her a nasty taste in the mouth and made her feel worthless. What sort of person would have these kinds of thoughts when her brave husband was fighting for his country?

She didn't like herself much at that moment. She had wanted Terry to kiss her again, and she'd wanted to tell him that she would leave Simon to be with him. Her conscience had prevented her from saying it, but that didn't stop her thinking.

She went upstairs and changed into her working clothes. It was better at work; she didn't have time to think – and although she'd told Terry she needed time to think, it was the last thing she wanted to do. When she came down, her landlady was answering the telephone.

'Ah, here she is – just a moment,' she said, and held it out to Emily. 'It's for you...'

'Thank you.' Emily took it, her brows raised, but the woman shook her head and walked back into the kitchen. 'Hello, Emily Searles – I mean, Emily Vane speaking.'

'Emily, my dear,' the voice said, and it was Amelia's. From the concern and huskiness of it Emily knew at once that something was wrong and her throat caught. 'I am so very sorry to tell you but Simon has been hurt.'

Emily could hardly speak for a moment. 'Is he...?' She broke off, unable to ask the question.

'No, not dead,' Amelia said, and there was a sob in her voice. 'His plane was brought down in the Channel. He's alive but' – she choked as though it was impossible to go on – 'they say he has received some nasty burns to his left side... Face and body.'

For a moment the world seemed to whirl madly around Emily. She thought she was going to faint, but made a grab for the nearest object, which happened to be the hallstand, holding on until the dizziness passed.

'Yes, I see,' she managed at last. 'Where is he?'

'He's at St Michael's, just a few miles from us. His father had him transferred from the military hospital, because he will get more attention here. Vane is bringing a specialist in to examine him and then we shall see.'

'When did it happen?'

Amelia hesitated. 'We were told last week. His father didn't want you to know until he had been assessed – in case it was too much of a shock for you. It isn't quite as bad as we had feared, Emily. The doctors here think he will pull through, though it is going to be a long haul.'

'But why wasn't I informed? I am his wife...' Emily felt a spurt of irritation. She was his next of kin, but his parents had been told first and they hadn't told her until almost a week after the plane came down.

Amelia sounded embarrassed as she tried to explain. 'Apparently Simon still had his father down as his next of kin, though how that happened I don't know. He must have told them he was getting married, but you know how these things happen. It's just an official mix-up again. I'm sorry, Emily. I thought you should have been told immediately, but Vane was worried for you in case—'

'I'm not pregnant if that's what you're trying to ask,' Emily said, a sharp note in her voice. She was angry that they had kept the news from her, and that Simon hadn't registered her as his next of kin. It reinforced her feeling that she was just a woman he had married for breeding purposes, and that she wasn't truly important.

'No, well, that can't be helped,' Amelia said. 'You will want to see Simon as soon as they allow visitors, of course. Shall we expect you tomorrow?'

'Yes, I'll come tomorrow if they will let me go.'

'I should hardly think they will refuse in the circumstances.'

'No, I don't suppose they will,' Emily said. It was awful of her but she was reluctant to give up her work to live with Simon's family, which would almost undoubtedly happen. 'I'll speak to my supervisor this evening and catch the first train tomorrow.'

'We shall expect you,' Amelia said. 'And I'm very sorry, Emily... About everything.'

'It isn't your fault,' Emily said, but she knew her voice was formal, cool. 'I'll see you tomorrow then.'

She put the phone down and sat on the bottom stair, hunching her knees up to her chest. She felt numb, confused, and her chest hurt. Tears were burning her eyes, but she held them back. Mostly, she felt guilty, as though it was her fault Simon had been hurt. She had been resenting him for not phoning her while he'd been lying in a hospital bed. It was almost as bad as if she had been directly responsible.

Why hadn't his father let her know immediately? More importantly, why hadn't Simon had her down as his next of kin?

Hearing her landlady hovering, Emily jumped up, grabbed her coat from the hallstand and went out before anything was said. She had money in her pocket, though she would walk most of the way. It would do her good.

10

Alice was walking home after returning from Ely with the shopping she'd done for her mother. It was a better day at last and there were signs that spring might be on its way – another reason to make her smile if she didn't have enough of them already.

She was almost certain she was having a baby, Daniel's baby. She nursed the pleasure of her secret to her as she remembered sitting up in bed eating chocolates and sipping champagne. It hadn't happened the first time they had made love, but she must have fallen on her wedding night or the morning after. They had certainly made the most of their brief time together, and she couldn't be happier if a baby was the result. She knew that Daniel had wanted to wait for a family at one time, but if it had happened, it had happened; they would manage somehow. Her father had promised her a nice present when they set up home, and she'd decided to save the money for rent by staying put for the time being.

'Why move when we've plenty of room for you?' her mother had told her when Henry took them to see the house in the fen. 'This place would be nice enough if Daniel were here to share it, but you'll feel lonely here on your own. Save the rent and wait until he comes home.'

Her mother's advice made a lot of sense, Alice decided. She didn't particularly want to live in a large old house in the fen when there were modern ones in the village that might come available in time.

'It was good of you to find it for me,' she told Henry, 'but I think I'll wait until Daniel comes home.'

'Sensible lass,' Henry said, and smiled at her. 'See how things go. Daniel will probably buy something better when he's ready – with a yard where he can do up his bits and pieces. We've got land he could build on if he wanted. I think you're doing the right thing. Save your money and wait.'

So Alice was going to keep living with her family for now. Her mother might frown when she discovered she was pregnant, but she wouldn't change her mind.

'Oh, Alice!' Frances called to her from across the street. 'Wait a moment, will you? I wanted to tell you something. I've had a letter from Emily.'

Alice waited for her to walk across the road. It was very quiet, hardly anybody about, and somewhere nearby a thrush was trilling its heart out.

'It's warmer today, isn't it?' Alice said, then she saw the look on Frances's face and felt chilled. 'Is something wrong – bad news?'

'Yes, it is,' Frances told her. 'Emily's husband was shot down over the Channel and he's been badly hurt.'

'That's terrible,' Alice said, immediately concerned. 'Poor Emily... But doesn't Marcus fly with him?'

'No, not for a while. They were moved to different crews a few months back. I'm not really sure why. Marcus said it was something to do with Simon – a disagreement between them. Simon asked for a transfer, I think.'

'Oh, I see,' Alice said, though of course she didn't. 'Does Emily know?'

Frances gave her an odd look. 'Marcus said I wasn't to tell her – he thought it might be awkward for me if she knew he and Simon had fallen out.'

'Oh, I see. So Marcus is all right then?'

'Yes, he's fine, fingers crossed,' Frances said, but her eyes were anxious and her hands worked nervously at her sides. You never knew who was next and the news had upset her. 'Emily says it was some time before they would let her see Simon, but she has visited now and she doesn't think the burns are as bad as they could have been. Simon is scarred but will recover with the proper medical care, and his father has brought in specialists – one of them flew over from America to consult with the English doctors on the best way forward. He might even go there to have some of the surgery he will need when he is well enough to undergo treatment.'

'To America?' It seemed such an impossibly long way away to Alice, and she could hardly comprehend that anyone would think of going there for surgery.

Frances nodded. 'They have some of the best hospitals in the world, Alice, especially for things like this. Marcus knows someone who had an accident in a training flight over there, just before the war really got going, and his family almost wrote him off, but the Americans pulled him round. He is home now but will never be able to fly again, though he's hoping for artificial limbs soon.'

'Let's pray Simon recovers,' Alice said, feeling the sting of tears. War was so awful! 'Emily must be terribly upset.'

'Yes, she is,' Frances said. 'She has asked me to go and

stay at the Vanes' place for a few days, and I shall of course – though it's a bit of a trek.' She patted her stomach proudly. 'Not much longer to go...'

'When are you due?'

'I think it will be April sometime,' Frances said. 'Marcus had a couple of short leaves close together so I'm not certain – but we think April.'

'Oh, well, you'll be home again before then, won't you?'

'Yes, I'll be home in a few days. But Emily seems so down – I've got to go and see her. She doesn't want to leave his parents while there's still doubt about Simon's recovery, you see.'

'She's given up her job, then?'

'I don't think she had much choice,' Frances said with a little frown. 'Lord Vane told her it was her duty to stay with Simon, so I suppose she had to ask for a discharge on compassionate grounds.'

'Yes, I expect so,' Alice agreed. 'Dan said she loved her job there. It's a shame, isn't it – but she didn't have much choice with Simon badly wounded, did she?'

'No, I don't think she could refuse in the circumstances. I'm glad she's with his family. I hated to think of her in Liverpool with all that bombing going on.'

'It just keeps on and on, doesn't it?' Alice shivered. 'Look at what they're doing to London. I don't know how the poor devils stand it.'

'I know...' Frances sighed. 'It's terrible; that's why I'm glad Emily is well out of it, though I don't think she feels that way.'

'No, but she'll be glad to be with her husband, won't she?'

'Yes, of course,' Frances said. 'When he comes out of the

hospital she won't want to be anywhere but with him. That's not likely to be for a while, of course.'

'No, I don't suppose so.'

Alice nodded, because it was bound to take time. She considered telling Frances about her baby, but decided to keep her secret a while longer.

She was thinking about Emily as she left her sister-in-law and continued her walk home. It was so sad that Emily's husband should have been badly injured. Alice knew how she would feel if it had happened to Daniel. She would want to be with him as much as they would let her. Nothing would have made her go back to work and leave him in the hospital. She thought about the precious love letter he'd left on the table beside the bed. He'd said it was things she needed to know, but it was really a passionate love letter. She kept it with her and read it whenever she was missing him too much.

Alice was still doing a few days a week on the land, but she might have to cut down soon if her hopes were proved right. She could keep on doing tractor work for her father and perhaps some milking for a while, but she would have to stop doing the hard labour.

She enjoyed her work too, but she wouldn't mind giving it all up if she was having Daniel's baby.

* * *

'It's so good to see you,' Emily said, and she hugged her sister, feeling the sting of tears behind her eyes. 'Thank you for coming. I really needed to see you.'

The emotion in her voice made Frances look at her. This wasn't like Emily at all. She was usually a well-balanced, thoughtful girl who kept her feelings under control, but of course she had more than enough to distress her now.

'Of course I came,' Frances said, and she kept an arm about her waist as they walked into the little back parlour that Emily had chosen to use. 'Have you seen Simon yet?'

'For about five minutes,' Emily said, choking back the sob that rose in her throat. 'He was still under sedation so he didn't know I was there, but they tell me he's doing well. They say he will recover, that he isn't going to die.'

'That's something,' Frances said, and looked at her face. 'Was it awful for you, love? I mean, the burns... Seeing them?'

'He had bandages covering his hands and part of his face, but I could see his mouth and his eyelids,' Emily said. 'They looked a bit swollen but it is early days yet. I spoke to one of the doctors and he said Simon is in better shape than a lot of airmen who come down like that, so perhaps we've been lucky.'

'Good, let's hope that's right, love.' Frances squeezed her waist. 'Besides, they can do wonderful things these days.'

'Yes, I know. I'm not worried about that – not for my own sake, anyway. It's dreadful for Simon. I keep thinking about the pain he will have to suffer and...' She shook her head as the emotion clogged in her throat. How could she tell her sister that she felt trapped? It was so awful of her to think of herself at a time like this, but she was confused and unhappy, and it didn't help that she was expected to live here with Simon's family.

'What is it, then? Something's wrong, I can see it.'

'Oh, nothing...' Emily blinked her tears away. She couldn't tell Frances that she believed she had made a mistake in marrying so hastily. It would look as if she was deserting Simon at the first sign of trouble, and her own sense of decency wouldn't let her do that, even if she knew what she wanted – and the trouble was, she didn't. 'It's just...' She couldn't find the words to go on.

'Yes, of course,' Frances said at once. 'You must be desperately worried, love. I wish there was something I could do to help.'

'You're here and that makes me feel better,' Emily told her, and smiled. 'Let's talk about something else. Tell me how you feel, what it feels like having the baby – and what you've managed to buy. Amelia gave me some baby wool she had put by yesterday and I've started to knit some coats for you, one in white and another in lemon.' She pulled a wry face. 'I'm not very good at knitting, though.'

'I'm sure they will be lovely,' Frances said. 'I've brought my knitting with me, and some sewing too. I'm making a christening gown.'

'I'm sure ours must be somewhere in the attic at Rathmere,' Emily said. 'Don't most families keep them from one generation to the next?'

'I think Henry had one and Clay gave Dorothy another,' Frances said, and pulled a face. 'I'm a bit worried about Henry, Emily. He had a terrible cough when I saw him last week, and I think he's finding it all a bit much without Clay. It wasn't too bad when Daniel was home, but now – well, he can't cope.'

'Have you heard anything from Daniel?' Emily asked.

'No, and I don't think Alice has either,' Frances said. 'But you know what it's like getting letters from over there...'

'From over where? No one knows where he is yet, do they?'

'No, but Alice thinks it might be Egypt, though of course she doesn't really have a clue.'

'I just hope he is all right,' Emily said, her eyes clouding. 'He and Alice had so little time together and she thinks the world of him, doesn't she?'

'Yes, well, it's the same for all of us,' Frances said. 'I worry about Marcus too, you know.'

'Yes, of course you do,' Emily agreed. 'But you're so lucky, Frances. You always have been. Nothing will happen to Marcus; it can't, because you won't let it.'

Frances laughed, laying her hands on her swollen belly. 'Well, if wishing and praying will keep him safe, we're doing our best.'

Emily smiled. Frances looked more beautiful than ever, even though she hadn't got much longer to go until her baby was born – but it couldn't be any other way for her. Lady Luck always smiled down on Frances.

* * *

Daniel sat in his tent writing his letter to Alice. It was the fourth he'd written to her, though none of them had been sent yet, because they were too busy settling into their new surroundings. He chewed the end of his pencil, wondering how he could tell her where he was without having the censor blue pencil it out. They had all been wrong, and the guesses they'd made had been wildly out. He wasn't in Africa or Malaya, but it was warmer than at home because this was Greece, and so far it was fine. The locals were friendly, and he'd been to a taverna with some of his mates a couple of times of an evening.

It's much better than I imagined. Not at all what we were
expecting – pleasant, in fact. So don't worry about me,
darling. I shall be as safe as houses here. The worst bit is
missing you.

He smiled as he finished his letter, tucking it into his
kitbag with the others. He would send them all together very
soon. He looked up as a soldier entered the tent, something
about his manner alerting Dan that all was not well.

'We're on the bloody retreat,' the soldier said. 'Orders are
to pack up and move out and look smart about it.'

'We've only just got here,' Daniel said. 'I thought the
Greeks were beating the Italians?'

'They were but the flaming Jerries are invading and we
ain't got enough men to do much about it. So get your kit
together and look sharp. We've got to fight our way out of
this or the buggers will 'ave us too.'

Daniel thought about the letter he had just written to
Alice, a wry smile on his face. By the looks of things he
might have been better off if they had gone to Egypt!

* * *

Emily stared out of the long window in the small back
parlour. The view of the park was just as beautiful as the first
time she'd seen it, but she was restless, unable to settle to
anything. It was all the uncertainty, the sitting around and
waiting. It hadn't been too bad when Frances was here, but
she was at home now, and her baby was due at any time. In
fact Frances thought she was late and had begun to get a bit
fidgety.

Emily knew her sister was being well cared for by her

husband's family. She had promised to visit as soon as the baby was born, but she thought she might go for a visit sooner, because she wasn't doing much good here. She wished she had been allowed to continue her work for the fire service, but Lord Vane had made it impossible for her.

'It is your duty as my son's wife to be here to support him,' he had told her when she had mentioned that she might return to work after a few weeks' leave. 'I do not know how you can contemplate such a thing. Simon needs you.'

If Simon had needed her it wouldn't have been so bad, Emily thought, but he didn't. His father was in charge of his treatment, and she wasn't included in the discussions with the doctors. It would be too painful for her and it wasn't her decision, was the message she'd received, though not in so many words. But words weren't needed in this case. Lord Vane intended to pull every string available to him to get the best treatment for Simon, and he didn't need her advice. Not that she would have been able to help – Emily was honest enough to admit that – but she would have liked to be consulted, to be treated as his wife and not just a guest. She realised that was the way she had always felt – a guest in their house. The Vanes were pleasant and friendly, but she didn't feel as if she belonged here.

'I know he looks a bit of a mess now,' Vane had told Emily when she had been allowed to see her husband for the first time after the heavy bandages came off. 'But these chaps can do miracles these days. You'll see, we'll have him looking nearly as good as new before you know it.'

'He doesn't look too bad,' Emily said. Simon had a nasty burn covering the left side of his face, but he hadn't been anywhere near as badly disfigured as Maura's boyfriend. 'I've seen worse burns, sir. Simon was lucky considering.'

'Indeed?' Lord Vane looked at her as if he thought she was mad, then nodded his head, apparently deciding to approve. 'That's it, Emily. Stiff upper lip. I knew you were made of the right stuff when Simon brought you home that first time. Told him to marry you. You can always tell good blood – and I didn't want him making my mistake. A lot of girls would have bolted faced with something like this. I am glad you know your duty.'

Of course it was her duty to be there for Simon. Not that she had much choice in the circumstances. Nor would she have thought of leaving him if he needed her at all, but she couldn't see that he did. Even when she visited him at the hospital he had little to say. He didn't tell her to go away as Maura's boyfriend had, but he wasn't interested. Most of the time he lay with his eyes closed, feigning sleep. She might have been a part of the furniture for all he noticed her. And there was absolutely nothing for her to do in this house, she thought, except sit here twiddling her thumbs like a useless dummy.

'Oh, there you are,' a voice said from behind her, and she turned to see her father-in-law watching her, a frown creasing his brow. 'Are you bored, Emily? I know there isn't a lot for you to do here, and you must be worried about Simon.'

'Yes, I am worried about him,' Emily admitted, because she did care what happened to Simon. Her feelings for him were confused, but even if she wasn't in love with him, she felt upset by the thought of him being in pain and distress. 'But I wish I had something more to do.'

'My project doesn't interest you, I suppose?'

'Not really, sir,' Emily said, deciding to be honest. 'I

would like something more – to do something for other people.'

'That's what I thought,' Lord Vane said. 'And I think I've found the very thing for you, Emily.'

Emily wasn't sure she wanted her father-in-law to solve her problems. 'I'm not certain what you mean, sir.'

'I wish you would call me Vane,' he said, a note of irritation in his voice. 'You are a part of the family, Emily, not a servant or a visitor.'

'Am I?' She couldn't help sounding bitter. 'Apparently you didn't consider it necessary to tell me the moment you heard Simon had been shot down – and he hardly cares whether I visit him or not.'

'That is ridiculous,' Vane said, looking grim. 'I was contacted as Simon's next of kin and thought it best to see how things were going before I got you here.'

'But you aren't, are you?' she said, angry in her turn. 'I am Simon's wife. Why wasn't I told first? Or let me guess – I'm just a woman, hardly important unless I produce an heir to carry on the family tradition.'

'This is really rather childish,' Vane said. 'Simon obviously forgot to update his details. He filled in my name when he joined up and didn't get around to changing it, that's all. And I was merely trying to protect you from unnecessary shock and pain.'

'Just in case I was pregnant, I suppose? The child would have been all important, wouldn't it – especially if it happened to be a boy?'

'What nonsense is this?'

'Isn't that why you told Simon to marry me? So that I could provide an heir for the estate?'

'Naturally I hoped—' Vane's mouth pulled into a thin

line. 'Simon married you because he loves you. You must know that, Emily.'

'I thought he did,' she said, 'but I don't know any more.'

'Are you making this up simply as an excuse to leave him?'

'No, of course not. I wouldn't leave him while he needed me – but I'm not sure that he does.'

'Of course he does. Stop all this nonsense, Emily. You are upset and bored with nothing to do but sit and worry, which is why I thought you might like a new job.'

'What kind of a job?' She looked at him warily.

'I have given one of my houses as a convalescence home for wounded soldiers,' he said. 'It has been standing empty for a while but I've kept it in good repair. The government requires us all to do our bit in this war, Emily. We are not the only ones being asked to make sacrifices. Almost every large house in the country is being considered, because we need all the available space we can get. There will be nursing staff on hand, naturally, though most who come here will be through the worst of it. They are likely to be long-term patients, and it will be their home rather than a hospital.'

Emily's interest was caught, but she didn't speak, waiting for him to continue, to tell her what he wanted from her.

'This is a privately funded home, Emily. I offered to provide and run it independently of government funding – and my offer has just been accepted. I thought you might like to take charge of the day-to-day running. Not the nursing – as I said, that will be provided – but there will be accounts, ordering, overseeing that everything runs smoothly – and that the men have everything they need. You'll need to provide visiting access for friends and relatives, help with writing letters for those who can't manage it

– numerous things I haven't even thought of. Amelia has her hands full with this house and the horses – but I thought you might like this project as your own.' His gaze narrowed, holding her fast. 'You will need something to occupy you until Simon gets on his feet again.'

He was offering her a bribe to keep her here, Emily realised. It seemed that he knew her well enough to understand that she would not be content to be idle, and this was his way of holding her. Perhaps he knew that she was telling the truth about Simon not needing her; he understood that she was unhappy. For the first time, she felt as if they were communicating – that he saw her as a person and not just as the means to an end.

If she agreed, it would mean she would have to stay here for a long time, perhaps years, because she couldn't just turn her back on something like that, and already she felt a stirring of excitement, a feeling of purpose. He was right. She had to be here in case Simon needed her one day – and this would help her to feel that she was doing her bit for the war effort.

'Do you think I could manage something like that?'

'I shall be here if you need to consult me.' His brows rose, challenging her. 'You seem a sensible woman to me, Emily. I wouldn't have thought it beyond your capabilities.'

'What about the construction work, the necessary plumbing and proper furnishings?'

'I can see you are already on top of it,' Vane said, a smile playing briefly across his mouth. 'I have had plans drawn up in readiness and the work is about to begin. If you wish to review the plans with me, your suggestions will be looked at and acted upon if they improve on what is already decided. I daresay you can sort out the beds and things from what is

already there or here in the house. We have attics bulging
with stuff we don't need, or you can raid the spare bedrooms
if you prefer. The idea is to make it a home, Emily, not a
hospital, so we want it as much like a country house as possible, though of course there will be certain medical require-
ments for some of the men. We shall be inspected before the
first guests come, and there will be meetings before that. The
first is set for early next week.'

He was looking at her, waiting for her decision.

'This is very sudden,' she said. 'May I have a little time to
think about it?'

'Of course. Shall we say tomorrow morning? If the idea
doesn't appeal I must look for my matron elsewhere.'

Emily knew that she was going to agree. She thought that
Vane knew it too, but she would keep him waiting at least
until the morning.

'All right,' she said. 'I'm going to drive over to the hospital
and visit Simon now. I'll think about what you've said and let
you know tomorrow.'

'Thank you, Emily,' he said. 'Please believe that I am
sincere when I say that I hope you will accept – and if I have
offended you over this business, it was unintentional. I didn't
realise that you had not been told immediately, and then I
thought it best to wait until he had been moved nearer
home. You see, I couldn't be sure that you would stand by
him.'

Emily felt her cheeks flame. He had guessed that there
was something not quite right between her and Simon!

'I couldn't leave Simon while he needs me,' she said, a
flicker of defiance in her eyes. 'But that doesn't mean I shall
stay for ever.'

'I am not the autocrat you imagine, Emily,' Vane said

with an odd smile. 'Simon needs you at the moment whether you believe that or not – but nothing is for ever, my dear. The young always think that today and now mean everything, but one day you will understand that life is full of endings and beginnings.'

She was silent as he inclined his head and then turned and walked from the room, leaving her to her thoughts.

* * *

Emily parked the car she had borrowed from Amelia in the grounds of the hospital. She thought how lucky they were that Vane seemed to be allocated more petrol rations than most people, but that was because his job was considered important. He never spoke about the meetings he went to every few days and she supposed they were hush, hush. He was a busy man and also very generous. She imagined he supported the hospital in which his son was receiving treatment. It was a small, discreet place, privately run and in pleasant surroundings. Even before the war it had been one of the foremost hospitals in the country for treating burns, and since then those patients fortunate enough to be referred here were certain of getting the best treatment available. However, Lord Vane remained determined to send Simon to America when he was feeling well enough to travel.

That wouldn't be for some months, of course. Apart from the burns, which Simon had sustained before he managed to eject, he hadn't been too badly injured. His ankle had been damaged and there had been some bruising and fractures, but because he'd come down in the sea, he'd been relatively lucky. A fishing boat had picked him up soon after ditching, and he'd been rushed straight to the military hospital nearby. He would be scarred on his face and body, but he would probably be able to live normally when he was fully recovered.

Emily had felt no revulsion when she'd seen Simon's scars. It hadn't made her want to run away as Maura had when she saw John. She was genuinely concerned for him, upset and distressed by the pain she knew he was suffering, and yet she wasn't sure she wanted to spend the rest of her life with him or his family.

As she approached the little private ward where Simon was being cared for, a man came out and began to walk towards her. He was wearing a dark lounge suit, his black hair waving off a high forehead, his eyes dark brown and his generous mouth topped by a neat moustache. He was actually a very handsome man, she thought, possibly in his early forties.

'How is my husband today, Doctor?' she asked, and saw an odd look in the man's eyes. 'He isn't worse, is he? He hasn't had a relapse?'

'No...' The man glanced at his wristwatch – gold and very expensive, she noticed. 'Excuse me, Mrs Vane. You've made a mistake. I'm not a doctor.'

He walked quickly away from her, seemingly in a hurry to escape. How odd, she thought. If he wasn't a doctor, why had he just come from Simon's room? Her heart quickened as she wondered if he had done something to harm her husband, and she opened the door without knocking.

Simon was propped up against the pillows. She saw that he was smoking, something his father and the doctors had absolutely forbidden, and as she approached the bed, she thought she could smell whisky.

'Should you be smoking?' she asked. Simon had opened his eyes but was staring at a point somewhere beyond her shoulder as he usually did when she visited him these days. 'Who did I just see leaving – that good-looking man with dark hair?'

Simon glanced at her then. He ignored her comment about smoking, putting the cigarette to his lips as she sat on the edge of the bed and inhaling deeply. It was a moment or two before he answered.

'You must have seen Philip. He's a sort of distant cousin. We've known each other for years.'

'Oh...' Emily felt vaguely dissatisfied with his answer, though she wasn't sure why, except that she sensed he was not telling her the whole truth. 'How are you feeling today?' He seemed more cheerful, so his cousin's visit must have done him good.

'Bloody awful,' he said, 'if you want the truth, but better than I have been, I suppose. The doctors tell me I was lucky.'

'I think they're right. It might have been worse, Simon.'

'You try it and see how it feels.'

'I'm not saying it isn't awful for you, but the doctors here are very good and your father is very hopeful that surgery will help.'

'My father doesn't have to have the bloody surgery,' Simon muttered angrily. 'But Philip says I should stop moaning and start thinking about the future...' A rueful expression came into his eyes. 'I suppose I have been rather a bore these past few weeks...'

'You were entitled to be,' Emily said with a smile. This was the first time he had been anything like his old self, which was understandable. 'Besides, they had you on drugs for ages. I came several times before you even knew me.'

'Poor Emily,' Simon said. 'I haven't been fair to you, have I?'

Emily's heart caught. When he looked at her like that she remembered how she'd felt at the start of their relationship, like a young girl in love. She wished she still felt like that but however hard she tried, she couldn't – because at the back of her mind there was always a picture of another man.

'You didn't ask to get shot down.'

'But I knew it could happen.' He reached out to stroke the back of her hand as it lay on the bed next to his. 'Do you want a divorce, Emily? I wouldn't blame you if you did.'

She couldn't answer him immediately. For weeks he'd ignored her and she'd felt like a bird, beating her wings uselessly against the bars of a gilded cage, but now there was an appeal in his eyes that held her fast. She must feel something for him despite all the doubts and suspicion that her marriage was a mistake. At the moment, she felt as if she were being torn in two, and it hurt like hell.

'What do you want, Simon? Do you want to be free?'

'I'm not going very far for the moment, am I?'

'You know what I mean.'

'Why do you ask? You're the one married to a man with revolting scars all over his body.'

'I don't find them revolting.'

'I bloody do,' Simon muttered. 'I'm a sodding freak.'

'That's not true, and I wish you wouldn't swear, Simon. I asked if you wanted to be free, because I wasn't sure that you liked being married to me that much.'

'I did warn you I have moods, didn't I?'

'Yes, but it was more than that. You know it was. Sometimes, at the start, it was all right but last time you were here... You were distant, Simon. You smiled at me, but you weren't really thinking of me. I sensed something – it was as if there was a barrier between us. I feel as if I don't know you. You're not the man I thought I'd fallen in love with that first day. Your eyes seemed to hold secrets. You never tell me what you're thinking...'

'That's a bit unfair, Emily. We haven't spent a lot of time together.'

'Marcus got home leave twice as often as you. I think you didn't want to come home to me. You didn't want me here when I came to visit...'

'I couldn't tell you... I was afraid of being shot down, of dying before—' He avoided her eyes. 'Whatever I am, whatever my failings, I love you as much as I am capable of loving any woman, Emily. I don't want a divorce. Please don't leave me.'

Emily looked down at her lap, twisting her wedding ring nervously. She knew that she was caught, that it was impossible for her to break through the emotional ties he and his father had woven about her.

'Vane wants me to run his convalescent home for him.'

'Yes, he told me he was going to ask you,' Simon said. 'It would give you something to do, Emily. I'll be tied up here for a long time, and after that I may go to America for treatment. I was going to refuse but Philip thinks I should go.'

'It's your choice,' Emily replied. Clearly this distant cousin had quite an influence on him. His visit had changed Simon's attitude completely. Before, he'd been morose, hardly speaking unless forced, and he certainly hadn't talked to her like this. 'You're the one who knows how important the treatment is for you. Successful surgery might make you feel better about yourself.'

Simon looked at her oddly, almost as if he were ashamed

of something. 'You've been very good, Emily. A lot of girls would have run away screaming. Father told me he is proud of you – that's quite a compliment. He likes you a lot.'

Emily was silent. If she could put aside her resentment at the way Lord Vane had taken over her life since his son had been shot down, she supposed she liked him too. It was considerate of him to offer a job, because most married women had to be satisfied with staying at home.

'I'm not going to run away because you have a few scars, Simon. It would take more than that to make me leave you.'

'Are you going to take on the job?' Simon ignored the comment on his scars, as if he didn't want to know. She understood, because he had been so very good-looking, and he must hate the thought of being scarred for life. Even though he had been luckier than many, he would still bear reminders of his burns for as long as he lived.

'Yes, I think so. I haven't told him yet. Your father gets too much of his own way, Simon. It will do him good to wait.'

Simon gave a short, harsh laugh. 'That's the spirit, Emily. Stand up to him. He will respect you for it.'

Emily bent down to kiss him lightly on the lips. She felt him stiffen, withdraw. When she moved away his eyes were closed, and she could see that he hadn't wanted her to kiss him. It was almost as if he found it distasteful to be touched by her.

'What's wrong, Simon? I'm sorry if I hurt you.'

'You didn't,' he muttered. 'I'm tired. Go away now and leave me to sleep, will you?'

'Yes, of course.'

Emily opened the door, glancing back for a moment before closing it behind her. Simon had asked her not to leave him, but he didn't want her to kiss him. When she thought about it, she knew that he had never truly enjoyed their lovemaking. Was there something wrong with her – something that made him reluctant to touch her – or was there some other reason? Something was nagging at the back of her mind but she didn't know what... There was nothing she could really put her finger on. Simon's attitude just made her more certain that he didn't truly love her.

If she stayed with him it was likely that they would never have a true marriage, not the kind she might have if she married Terry – and yet what could she do about it? Terry would urge her to leave Simon, but she knew she couldn't bring herself to do it. She was going to give in to Lord Vane's emotional blackmail and take the job he had offered her.

* * *

Daniel heard the truck's engine splutter and die, and he knew that there was no way he was going to keep up with the rest of the convoy. He glanced at his mate and saw the fear in his eyes. From the information they had, the Germans were half an hour or less behind them, and if they couldn't get this damned truck going pretty sharpish, they could be in trouble because it was packed with explosives.

'Look, grab a lift with one of the other trucks, Ted,' Daniel said. 'I'll have a go at getting this running and I'll catch up with you at the other end.'

'I don't like leaving you, Dan,' his mate said. But there was a nervous look in his eyes as they heard the sound of gunfire somewhere in the distance. It was probably an attack from the air on another convoy. 'I wouldn't mind if we were dug in somewhere, but we're sitting ducks out here.'

'Go on, get going,' Daniel said, and he gave him a little

shove. Just before Ted obeyed, Dan took a packet of letters from inside his jacket and shoved them into his friend's hand. 'If you get off safe, send these for me, will you?'

'Yes, of course. Good luck then.'

Daniel nodded. He jumped down from the cab and opened up the bonnet, peering inside. The carburettor was playing up again by the looks of things, but he had a spare in the back; it wasn't much better than the one that had just given up the ghost, but he'd been going to swap them over before the order to retreat had come through. He cursed as he started work, watching the convoy retreating into the distance. Maybe he was a fool to try and get this bloody thing going; he could have simply abandoned it, and yet he felt it was his duty to get as much equipment out as he possibly could. They were going to lose too much stuff as it was, to say nothing of the men.

Like Ted, he hated being stuck on this open road. The truck made too good a target, and besides, once he got going again he had no idea where he was headed. It had been a case of follow my leader, and take out as much as you can; those were their orders.

It took him nearly twenty minutes before there was a flicker of life in the tired engine, and then, just as it began to spark, a man came running towards him at full pelt.

'The Germans come,' he said in a heavy Greek accent. 'You go quick.'

Daniel could hear the roar of motorbikes in the distance, and he knew it must be the advance patrol that so often preceded heavier armaments.

'They're not having this damned thing,' he muttered. 'I'll blow the bugger to kingdom come first!'

The Greek raised his brows, lifting the flap at the back of

the truck to peer inside, and then grinned. 'You come. We go quick,' he said, and he jumped into the driving seat, leaving Daniel to scramble into the passenger side as best he could. 'We don't let the buggers have it. We have better uses, eh, my friend?'

Daniel saw his grin, realising that he was dealing with more here than he had imagined at first. He knew that it was his duty to follow the convoy, but the Greek was in command now, and they were headed down a steep incline. The lorry was bumping and shuddering danger-ously as they hurtled at terrifying speed, making Daniel shudder as he imagined the ammunition exploding at any moment. Finally they stopped behind a huge clump of boulders further down the ridge. It was only just in time, he realised, as the motorbikes went roaring by, and a few minutes later they heard the rumble of tanks and heavy armour.

Daniel thought they were sure to be discovered, but the rumbling went on and then, suddenly, it was quiet. He turned to look at his companion, who was grinning at him.

'So now what do we do? I can't get this thing through to the coast now. Unless you know another route?'

'I have the better idea.' The Greek held out his hand to Daniel. 'I am Mikkos, yes? You British Tommy, no?'

'Name is Daniel. Pleased to meet you, Mikkos.'

'The British go and we surrender,' Mikkos said, and he spat out of the open window. 'But we are not finished. There are some of us who will not lie down and play dead. We make the buggers pay, yes? Your lorry has what we need to blow them up, yes?'

'Yes...' Daniel looked at him warily. 'Are you suggesting you take this stuff for sabotage purposes?'

'We make things bad for them for a while, yes?' Mikkos raised his brows. 'You stay and help, no?'

The sensible thing would be to hotfoot it after the retreating British troops, Daniel knew. It was stupid to get involved with Mikkos's plans, and yet somehow it appealed. He'd felt like a scalded cat, having to run from the Germans again, and only a few weeks after he'd arrived. Besides, ten to one if he tried to make it through to the coast he would get picked up by the Germans. If it was a straight choice between working with Mikkos, who smelled like a goat but had saved his life, or sitting the war out in a German prisoner of war camp, then there was only one choice.

11

———

Alice stared at the telegram waiting for her on the kitchen table when she came in from shopping. It had an official look about it and she was reluctant to open it. She'd had this strange, heavy feeling for several days now, and it was nothing to do with the fact that she was five months pregnant.

'Do you want me to open it for you?' her mother asked.

Alice hesitated and then shook her head. 'It won't change what it says, will it?'

'No, nor will just staring at it.'

'No...' Alice reached for the telegram. She felt sick and reluctant. It had to be bad news. Forcing herself, she ripped it open and read the brief message. For a moment the letters blurred into a jumble as the tears stung her eyes.

```
Regret to inform you, Corporal Daniel
Searles has been reported missing in
action…
```

She sat down at the table as her knees turned to jelly. Daniel was missing, her lovely Dan with his wonderful smile and teasing eyes. Something had happened to him. She had known it inside herself for days but she hadn't wanted to admit it.

Mrs Robinson took the telegram and read it for herself.

'Well, there's a thing,' she exclaimed in disgust. 'What are we to make of that? Why don't they say what happened?'

'I suppose they have to be careful – you know what they're always telling us, Mum. Careless talk costs lives.'

'As if we know any spies! Daft, I call it. What we need is to be told exactly what happened.'

'Daniel is missing.' Alice felt numb, as if this was a dream, unreal. Surely she would wake up and discover it was all a mistake. 'They don't know he's dead, just missing. I might get a letter to say it's all right… That he was just lost or wounded or something.'

Mrs Robinson thought that pigs might fly first, but she didn't say anything. This was exactly what she'd feared when Alice had rushed into marriage. Her lovely, happy daughter was probably a widow and she was going to have a child in a few months.

'We would be better off knowing.' She threw the telegram down in frustration. 'It's neither one thing nor the other.'

Alive looked at her mother, her eyes pitiful. 'At least I've still got hope, Mum. Missing isn't dead. It isn't final. Sometimes men come back when they've been reported lost and it turns out to have been a silly mistake.'

She got to her feet and walked to the door.

'Where are you going?' Mrs Robinson was alarmed. 'You're not going to do anything silly, are you?'

'I have to tell Frances,' Alice said.

What she really wanted was to be alone. She was holding back the tears, refusing to let herself believe that Daniel was missing in the true sense of the word. It was surely a mistake. She knew it was one of those official mix-ups that Daniel had told her about. She wouldn't let herself think anything else, because that would hurt too much.

* * *

Emily walked back from the Dower House. It was a beautiful spring morning, really warm for the first time, the sky blue and the garden beginning to look its best. It was wonderful how Amelia kept it looking so nice, but that was only because she did so much of the weeding and planting herself. Emily sometimes gave her a hand these days, but today she had spent the morning talking to plumbers and builders and measuring the windows. Because the house had been unoccupied, the blackout regulations hadn't been followed and that was just one more job added to her growing list. It was good to keep busy. Then she didn't have to think about poor Daniel, missing in action – or about Terry and the happiness she was walking away from.

'Ah, there you are,' Amelia said as Emily entered the hall. 'I was just about to have some coffee. Would you care to join me?'

'Yes, thank you.' Emily saw two letters waiting for her on the silver salver on the hall table. She recognised the handwriting on one immediately, because that was her sister's, but the other was new to her. 'I'll read these later.' She pushed them into her skirt pocket. 'I wanted to talk to you about linen, Amelia.'

'You're wondering if we have any to spare, I suppose?' Amelia looked thoughtful. 'I should imagine there is a load in the linen cupboards. We haven't used much of it for years so it will probably need freshening up. I'll have a look later and let you know. How many beds do you need to make up?'

'We shall have about ten guests to start with,' Emily said. 'We could take another five at a pinch, but it depends on the nursing staff they send us, I expect.'

'It's hard to get any kind of staff these days,' Amelia said with a grimace. 'If it wasn't for Mrs Morris, Bailey and Jenny I'm sure I don't know what we would do ourselves.'

Emily found it amazing that such a large house functioned at all with so few staff, but of course half the rooms were closed up these days, the furniture covered with dust sheets. She sometimes thought it would have been better to move into the Dower House and give the mansion to the government, but she knew Vane would never agree. He clung to his house and traditions despite the discomfort, shortages and restrictions the war had imposed.

'Well, I've found two cleaners, a middle-aged couple from the village,' Emily said, looking at her list. 'They were keen to take it on and I've given them a trial. I might have to find more help once the guests arrive but it's a start. We shall need a cook. I was considering running an advert – a national newspaper would be best, don't you think?'

'Yes, I imagine so.' Amelia gave her an odd look. 'You're enjoying this, aren't you?'

'Yes, I am. I hate to be idle and this is time-consuming. I don't have time to sit about and feel sorry for myself.'

'I can't imagine you ever doing that. Simon is the one for sulks.' Amelia frowned. 'We hoped all that stuff was over when he married but...'

'What do you mean?' Emily asked when Amelia faltered and looked conscious, as if realising she'd said too much. 'What kind of stuff?'

'Oh, nothing. Vane was disappointed in him that's all. He had such a bright future and then it looked as if he might throw it all away. I blamed that friend of his, but—' Once again she was silent as her husband walked into the room. 'Ah, Vane. We're having our coffee. Will you join us?'

'Thank you, my dear.' He bent to kiss her cheek. 'Is everything going well with the building work, Emily?'

'Yes, I believe so. There was a problem with the plumber but it's sorted now. We should be ready to move the beds in next month as we planned.'

'Good. Well done. Excellent.' He sipped his coffee, grimacing over the taste. 'This is awful, Amelia. If this is the best Mrs Morris can do we should give it up for the duration.'

Amelia smiled. 'I know, it is rather awful. I'll speak to her and see if it can be improved, but you know how things are. It's so difficult to buy anything worth having.'

'Of course I understand, but there are limits.' He glanced at his paper. 'The news just gets worse. Not content with destroying the heart of London last month, the damned Germans overran Greece and we had to withdraw and now they've launched an attack on Crete.'

'But there was some good news recently,' Amelia pointed out. 'Did I read somewhere that we had sunk the Bismarck?'

Emily stood up as they began to argue in a gentle fashion. 'I have some things to do. If you will excuse me.'

She walked from the room, going quickly up to her own apartment. She wanted to read Frances's letter and she was curious to discover who had sent the other, though in her heart she thought she knew.

* * *

Emily frowned over her sister's letter. Frances had rung her earlier in the month to tell her that Daniel was missing, of course, but it was clear that she was worried about Alice.

She seems to be in a state of denial. Her mother is very worried about her but there isn't much any of us can do until we know more.

It wasn't surprising that Alice didn't want to believe that Daniel might be dead, Emily thought. She knew that Alice was very much in love with her husband, and she must be feeling terrible, especially with a baby on the way. Emily felt a choking grief whenever she thought her brother might be badly wounded or dying, so she could imagine how her sister-in-law must feel.

Most of Frances's letter was about her own baby. She had a beautiful, healthy boy she intended to call Mark Robert Danby, and was naturally very happy. Marcus had been given a seventy-two-hour pass when the baby was born, and Frances, feeling very contented, wanted to know when Emily was coming to see them.

I know Alice would like to see you. Perhaps you could talk to her? And we are having the christening in August, so if you can't come before, perhaps you can manage a weekend then?

Emily put the letter away in her drawer and picked up the second. She wasn't sure why she felt sort of excited and yet nervous, but even before she opened the envelope, she half expected that it was from Terry.

His first words asked her to forgive the liberty he had taken in writing to her. He had done so because he was worried about her and wondered if she had settled down. He told her that he had been accepted back on regular duty and would be working in London from the beginning of next month.

My hands aren't quite as they used to be, but I can do my work and that's good enough for the powers that be. I volunteered for work in London. Those poor devils have had a rotten time and I shall be needed there. At the moment I don't have much to worry about except myself, and there are others, married men, who could do with a quieter life. I think about you often, Emily. If ever you need me, I'll be there. I'm giving you an address. A postcard will reach me.

Take care of yourself.

I love you, Terry

Emily read the letter three times and then put it away in her writing box, locking the drawer in which she kept personal papers. It lay on top of her marriage lines, mocking her. Terry hadn't expected an answer unless she was in trouble, and she thought it best not to reply. She couldn't give him the answer he wanted, and it might be kinder to make a clean break.

She felt a pang of regret for what might have been, knowing that she could have been happy with Terry in a way she sensed she never would with Simon. Yet she had begun to settle here at last, to find pleasure in her surroundings, and she enjoyed her work. Once the Dower House was ready and they had guests, she imagined she would be busy most of the time.

She decided that she would visit her sister before the first guests arrived. Vane could oversee anything to do with the construction work while she was away, and once the home was up and running she wouldn't want to leave for a while.

Having made up her mind, she tidied her hair and went downstairs. She would drive over to see Simon after lunch, and then there was a pile of paperwork waiting for her in her office. It was a good thing she didn't mind filling in forms and keeping accounts, Emily thought, and she smiled wryly as she remembered Frances saying Henry had made a muddle of the farm accounts again. She would have to have another go at them for him one day...

'You won't mind if I'm away for a few days, will you?' Emily asked as she handed Simon the book he had requested her to bring in. He was sitting out in a chair now and taking more of an interest in things. The book was about Greek architecture of ancient times, and had lots of fascinating pictures. 'It's my last chance before the home is ready to receive guests.'

'No, of course I shan't mind,' Simon said, giving her an odd look. 'And you mustn't let Father bully you, Emily. He gave you a job but you're free to do as you want with your life.'

'Yes, of course. I didn't want you to feel I had deserted you, that's all.'

'Don't be ridiculous. I don't need you to run around after me all the time. Besides, I'm getting better. They say I may be able to come home soon, at least for short periods, though I've got to come back here for treatment.'

'Yes, I know. It will be nice for you to get out of here for a while at least.'

'Thank God,' he said. 'It's driving me mad. I can't see why I should stay here now that I can hobble about.'

'You still have pain, don't you?' She looked at him doubtfully. He didn't talk to her about these things often and she didn't really know the situation. Vane had told her he was improving, and Simon said he felt better, but neither of them told her anything that mattered. What little she knew came from one of the doctors she met occasionally.

'If I do I can manage it with pills or an injection,' he said, and frowned. 'It's nothing for you to worry about. Anyway, once I'm able I shall probably go to America, have most of my treatment there.'

Emily looked at him doubtfully. 'That will be rather awkward for your father. He will have to find someone to look after the home while I am with you.'

'I shan't need you to come with me,' Simon said. 'You would be miserable sitting around waiting for me while I was having treatment. No, Emily. You will stay here, of course. I wouldn't dream of asking you to come with me.'

'I see...' She looked down at her lap. It was obvious that Simon neither wanted nor needed her. He had asked her not to leave him, but it was for the sake of appearances. He wasn't interested in renewing their marriage in any shape or form. She wondered why he'd asked her, because it was obvious that she meant very little to him. 'That's just as well, isn't it?' She stood up, feeling that it was pointless to sit there with someone who obviously didn't want her company.

'You haven't stayed long,' Simon said. 'Have I upset you? It isn't that I don't want you around, Emily. But you would be bored just waiting for me all the time.'

'Yes, perhaps I would be,' she said. 'I'm rather busy for the moment so you won't mind if I don't visit for a while.'

'Emily...' Simon said in an exasperated voice as she walked towards the door. 'I was only thinking of you.'

Emily didn't look back as she went out. She was feeling angry and upset, even though she knew in her heart that it was better if Simon went away to have his treatment without her. There was no point in pretending that they were a happily married couple, because it just wasn't true.

As she got into the car she had once again borrowed from Amelia, she saw a man getting out of what she thought was an expensive Rolls Royce. He was immaculately dressed in a grey striped suit, and his shoes looked handmade. She knew him as the man Simon had called Philip – some sort of a cousin. Well, perhaps her husband would be more interested in his next visitor than he had been in his wife.

* * *

Alice picked up the small packet of letters with shaking hands. There were four of them and they had arrived together that morning – four letters from Daniel. Surely it meant that he was alive and well? She saw that they all had the same date on the envelope, and she opened them at random. They had all been written within a couple of days. Daniel was telling her that they had arrived at their new billet and were settling in. He said it was nicer than he'd thought, and that he'd been out for a drink with the locals at... The next bit had been blue-pencilled but looking at the back of the page, Alice could just about read the word.

What was a taverna? She puzzled over it for a moment, and then realised it must mean the same as a tavern or an inn. It might be somewhere like Spain or Italy... No, not Italy – Greece! It clicked in her mind suddenly, and she remembered the reports about the British having to retreat from Athens; that was about the time when Daniel went missing, just after these letters were written. He must have sent them just before... whatever happened.

Alice closed her eyes, trying to picture the scene. What was it like when men were being forced to retreat before a stronger enemy? She had read reports about how the New Zealanders and Australians had fought so bravely to try and repel the invaders, and how the Greeks had covered the retreat of as many men as they could, cheering the British troops as they marched out.

There must have been lots of shelling, gunfire and explosions. She could see Daniel in the middle of a battle, see the men falling all around him, and then... it all went blank. She couldn't see Daniel being dead, because it didn't feel to her as if he were dead.

Her mother said she must start to accept that he probably wouldn't be coming home. Even her father had told her to cry, to let her grief out, but she had cried and the grief was still inside her, gnawing at her. Yet she couldn't believe that Daniel was dead. She would feel empty if that were so, but she didn't, she just felt worried and on edge.

'You won't do the baby any good mithering over Daniel,' her mother had told her when the letters were delivered.

'You've got to pull yourself together, Alice. You've got the baby to think of now.'

She was thinking of the baby, of course she was. She had knitted coats and bonnets and bootees, and she'd made some nightgowns from material she'd found on the market, but that didn't stop this ache inside her. It never went away, whether she was waking or sleeping; it just stayed there like a heavy lump in her heart.

Frances had told her that Emily was coming to visit that weekend. She would be pleased to see her sister-in-law, and she hoped that in Emily she would find a believer, someone who wasn't prepared to just write Daniel off as if there wasn't a shred of hope.

* * *

'Oh, isn't he beautiful!' Emily said as she bent over her nephew. He looked pink and chubby, his fat little fist waving at her, and he smelled of baby talcum. 'You must be so proud of him and so happy.'

'Yes, I am,' Frances said. 'He is lovely, isn't he?'

'Gorgeous,' Emily said. 'I wasn't sure I wanted a baby just yet but looking at your little Charles makes me broody.'

'It's a pity—' Frances stopped abruptly, seeming awkward. 'I mean – will you... Will Simon be able...?'

Emily took pity on her. 'He wasn't damaged in that way, if that's what you mean. I'm not sure if we shall ever have a normal marriage again, but I don't think he's incapable.'

'Surely it will be all right between you when he's over all this?'

Emily shrugged her shoulders. 'I'm not sure. Simon seems to have withdrawn. He says he doesn't want me to go with him when he goes to America for treatment so I shall stay here and do my job.'

'Not go with him?' Frances looked shocked and then upset. 'But surely you will? Oh, Emily, I think that's awful. You must go with him, of course you must.'

'Not if he doesn't want me to. Besides, I have plenty to do here. They need me at the home, and I'm doing a worthwhile job.'

'But Simon is your husband!'

'Yes – but not all husband and wives live in each other's pockets, Frances.'

'Well, I know some don't,' Frances admitted, 'but if you love each other...' Her eyes narrowed as she looked at Emily. 'You do love him, don't you?'

'To be honest, I don't know,' Emily admitted. There was no point in hiding it any longer, because she wasn't sure how long her marriage would continue. 'It was all such a rush when we got married. I wasn't sure it was right then, but Simon was so down and I thought...' She sighed. 'I probably made a mistake, but I'm stuck with it so there's not much use in complaining.'

'Oh, Emily!' Frances looked shocked, as if she would burst into tears at any minute. 'I don't know what to say to you.'

'There isn't anything to say. I can't leave Simon the way things are, and I've taken on this project for Vane. I shall just have to grit my teeth and put up with it, shan't I?'

'But that's a horrible way to live.'

'It's all I can do for the moment,' Emily said. 'I've accepted it and that's that as far as I'm concerned.'

'But when Simon is over this...'

'Perhaps,' Emily agreed. 'I shall have had time to think

things over. I do care about him, Frances. I don't love him, not as you love Marcus – or as Alice loves Daniel – but I do care, of course I do.'

'Have you seen Alice yet?' Frances frowned. 'Her mother told me she'd had some letters from Daniel. Apparently, she just refuses to accept that he is dead.'

'Has the War Office confirmed it, then?'

'No, not yet. But he must be, mustn't he?'

'I don't see that follows,' Emily said, her heart aching. 'Don't give up on him, Frances. He might be wounded – or even a prisoner.'

'They get lists of prisoners, don't they?'

'Yes, but they aren't always accurate, and sometimes it is ages before names get listed. I think Alice is right not to give up yet. Besides, it will be easier for her to accept as time goes on.'

'Well, perhaps you are right,' Frances said, and she picked up her son as he started to whimper. 'I wish you would talk to Henry while you're here, Emily. He isn't at all well, but he won't listen to anything we tell him – and Connor is playing me up. He's been moody ever since he heard about Daniel. He stays out late and I can't do a thing with him.'

'I'll see if I can talk to him,' Emily promised, and sighed. Everything was so complicated and so distressing, and even Frances looked tired to death. Why couldn't it be like it had been before the war – before her father died? If he'd still been here he would have sorted them all out, she thought, and she felt the ache that had never quite gone away stir inside her. 'I expect he's just upset over Daniel.'

* * *

'I'm really glad you came,' Alice said as she served Emily a slice of her seed cake and refilled her cup with tea. 'It's been good having a long talk to you, and I feel much better.'

'I know everyone thinks we have to accept that Dan has gone,' Emily told her, 'but I'm like you, Alice, I don't feel that he is dead. I know something is wrong, but I can't believe he won't come back to us one day.'

A tear trickled down Alice's cheek, but she brushed it away with the back of her hand. 'Thank you for saying that, Emily. Mum thinks I'm laying up trouble for myself by refusing to accept it, but I can't believe he's gone – I just can't.'

'Well, you may be right. You hang on to that thought until we know for certain,' Emily said, and reached across to kiss her cheek. 'How are you, love? You look as if you're blooming. Frances got very tired towards the end of her term, but you seem to be carrying well.'

'I am,' Alice said, and patted her stomach. 'He's very good. I'm determined to have a boy for Dan. I was hardly sick at all, and I haven't had some of the troubles other girls have. That poor Millie Richardson up the lane, for instance – she's having her third in three years and she looks terrible, all kinds of problems. Mum has gone up to her today to see if she can do anything to help her.'

'Is she having another?' Emily shook her head over what had been a scandal in the village for ages. 'She isn't much older than you, Alice. Who is the father this time?'

'She says she doesn't know, but Mum swears it's Millie's father. She thinks he's to blame for all her children.'

'That's horrible,' Emily said. 'He should be ashamed – his own daughter! Someone should tell the police.'

'That's what Mum thinks,' Alice agreed. 'But Dad told

her she isn't to do it and nobody else wants to get involved either. Everyone knows what's going on, but the poor girl doesn't have much now and if he was tried and sent to prison it would be even worse for her.'

'Yes, I suppose it might,' Emily agreed. 'But it isn't right, Alice. You would think her mother would do something – or her brothers.'

'Maybe they think it keeps it in the family,' Alice suggested. 'But her last child isn't right in the head. I think it's time someone did something, but I doubt if anyone will. Especially at the moment. They all have too much to worry them. Sally Johnson's eldest son was killed at Tobruk earlier this year and now her youngest has joined the Army.'

'Oh, the poor woman,' Emily sympathised. It wasn't just their family that had suffered; everyone was having their own troubles. 'It's this rotten war. At the start they thought it wouldn't last long, but it just keeps on, and we don't seem to get anywhere.'

'Oh, don't,' Alice begged. 'Please don't talk about it. I try not to think about it more than I have to.'

Emily understood how she felt. Alice must be miserable over not knowing what had happened to Dan, but she was being very brave, facing it in the only way she knew how.

'Let's talk about the baby then,' Emily said. 'What about a christening gown? Amelia told me there was one in the attic I could have. I've brought it for you to see. It is beautiful old lace, though it will need a bit of blue to make it white again. I offered it to Frances first but she has made her own so I thought you might like it?'

'But won't you want it for your own children – when you have them?' Alice blushed faintly. 'Sorry, perhaps I shouldn't have asked that...'

'It doesn't bother me,' Emily said. 'Seeing little Charles, and you having Dan's baby, makes me a bit broody, but it isn't likely to happen for a while. I've accepted that and I have lots of other things to occupy me.'

'I should love to have the gown – if you're sure?'

'Yes, of course. I thought I would ask first, but I'll drop it in tomorrow before I leave.'

'Are you leaving so soon?'

'I only came for the weekend,' Emily said. 'I've seen Frances and the baby, and you – and I'm going to Henry's for dinner this evening.'

'He hasn't looked at all well lately,' Alice said with a frown. 'And Connor has been up to a few tricks recently. He and Peter were in trouble with Mr Wright last week. They let his boar out and he had a problem getting it away from the sows – and they do other things that would give Mum a fit if she knew.'

'What kinds of things?'

'They go and lie in the ditches around the drome to count the planes in and out,' Alice told her. 'Sometimes they are out until it's almost light. I caught Peter sneaking in the other night. He pleaded with me not to tell Dad and I haven't, because he would get a thrashing if I did. But it could be dangerous for them if the drome was bombed, and it has been a couple of times, although they were daylight raids and didn't do much damage really.'

'Frances told me he was getting out of hand. I think he's upset over Daniel.'

'Yes, I am sure he is,' Alice agreed. 'I've tried to talk to him, but he just backs off and gives me an accusing look, as if he were blaming me.'

'I'm sure he doesn't blame you. He just feels miserable,'

Emily said. 'He will be coming to Henry's with me this evening so perhaps I can talk to him then – not that he will listen to me.'

'I think he listened to Daniel more than anyone else,' Alice said. 'And I know Dan is fond of him. He talked about Connor living with us until he was old enough to get his own place.'

'Perhaps that's what is upsetting him,' Emily said. 'I know he resented Frances getting engaged and married so soon after Father died – and he said Henry and Clay wanted their own way on the farm. It wasn't so bad when I was at home but now... He must feel abandoned by his family.'

'Yes, perhaps he does,' Alice agreed. 'But he is always welcome here, Emily. Mum would let him share Peter's room if he wanted to stay, though he's got his own room with Frances, of course.'

'I don't think he has ever felt close to Frances. I was closer to him, and so was Dan. But it might help him if you told him he could stay here sometimes, Alice. He is always talking about you and your seed cake, so he obviously likes being here.'

'He will be welcome to live with us when Daniel comes home.'

Emily nodded. Alice was determined to be positive, and perhaps she was right. After all, no one knew for sure where Daniel was or what had happened to him.

* * *

'You come now,' Mikkos said, grabbing Daniel's arm. 'The Germans come, we hide in the cellars.'

It wasn't the first time they'd received a visit from a

German patrol. Mikkos and his friends had been causing some trouble in the area, blowing up a train carrying German supplies and attacking a convoy. Daniel had helped in the attack on the convoy. He had enjoyed being a part of it, but he knew they were playing on dangerous ground. You didn't do things like this without risk. After all, they were breaking the terms of the Greek surrender, and the consequences would be harsh if they were caught.

'We are endangering your family staying here,' Daniel said as Mikkos took him down into the dark cellars that connected to tunnels that ran beneath the mountains for some distance. Wine had been stored here before the war and it was very cold but dry. 'We should find somewhere else to run the group from.'

'They know the risks,' Mikkos said. 'Besides, the Germans are stupid. They will never find us here.'

It was true enough, because the tunnels emerged at a secret location further down the hillside, and by the time a patrol found their hiding place they would be long gone – but the Stavros family were left behind at the ancient farmhouse to bear the brunt of the German anger.

Daniel knew that other men and women had been shot for helping the saboteurs. He just hoped it wouldn't happen to the family he had begun to know and like.

Sometimes, when he thought of his own family, of Alice and the way it had been on their wedding night, he wished that he had simply abandoned that damned truck and caught a lift with the retreating troops. He wondered how his wife was coping, and whether they had told her he was missing. What would she do if she thought he wasn't coming home? His worst nightmare was that one day he would get home and discover that she had found someone else.

* * *

'Frances has been worried about you,' Emily said as they were having dinner that evening in the big warm kitchen of Henry's ancient farmhouse. It had huge pine dressers at either end and a homely, comfortable feeling. 'Is your cough any better?'

'No, he sometimes keeps us awake all night with it,' Mary said, and pulled a face at her husband. 'I've tried making him go to the doctor but he won't. Stubborn as a mule, our Henry.'

'I can buy a bottle of cough medicine from the chemist for all the good it will do,' Henry said, and frowned. 'It's just a chesty thing I picked up last winter, Mary. It will clear up in time.'

Emily thought it ought to have cleared up now that the weather was so much better, but there was no point in nagging her brother.

'Is everything all right with the farm?' she asked. 'Any forms you want me to fill in for you before I leave?'

'Things are all right for the moment. There are a couple of forms you could do for me,' Henry said, giving her a grateful look. 'And you could write to the bank for me, tell them I can't manage to pay all the interest this month but I'll make it up when the harvest comes in.'

'Yes, of course,' Emily agreed. 'I haven't seen Clay for months – is he managing all right?'

'I don't know and I don't want to,' Henry said, and looked annoyed. 'He took advantage of us and I haven't forgiven him for it, Emily. That land was the best we had and if we'd kept it all together we might have broken even this year. He got off scot-free and it isn't fair.'

'Now you've got him off,' Mary said bringing them a cup of tea. 'We don't mention Clay in this house, Emily. It's off limits for Henry.'

'Sorry.' Emily got up to help her sister-in-law carry the dirty plates to the scullery for washing. 'I thought that was all sorted out?'

'It never will be as far as Henry is concerned,' Mary said. 'He blames Clay and Margaret for all his troubles, though that isn't quite fair. To be honest, Henry isn't a manager. He works all the hours God gives, but he can't handle the business side. Your father was the one who did all that.'

'Yes, I see,' Emily said. 'It isn't easy for Henry with all these restrictions and regulations, Mary. But if he can hang on it will get better when the war is over.'

'If he can,' Mary said, and looked worried. 'I suppose he'll manage somehow – but sometimes I think it will be the death of him – and then what shall we do?'

Emily didn't know how to answer her. It was clear that things were far from right with her brother and his family, but there wasn't a great deal she could do about it at the moment. Perhaps she would have more luck with her younger brother.

* * *

'We are all worried about you, Connor,' Emily said as they walked back to the house later that evening. 'Frances, Alice, and me – and you don't want to give Henry more grief, do you? He already has too much to do.'

'You might have been concerned, and perhaps Alice,' Connor said, 'but the others don't care what I do. Frances is only bothered about the baby, and Henry has Mary and his children.'

'But you know he is worried about the farm, don't you?'

'Yeah – that's Clay's and Margaret's fault,' Connor said. 'She was greedy after Dad died, and Clay helped her. He wanted her knickers off... That's why he took her side.'

'Connor!' Emily stopped and looked at him. 'Where did you get that from?'

'I heard one of the men talking to Henry about it. They saw Daniel and Clay having a fight and it was over Margaret – because Clay made her do it against her will and she made Daniel pay her money to keep quiet.'

'That's a wicked thing to say, Connor!'

'It's the truth. Henry told him he'd known something was going on and made him promise not to repeat it to anyone else.'

'Are you sure you heard right?'

'Yeah. I was behind the hedge. They didn't know I was there. I was trying to catch a frog and I'd got down in the ditch, and I heard it all. Clay raped Margaret and she was going to have him arrested so Dan paid her to let him off.'

Emily was silent. She'd always known that Dan had changed his mind about the house for a reason, and she'd suspected it had something to do with Margaret and Clay, but she hadn't realised it was anything like this.

'That is horrible,' she said at last. 'I don't know if it is true, but even if it is we don't want anyone else to know. I want you to promise me that you will never mention it to anyone – not even Peter.'

'I haven't,' Connor said. 'I wouldn't care about Clay but I thought it might get Dan into trouble.'

'Yes, it might,' Emily agreed. 'If he covered up something

like that... But it may not be true, Connor. You know what people are like for tales in a village.'

'This one is true,' Connor said. 'But I shan't tell. I care about Dan.' He looked at his sister and she saw a suspicion of tears in his eyes. 'Everyone says he's dead but he isn't, is he?'

'I don't know,' Emily admitted. 'Alice doesn't think so and I'm praying he isn't, Connor. It is possible that he is a prisoner of war or something. It is possible that we shall hear he has turned up one of these days.'

'Dan said I could live with him and Alice when he came home.'

'I know, Alice told me something like that,' Emily said. 'Are you unhappy living with Frances?'

'I don't mind it,' Connor said. 'But I would rather be with Dan or you.'

'Would you like to come and stay with me in the holidays? I'm setting up a home for wounded soldiers and we need lots of help. Would you come and help me for a few weeks, Connor?'

'Can I really?' He stared at her, and she saw his eagerness.

'Yes, of course you can. There are lots of things you can do if you are willing to work.'

'I don't mind working. I used to help Dad on the land, and sometimes I give Henry a hand on the farm – but he nags all the time.'

'I shan't nag you,' Emily promised. 'But I shall be grateful if you can help me during the holidays.'

'Thanks, Emmy,' Connor said, and grinned at her. 'And I'll try not to worry Frances if I can help it.'

Emily smiled as they started walking again. 'Well, I don't

suppose you do anything very terrible,' she said. 'Is it fun watching for the planes to go out and come back?'

Connor gave her a conspiratorial look. 'We know which are Peter's lodgers,' he told her, 'and they waggle their wings to us when they come back so that we know they are safe.'

'That's nice,' Emily said. 'Our home will be ready very soon now and I dare say you will like meeting our soldiers when you come and stay.'

12

Alice felt the ache in her back intensify. She'd had a niggling pain all night in her stomach but she hadn't thought it was the baby. Now, suddenly, it ripped through her and she gasped. She'd known it had to be any day now, but somehow she hadn't expected it to hurt quite as much. She went into the kitchen, where her mother was scrubbing potatoes at the sink.

Mrs Robinson turned to look at her and frowned. 'Started, has it?' she said, and began to wipe her hands. 'I'd best get some kettles on the boil then, and I'll give your father a shout, tell him to fetch the doctor and the midwife.'

Alice gasped, perching on the edge of a chair. She hadn't been able to sit properly for days. 'Does it always hurt this bad, Mum?'

'Pretty much,' her mother told her in a no-nonsense way. 'You'll be worse before you're better, but no sense in worrying over it, Alice. Babies come when they're ready and not before. You might as well walk about a bit. It will be hours yet and it won't help going to bed. I found it better to walk, it takes your mind off things.'

Alice bent double as she felt the pain rip through her again, and then there was a warm, stinging sensation between her thighs. She could feel something trickling down her legs.

'I think my waters have burst, Mum.'

'Right, that's a good sign,' Mrs Robinson said. 'Maybe it's going to be quicker for you than it was for me, love. Here, take these towels and go through on the bed. I'll give your father a shout.'

Alice took the towels her mother had given her. She'd had a rubber sheet on her bed for days now, and the towels wouldn't be needed, but she instinctively did as her mother told her. She just hoped that it would all be over soon, and she would have Daniel's son to hold in her arms.

Oh, God, she wished he was here now. She had never felt such pain in her life, and she was terrified, even though she knew that what was happening to her was natural. But no one had told her it would hurt this much.

It seemed to Alice that the pain was never ending. Her screams had made her hoarse and she was exhausted by the time the baby was finally born, even though her mother and the midwife kept telling her how quick and easy it had been, and how lucky she was.

Alice didn't feel lucky until she looked at the child they had put into her arms, and then a flood of love poured out of her and tears trickled down her cheeks as she kissed him. It had been worth the pain to have him, to know that she had Dan's son to love and care for. He was hers, and she would have a part of her husband for ever, even if Dan never came back.

But he would, he would, she told herself, cradling the child to her protectively. She didn't know where Dan was or what he was doing, why the Army didn't seem to be sure what had happened to him, but in her heart she knew he was alive and thinking of her.

'Wherever you are, I love you,' she whispered, 'and our son loves you, too. Come home to us, Dan. Please come home. We need you. We need you so much.'

It was September now and Dan had gone missing in May, and still she didn't know for sure what had happened to him. The letter from his commanding officer had told her that he had been driving a truck behind a long convoy of retreating British soldiers, but when the men were taken on board ship, he wasn't there. No one seemed to know what had happened, except that there was a report that his truck had broken down and when last seen he had been trying to repair it.

No one had seen him killed. He had simply disappeared.

Oh, Dan, Dan, she thought, kissing her child. Where are you, my love? Where are you? She had been married just after Christmas in 1940, and in a few months it would be Christmas again. How long would it be before she knew whether she was a wife or a widow?

* * *

Dan smoked a cigarette as he lay on his back, looking down at the fertile valley below. The hillside was barren in places, but he was sheltered from view by some scrubby trees that somehow clung to the rock. Before the retreat from Athens, he had found Greece rather lovely, a place he might like to bring Alice to one day, but here on this remote farm he had learned how hard the people lived, and how easy he'd had it before the war. He was beginning to feel as if he'd been here for months, picking up enough of the language to understand a bit of what was going on around him.

Sometimes they gave him news of the outside world. He wondered how they discovered the things they did since the Germans censored everything they could. The Greeks were having a pretty rough time of it since the surrender; shortages of food and other goods were the least of their problems. Mikkos and his group were not the only ones to fight a fierce Guerrilla campaign against the invaders, and the Germans could be bloody in revenge. Daniel heard that in one part of the country they had destroyed hundreds if not thousands of homes.

The war seemed to be going the Germans' way, from what he heard, and sometimes he feared that the Allies were losing the war. At those times the depression set in and he wondered if he would ever see his wife or family again.

In a few weeks it would be Christmas and he would have been married for a year. One bloody night and a few hours in bed with his wife. He pulled a face and threw away his cigarette. This damned war had a lot to answer for. When he got home – if he got home – he was going to stay put! He'd had enough of being stuck in some foreign hole to last him a lifetime.

* * *

Connor loved the train journey to Hampshire. It was the first time he'd been away on his own and he was excited at the prospect of seeing where Emily lived now. She collected him at the station in a large black car that she told him belonged to Lord Vane.

'He lets me use it sometimes, because he gets more petrol coupons than he needs. He seems a bit severe when you first meet him, Connor, but he's not too bad.'

'I can't stop too long,' Connor told her. 'Henry needs me to help with the harvest before I go back to school, but he said I should come because it would be good experience for me.'

'Well, I am really pleased to have you. You can do lots of things to help me – if you don't mind visiting the men?'

Connor nodded. He was a bit worried about seeing some of the men. He'd seen one soldier in the village with a leg missing. Some of the other boys had stared but Connor had felt sorry for him. He'd asked if he could so anything to help but he'd been told to clear off. He hoped he could do something useful, because he couldn't help thinking about Dan. Maybe he was in pain and needing help...

'Oh, Emily,' the nurse said as she saw her coming from her office one morning some weeks later. 'Those medical supplies we ordered last week still haven't come through. I wondered if you could telephone and ask what has happened? We're getting short of the drug we need for one of the men.'

'Yes, I know,' Emily said, and smiled. 'I checked to see if

anything had arrived this morning, and when I saw that it hadn't I rang through to ask why. Apparently there has been a shortage because of some mix-up again, but they have a new batch in now and they've assured me we are first on the list.'

Nurse Rose Baines smiled at her. She was a pretty girl with dark curly hair and popular with the men. 'I might have known that you would be on top of it,' she said. 'You run this place like clockwork, and it certainly makes our lives easier.'

'That's what I'm here for,' Emily said. 'I know we have another month to go yet, Rose, but I'm planning the Christmas entertainment for our guests. I've secured the talents of a semi-professional piano player, and I've been told you sing.'

Rose blushed and waved her hand in dismissal. 'I sing a bit,' she said. 'But I'm not a professional.'

'That doesn't matter,' Emily assured her. 'I've got a conjuror for the children. We decided to have some of the village children at our party. The people have been good to us since we opened, bringing flowers and vegetables from the garden, and doing odd jobs about the place, and the men enjoy seeing the children sometimes. I've also found a stand-up comic. He has entertained the troops on these special tours they do overseas, and he was on stage with Vera Lynn once, something he is very proud of.'

'I sing her songs,' Rose admitted. 'Just don't expect me to sound the way she does!'

'The men won't mind, they all love you anyway,' Emily told her. 'It's just to give them a party, to help them feel they are part of a family, for those who can't go home. Some of their loved ones will be coming to stay, of course. We are putting three up here and another three will be staying up at the house.'

'I think it's wonderful the way you look after them,' Rose said. 'You've really made this place a home – and it's you most of the men are in love with, Emily.'

Emily laughed and shook her head. 'No, I don't think so. Anyway, I'll put you down for three songs, all right?'

'Yes – since it's you asking,' Rose agreed, but she was looking pleased as she went off, already humming a tune in her head.

Emily checked her list and then her wristwatch. She had been here for three hours and she was finished for the morning. She was going to pop back to the house now to see if the post had arrived, and then she was going to the hospital to fetch Simon home in the car. He was being allowed home for three days, and after that he was due to have an assessment. His condition had improved greatly throughout the summer and autumn, and now the doctors were saying that he was ready to have the first of a series of operations on his face. The previous day, Vane had told her that he was making arrangements to fly his son out to America for the necessary surgery.

'We can't really spare you, Emily,' he had said, a little frown creasing his brow. 'Besides, Simon says that you've talked it over and agreed that it would be a waste of time you going out there when you're needed here.'

'Simon doesn't want me to go. So I shall stay here where I'm needed.'

Vane had looked at her oddly but he hadn't said anything more. She knew that he was aware that there was constraint between the two of them, but apparently he had decided to ignore it.

Emily picked up her letters from the salver in the hall when she got home. There was one from Frances, and also a fat packet from Alice, which, when she opened it, turned out to have several photographs of Alice's beautiful baby inside. He was seven weeks old now and wearing the christening gown that Emily had given Alice. She thought there was a definite resemblance to Daniel, though she could see a bit of Alice too.

She read the brief note that accompanied the pictures. Alice hadn't heard anything more from the War Office, although she had recently been asked to fill out a form that seemed to imply she was going to be paid a widow's pension. She hadn't sent it back, because as she said, it would mean admitting that Daniel was dead, and she still wasn't ready to do that.

I've been getting part of Dan's pay all the time. I don't need much of it, except for the baby, because Dad won't take anything for my keep. He says I'm his girl and he'll look after us until I know what I'm doing. He goes daft over little Dan and so does Mum. He'll be thoroughly spoiled before long.

Emily smiled as she put the pictures to one side. She decided that she would read Frances's letter when she came back later that afternoon. She wanted to be early at the hospital just in case there was anything the doctors needed to tell her concerning Simon's home visit. He was due to leave at two o'clock, but she would be there by half past one, she thought as she got into the car Vane had recently bought for her use.

'It's time you had your own, Emily,' Vane had told her as

he gave her the keys to the small Ford. 'Amelia doesn't mind you using hers, but this will make you independent. Besides, you deserve it.'

Emily wasn't sure that she did deserve the gift, but she wasn't going to turn it down. It made it easy for her to drive into town to do her shopping, and saved any conflict of interest if Amelia wanted her own car at the same time as Emily needed it.

Parking in the hospital grounds, she frowned as she saw the expensive car drawn up a few feet away. Unless she was mistaken, that belonged to Philip, Simon's friend or distant cousin, or whatever he was. She hadn't bumped into him since that first time she'd seen him leaving her husband's room, and she wasn't sure that she wanted to see him now, but it hardly mattered. She was here to collect Simon and take him home, and she was a little before her appointed time.

She walked through the corridors to the small side ward that had been Simon's home for so many months. It seemed to her that they had been married much longer than a year, but it was only a few weeks past their anniversary. Of course they had never truly known what it was like to be married, having just brief times together, and then had come the crash which had changed everything.

She hesitated outside Simon's door, wondering whether to knock, and then changed her mind and went straight in. Afterwards, she wondered if her subconscious mind had suspected it long before, but it was a shock when she saw the man bending over to kiss Simon on the lips. It wasn't the kiss someone might give a man he was mildly fond of in a brotherly way – it was a lover's kiss.

Emily stood as if turned to stone, watching the little

scene and hearing the soft words as Philip drew back, stroking Simon's scarred face with his hand lovingly. She didn't need words to understand what was going on, and everything slotted into place. Simon had married her because he needed a son for his father, because Vane wanted an heir to the estate, but he hadn't been in love with her. The tender scene she had just witnessed was love. Philip and Simon were lovers. She knew instinctively that this wasn't a sordid sexual thing, though many would call it that if it were known outside the family; it was, she firmly believed, love.

Suddenly, the two men became aware of her presence, and the guilt on their faces would have been laughable if it hadn't been so heartbreaking, because of course theirs was a forbidden love – forbidden by the law and in the eyes of a judgemental society.

'Emily...' Simon was staring at her in horror. 'I wasn't expecting you yet... You're early.'

'Yes, I am, and I am very sorry,' Emily said, walking towards the bed. She saw that Philip was looking slightly green, clearly imagining that she was about to make a fearful scene. And of course she could if she wished. 'I should have knocked before I came in. Please accept my apology. I would go and leave you together, but I think we ought to get a few things straight – don't you?' She felt remarkably calm about the situation, almost relieved, as if this vindicated her own feelings.

'It isn't...' Simon faltered, seeing the clear light in her eyes and realising that it was useless to lie. 'We didn't mean to hurt you, Emily. Philip and I... It ended between us before I married you. I meant to be a proper husband to you, but then I had the crash and...'

'You needed the person you love,' Emily said, speaking calmly and precisely, because she wanted to get it straight in her own mind. 'Yes, I do understand, Simon. I have known for some time that you didn't really want me – not as a newly-wed husband should want his wife. Oh, you did your best, and if you drank enough champagne you managed to make it fun for us, but it wasn't what you wanted in your heart. You were never in love with me. I was just a means to an end.'

'You make it sound so cold, so calculating,' Simon said, frowning now. 'It wasn't meant to be like that, and I was fond of you. I intended to be a proper husband to you, Emily. I really did want to have a family, and I admire you very much. I never meant to hurt you.'

'Yes, I know that too,' Emily said. 'But the road to Hell is paved with good intentions, Simon. You were unkind to deceive me as you did. I was fond of you. I married you because you seemed to be so desperate, but I wasn't sure even then if it was right for either of us – and now I know that it was a mistake.'

'Do you want a divorce?'

'I don't know,' Emily said thoughtfully. 'I shouldn't have done, but this has come as a bit of a shock. I shall have to think it over, decide what is best for all of us.'

'Forgive me, Mrs Vane,' Philip said, finding his voice at last. 'I daresay you hate the sight of me, but please believe Simon when he tells you that we did try to make a clean break.'

Emily's eyes went over him, seeing all the signs that she ought to have recognised that first time and hadn't. 'I don't hate either of you,' she said. 'If anything, I pity you because

the cards you've been dealt can't be easy for either of you.'
She looked back at Simon. 'I presume you would rather I
didn't mention this to your father?'

'Please don't,' Simon said. 'He would be upset and angry.
He wanted our marriage to succeed, and he thinks the world
of you, Emily. Every time he visits he tells me how lucky I am
to have you.'

'All right, I shan't tell him. I don't see the need to cause a
fuss. So what happens next?'

'Philip is coming to America with me,' Simon told her.
'He'll be there for me while they do whatever they have to,
and then… We could get a divorce in a few years' time, I
suppose. I'll give you grounds with someone out there and it
will all blow over.'

It would be the easy way out for them all, Emily realised.
He was asking her to put her life on hold because it suited
him, and that was selfish, but for the moment she wasn't sure
what she wanted either.

'I'm not sure that's what I want,' she said. 'But I shan't
make waves for you before you leave, Simon. Things are
difficult enough for your father at the moment without
more trouble, so I'll leave it for now. If I want a divorce I'll
write and let you know. You will let me know where you
are?'

'Of course. We'll keep up appearances for now,' Simon
said, and then gave her the wry smile that had once made
her heart turn over. 'I'm a selfish devil, aren't I? It must seem
to you that I want to have my cake and eat it too?'

'Yes, it does rather, but I happen to be fond of your
father.'

'Yes… Well, thanks,' Simon said awkwardly. 'You've been
very good over all this.'

'Extremely reasonable,' Philip said, and offered his hand to her. Emily ignored it. 'Forgive me.'

'As I told you, I don't hate you,' Emily said, 'but don't expect me to like you either. I shall go and wait in the foyer downstairs, Simon. Come down when you're ready.'

She left the room, shoulders squared, head high. She was still feeling very calm, because of course it didn't matter. Simon had made a fool of her, deceived her, let her ruin her life to cover his illicit love affair, but it didn't matter. She felt as if a burden had fallen from her shoulders. Knowing hadn't changed anything, because instinctively she had recognised that their marriage had never been a true marriage. She had felt vaguely guilty because she had feelings for Terry that she knew were wrong, but now it was different.

She could see Terry now if she wanted. She could talk to him about getting a divorce one day in the future. She would wait a little longer, but then she would write to him, suggest that they meet in London. There were things she needed to do in town concerning the convalescent home, things that she had deliberately avoided because she knew that she would be tempted to see Terry. Now at last she was free to do exactly as she wanted.

She wasn't going to make a fuss over this, and she would be civilised with Simon while he was home for this weekend, but as far as she was concerned, her marriage was over.

* * *

Alice was wheeling her pram along the High Street when she saw Jim Wright coming from the baker's shop. He saw her, smiled, and then crossed the street to speak to her.

'You're looking well,' he said, and glanced down at the

baby. 'He's a lovely lad, Alice. You must be very proud of him. Keeps you busy, I expect?'

'Yes, he does,' Alice agreed, and laughed. 'Had me up half the night, the young beggar. He's good most of the time, but sometimes he cries a lot at night.'

'They do that sometimes,' Jim said, and nodded. 'I don't expect your parents mind, do they?'

'No, though I have wondered if I should look for a cottage of my own. If he keeps this up I might have to. It isn't fair on my father. He has to get up early, and then there's the lodgers...'

'I've got a cottage you might consider,' Jim said after a moment for thought. There was a hesitant, hopeful expression in his eyes. 'It's down by the station and it has been empty for a while. I could do it up for you, if you like?'

'It's kind of you to offer,' Alice said, and frowned. 'I'll have to think about it, Jim.'

'Yes, well, it's up to you. I suppose you haven't heard any more yet?'

'No... Nothing definite.'

'These things take time,' he said, and hesitated again as if he wanted to say more but couldn't make up his mind to say it. 'Well, I'd best get on then. Shall you be at the church social this weekend? I thought I might take a look in.'

'Frances asked me if I wanted to go,' Alice replied. 'Mum will look after Dan, so I might. It would make a change.'

'You don't want to stay at home all the time,' Jim told her. 'It's a bit soon yet, lass, but life goes on.'

'Yes...' She felt the sting of tears and wished he hadn't said anything, even though she knew he meant well. 'Bye, then.'

She walked off, keeping her tears at bay. She knew what

Jim was getting at. He had always liked her, and she was pretty certain that he was thinking they might have a future together. But that would mean that Daniel was dead, and he wasn't. She knew he was alive somewhere. He had to be, because she couldn't bear it if he were dead.

* * *

Emily's heart was racing as she got off the train that afternoon. It was early still and there were a lot of people about. She looked along the platform, seeking the person she had come to meet, feeling a sweep of disappointment when she couldn't see him, and then a rush of excitement as he was suddenly there, striding towards her through the crowds.

'Emily!' he cried, and he closed the distance between them, catching her in his arms. He was so big and strong and reassuringly masculine and she felt her heart leap as his arms surrounded her. 'I couldn't believe it when I got your letter.'

'I wasn't sure you would come...' She was breathless, lifting her face for his kiss, which was tender and sweet and so hungry that it took her breath away. Her eyes searched his face eagerly. 'I thought you might be angry because I didn't write earlier,' she said as he released her.

'How could I be angry after I had your letter?' He touched her cheek, his eyes caressing her. He was infinitely tender, infinitely loving, banishing her fears. 'Do you know how often I've dreamed of seeing you, of holding you in my arms? I love you so much... Want you so much, my darling Emily.'

'You do understand that I'm not free to leave my job and

come to you immediately?' she asked anxiously. 'I want to carry on with my work for now – and it will be a while before I can get my divorce.'

'Of course I want you to stay with me for ever,' Terry said honestly, his voice husky with emotion. 'I want you to be my wife, to wake up beside you every morning, and to see my son in your arms. But I know that you have commitments. After your husband was injured I promised myself I would wait for as long as it took – and I haven't changed my mind. I'll wait until you're ready, Emily.'

'We don't have to wait for some things,' she told him, and there was a hint of mischief in her eyes as she gazed up at him. What she was doing was reckless and forward of her, but she had made up her mind that she would tell him at once. 'I came here to be with you if you want me, Terry. There is nothing to stop us being together – if it's what you want.'

'If it's what I want?' Terry stared at her in disbelief. 'How could you doubt it? I've been wanting to make love to you since the second time you visited me in hospital.'

Emily laughed as she moved closer. 'In that case, I suggest you take me somewhere so that we don't waste a moment longer...' She laughed as she saw the flame leap up in his eyes. 'And if that makes me a scarlet woman I don't mind one little bit.'

'What it makes you is warm and loving and mine,' Terry said, his arm about her waist. 'I've been living in a hostel since I came to London so I'll book a hotel suite for us. If you're going to make this a regular thing I shall look for a flat of my own.'

'You had better start looking then,' she said, and giggled

as his arm tightened about her. 'You're stuck with me, Terry Burgess, whether you like it or not.'

'It's what I've longed and prayed for,' he told her, and the look in his eyes left her in no doubt that he meant it.

* * *

If Emily had doubted her reception, she learned to forget her doubts in Terry's arms that night, finding more pleasure than she had ever dreamed existed in loving and being loved. Terry didn't need a drink to make love to her – not just once but constantly throughout the three days she spent with him.

She had intended to stay just two days, but he had wangled three days of leave and she knew it might be some time before she could get away again so she stayed on. They talked as she lay snuggled up to his side, relaxing in the aftermath of loving.

'It's going to be harder to leave you than I thought,' she said as his hand stroked her thigh. 'I knew that I wanted to be with you like this so I came, but I didn't know it would be so hard to go back.'

'I would say that you don't have to go back,' Terry told her as he kissed her neck, 'but I know that you do. You're not the kind to break your promise easily. Besides, I would rather you were down there in the country. The Blitz is over for the moment – the Germans were losing too many of their bombers and they gave up in the summer – but it could start again at any time.'

'The bombs don't worry me,' Emily told him as she snuggled up to the firm, hard length of him. It felt so good to be here with him like this! 'I wouldn't let the thought of that kind of danger stop me being with you – but I have promised Vane I will stay until things are more settled. And I have to wait until Simon has had his surgery. I know it's asking a lot of you...'

Terry silenced her with a kiss. It was quite a long time later that they had time to talk again.

'As long as I know you love me, and we can be together sometimes, I can wait,' he told her. 'But you won't change your mind? You won't let him persuade you to stay with him?'

'I shan't do that,' Emily promised. 'My marriage is over. I shall ask Simon to give me grounds for a divorce as soon as it is decently possible.'

Terry smiled and stroked her cheek with the tips of his fingers. 'In that case, I promise to be patient. After all, a few days ago I had nothing to look forward to; now I have all I could ever want. I just have to be patient for a while.'

'I'm going to be busy over Christmas,' Emily told him. 'We are having a party and I'm committed to organising it. But I shall telephone you once you have your own place, and I can find some excuse to come up again soon after Christmas.'

Terry held her to him, his strong arms enfolding her. She was so beautiful, so warm and exciting, so loving. He wanted more than this, more than a few fleeting hours in a hotel, but if this was all he could have of her for the moment he would take it and thank his lucky stars. He had loved her for a long time and believed she was lost to him, and he couldn't believe his luck. Emily loved him, had come to him, and she would marry him when she was free of her husband. His dreams were all coming true. All he had to do was be patient.

* * *

Sitting in the train going home, Emily felt a surge of rebellion. Why was she doing this? Why hadn't she simply told Vane the truth about his son and Philip, given in her notice and told Terry she would stay with him until her divorce came through?

She was tempted to get off at the first station after leaving him, but she didn't; she just stared out of the window at the rain, feeling miserable. It hurt to leave Terry in London and to know that she wouldn't see him for several weeks. He hadn't wanted her to leave, but he hadn't begged her to change her mind, either. She knew he would hold to his end of the bargain, and in a way she wished he had told her she must leave her husband, now, at once.

She had chosen what seemed to be the easy way, Emily realised. Simon had suggested it because it suited him, but it also made things more respectable. There would be considerable scandal when the divorce happened, especially amongst the people of Stretton Village. Frances and Henry would be upset, though she didn't think Connor would mind. He had enjoyed staying with her in the summer, and he'd spent a lot of time down at the convalescent home with the men, talking to them and fetching things for them from the shops. She'd been really proud of him and she'd told him so.

'You're growing up,' she'd said when she found him sitting with a soldier who had lost both hands, feeding him strawberries and cream. 'It's the nurses' job but they don't always have time for treats.'

'I brought a basket of strawberries from the gardens in

with me, and Nurse Baines told me to bring some to Jock. She's a great girl, Emily. All the men love her.'

'Yes they do – and I love you.'

He had gone red and looked embarrassed but she thought his visit had brought them closer again. She had missed him when he went home. Yes, Connor would like Terry, she thought. He could live with them if he wanted to, because she was sure Terry would agree if she asked. He would do anything she wanted, because he really loved her.

She hadn't been certain of that when she wrote and asked if he would meet her off the train that weekend, but she knew it now. He was so different to Simon, wanting her, needing her – and she needed him. It was a very different kind of love to what she had imagined she'd felt for Simon at the beginning. She had been young and naïve. What she had felt then had been infatuation. She had been flattered by Simon's attention, believing his profession of love – but she knew the difference now.

Terry loved her. She didn't need words to tell her that, though he had said it many times and in many ways, but it was there in the way he touched her, in his eyes.

She smiled as she remembered lying in his arms just whispering. It gave her a warm feeling inside, and it was something she would never forget. She must wait for a little longer, but then she would speak to Vane, tell him that she was thinking of leaving, moving on. He would be upset, angry, but she must be prepared for that. If he demanded that she worked six months' notice she would do it, but after that she would leave.

Her decision made, Emily relaxed. She would write to Terry and tell him in the morning.

* * *

Emily found her car waiting for her where she had left it in the station yard. It started immediately, even though it had been frosty overnight. She was still feeling the warmth of her lovely weekend away when she parked her car and walked into the house, but then, quite suddenly, she knew something was wrong.

'Where have you been?' Amelia demanded as she came hurrying into the hall. 'I've been phoning everywhere and couldn't find you.'

'Has something happened?' Emily asked, a cold knot forming in her stomach as she saw that Amelia was both upset and angry.

'Simon had a sudden relapse,' Amelia told her, her tone accusing. 'Apparently there was a blood clot somewhere and it went to his lungs. He died two days ago.'

'Simon died...' Emily stared at her in shock. The cold had spread all over her and she felt numb. This couldn't be happening! 'But everyone said he was better! He was going to America with—' She could hardly believe it. Simon was dead? It didn't seem possible after he had seemed to be doing so well.

'Where were you? I rang your sister at her home but she had no idea where you might be.'

'I stayed with a friend,' Emily said, trying to gather her thoughts. 'I am sorry if you've had a worrying time, Amelia – but it couldn't have made any difference if I'd been here. It must have been quite sudden.'

'That isn't the point,' Amelia said, and now her eyes filled with tears. 'Vane was terribly upset when we couldn't reach you, and... he had a heart attack and collapsed.'

'Oh, Amelia, no!' Emily said. The news of Simon's death was shocking, but Emily realised this was more distressing. She hadn't truly liked Vane for a start, but she had come to admire him – and like him too. 'I am so very sorry. How is he? He isn't...?'

'No, thank goodness,' Amelia said. 'He was at the hospital when it happened and they rushed him to their special unit. It was only a mild attack and he is recovering now. But he has asked to see you. He is worried about things here, about the home – he seems to think you might be considering leaving us quite soon.'

Again there was that accusing look in Amelia's eyes, as if she were blaming Emily for everything that had happened.

'I wouldn't leave Vane while he is ill,' Emily told her.

'But I don't see why you have to leave at all,' Amelia said, looking a bit sulky. 'You know how we all rely on you.'

'You don't need me,' Emily told her. 'You manage this house so well, Amelia.'

'But you help in small ways, and I like having you here. I should miss you if you left.' Amelia gave her a look of appeal. 'I don't see that it makes a difference just because Simon is dead...' She bit her bottom lip. 'Oh, that sounds awful. Of course you must be upset over all this but it doesn't mean you have to leave.'

'Yes, of course I am upset, but I think you know our marriage wasn't all it should have been, don't you, Amelia?' Emily looked her in the eyes and she blushed. 'You know why Simon asked me to marry him – and why it could never have worked.'

'Yes, well, we thought it might change him, being married,' Amelia admitted as she led the way into the front sitting room. A huge bunch of fragrant hothouse lilies was overpowering the air with its heavy scent, and the fire was throwing out a great deal of heat. 'I had guessed something was wrong a while ago and then I saw Philip at the hospital when I visited. I wasn't sure if you knew or not and I almost told you. I'm sorry if it was a shock to you.'

'It was certainly a shock,' Emily said as she helped herself to a glass of sherry from the sideboard. She might not have been in love with Simon, but the news had still made her feel shaky and it was very warm in here. 'It's a bit early but I could do with this – will you have one?'

'No, thank you,' Amelia said. 'I've had a few since it happened, I can tell you. I thought Vane was going to die and it frightened the life out of me.'

'Yes, it must have been awful, coming on top of Simon's death like that.' Emily sipped her drink as she stood in front of the window. It had stopped raining now and looked as if it might turn foggy that evening. 'Have any arrangements been made yet?'

Amelia looked awkward. 'I didn't know what to do, and Vane couldn't tell me – so when Philip asked if he could do everything I said yes. I hope you don't mind? It's going to be a quiet service here at our own church in the village, and he will be buried in the family plot.'

'Good, as long as everything has been done that needs to be done,' Emily said. She felt relieved that Philip was seeing to things; it seemed fitting, somehow. 'Will there be an inquest or anything?'

'I shouldn't think so. Apparently, these clots do occur quite frequently when someone has been through an experience like Simon's.' She dabbed at her eyes with a scrap of lace that wafted lavender water towards Emily. 'To think of it happening like that after all Vane has done – all those specialists and doctors – and he dies like that.'

'Yes, it must have been terrible for Vane. Simon meant so much to him.'

'It means there won't be an heir for all this...' Amelia waved her hand to indicate the house and grounds. 'He hoped for so much when you and Simon were married.'

'But you're still young...' Emily stopped as Amelia shook her head.

'Impossible, I'm afraid,' she said. 'I daresay Vane hoped I might give him children. I am a lot younger than he is and it might have happened but it didn't; apparently one of us can't. The doctors haven't gone into it thoroughly because we didn't want that, but they incline towards it being less my fault than his...'

'Oh, I'm so sorry,' Emily said. 'Were you very disappointed when they told you?'

'It stung a bit, because it was what Vane wanted,' Amelia admitted. 'I don't mind much for myself – always been fonder of horses and dogs than babies, though if you and Simon had had one I might have enjoyed being a grandmother. All the pleasure and none of the bother.'

Emily smiled, though she sensed that Amelia was putting a brave face on things and that she minded more than she would admit. 'I'm sorry I wasn't able to oblige, but we didn't really have much chance.'

'No, I suppose not. It has been a pretty rotten go all round, hasn't it?' She got up and went over to the sideboard. 'I think I will have that sherry after all.'

'Yes, it has,' Emily agreed. 'So where do we all go from here?'

'I have no idea,' Amelia said. 'If Vane recovers we all

soldier on as best we can, I imagine. If he dies his private fortune goes to whoever he has named in his will, but the estate and title carries over to a distant cousin I expect.'

'It is odd that neither his son nor daughter had children,' Emily said. 'If there had been any kind of heir...'

'Vane says it's his curse,' Amelia said, and laughed oddly. 'I used to say he was imagining things, but now I wonder...'

'Oh no, I doubt that,' Emily said. 'It is just all rather sad.' She put her glass down. 'I think I shall take a little walk.'

She felt restless as she left the house and began to walk towards the lake. It was bitterly cold but she had put on a thick coat, scarves and a wool hat that covered her ears. She walked with her head down, deep in thought, hardly noticing the beautiful grounds, or the ancient trees with branches that dipped down to sweep the earth. In the distance a heron fished at the side of the lake, and a squirrel bounded ahead of her, racing for safety to the tallest branch of an ancient oak, but Emily was lost in her thoughts. She shivered as the mist started to curl through the park, giving it an eerie feel.

Simon's death was a terrible shock, even though she had accepted that their marriage was over. Divorce was one thing, but death was so final. Now she was remembering the good things, the way his smile had made her heart leap in those first days when she had thought they were falling in love. She wished that things had been different. Why hadn't he been the man she'd imagined when they married? It all seemed so sad and unnecessary. Why couldn't his family simply have accepted the way he was and let him be happy? He had been trying to please his father and in the process he had denied his own nature. What a mess! Poor Simon. He'd tried to be a proper husband the few times they'd been together, but it would never have worked in the longer term.

She discovered that all the bitterness had gone now, the regret and hurt had melted away, and she was able to shed a few tears for Simon, to pity him for a wasted, unhappy life. He had tried to do his duty towards his father and the estate, and perhaps he had cared for her in his own way.

He had been tired to the point of exhaustion when he came to her that day in Liverpool, desperate to give his father a grandson because he knew that he might be killed at any time. And perhaps he had been lonely, feeling at least a kind of affection for her in his need. No, Emily couldn't hate him, and she was glad that the feeling of resentment had gone away.

Despite everything that had happened to her, she was lucky. She had Terry and so many women had lost the men they loved. She thought about her brother, Daniel, missing in action, and about his wife. Alice was so young. Too young to be a widow.

* * *

Alice saw Jim Wright at the social straight away that evening. He was talking to some of the other men, having a glass of beer and laughing, but when he saw her he smiled, made an excuse and came over to where she and Frances were standing.

'Can I get you two lovely ladies anything?'

'Oh, yes please, I'll have a glass of lemonade,' Alice said. 'What about you, Frances?'

'I'll have a sherry if there's any going,' Frances said. 'Oh, there's Millie Richardson over there. Excuse me, I want a word with her.'

'I'll get your drinks then,' Jim said. 'They're having a bit of a dance here later, just to records, you know – or there's the whist, if you fancy that?'

'I'm not much good at playing cards,' Alice said. 'I'll just sit and watch you play if you like, have a good gossip.'

He nodded and went off to fetch a drink for her and Frances, but he didn't join in the card game that soon got going in the smaller room. Instead, he sat with Alice and several others, talking about things in general until someone put a record on the gramophone.

'Would you like to?' he asked. 'This is a barn dance. I can just about manage that. I shan't tread on your toes, Alice.'

'Oh, I don't know. I don't think I ought...'

'Go on,' Frances urged her. 'Dan would want you to enjoy yourself, and the barn dance is fun.' One of the older men came to ask Frances for a dance and she got up with him. Faced with her desertion, Alice decided she might as well join in.

She enjoyed the dance, which was a progressive and meant that she passed from one partner to the next. Some of them were men she had known all her life, some old enough to be her father, and some of her partners were women, because there weren't enough men to go around.

Alice relaxed as she got into the swing of it. She wasn't doing anything wrong, and Dan would understand that she couldn't sit at home all the time, wouldn't he?

She danced three progressives, because it was good fun and everyone was joining in, but when it came to the waltz she sat it out. Somehow it wouldn't be right to do that with anyone but Dan.

She couldn't help thinking about him, wondering where he was and whether he was thinking of her.

* * *

When the German patrol suddenly swept into the farmyard it took them all by surprise. It was early in the morning, the household just beginning to stir, and no warning had come this time. Daniel was in the sheds tinkering with a truck he had rescued from an old barn, using parts from the British Army lorry which they had sent crashing into a ravine after unloading its dangerous cargo. He was dressed in clothes that smelled of goats and looked as much like a Greek farmer as it was possible to achieve, his hair greasy and hanging about his ears, but he knew he would never be able to fool the Germans if they questioned him.

Mikkos put a finger to his lips, pointing to a pile of straw, meaning that Daniel should crawl under it and hide. He was about to do so when he heard the shots from outside, and a woman's scream. The bastards were killing indiscriminately!

Daniel knew they were looking for him. Mikkos had told him that reports of a British soldier hiding out had reached the Germans, and they must have been told to come here. He walked towards the barn door. Mikkos tried to catch his arm, to hold him back, but Daniel shrugged him off.

'Do you want them to kill all your family?' His eyes met and clashed with those of the young Greek, and then Mikkos let him go. He walked out into the yard with his hands above his head, seeing the bloody bodies of a young woman and a boy lying on the ground, his stomach churning. 'I'm the one you want,' he said. 'Kill me, you pigs, not women and children. I'm the one who has been causing you trouble.'

'Britisher?' A German officer moved towards him, his eyes going over Daniel, his nose wrinkling in disgust as he caught the stink of him. 'You stink like a goat, Britisher. So you are the one we want. Good! You are a spy and a saboteur and an enemy of the German people.'

'I'm a soldier left behind in the retreat from Athens,' Daniel said. 'And I demand to be treated as a prisoner of war under the Geneva Convention.'

'You demand nothing,' the officer said, and he took a pistol out of the holster at his waist. 'We shoot spies and saboteurs.'

Daniel knew he was going to die. It was in the officer's eyes and he clenched his mouth shut hard, refusing to scream or beg for mercy. All he could think of was Alice, his lovely Alice, who had been his for such a short time. The officer's finger was on the trigger when the shot came from behind Daniel. He saw the German shudder and fall face down in the farmyard mud, blood pouring from a hole in the side of his head. All hell broke loose suddenly as the men tried to fight their way out of the yard, and several shots were fired.

Daniel had no weapon, but he used his hands, picking up a spade and going for the nearest German soldier. He never knew what hit him, simply felt the blow to his head seconds before everything went black and he too fell into the mud close to the body of the German officer. He was unaware when more German soldiers arrived with a new young officer in charge, and he didn't feel anything when his body was piled into the truck carrying the prisoners away. The knock on the head that caused his unconscious state would bring on an illness that kept him wandering in his mind for a long time, and it was also what saved his life. It was only weeks afterwards that he began to be aware of his surroundings once more, to know who he was and to remember Alice.

* * *

The first few days after her visit to London were too busy for Emily to have much time to think about her own life. She wrote to Terry to tell him that Simon had died suddenly, explaining that it hadn't changed things as far as her commitments went for the time being. She couldn't leave while Vane was ill, because she knew she was needed. The very least she could do was to continue in her post until Vane was on his feet again, and then she would have to find a replacement to take over her job.

Amelia seemed to rely on her far more than she ever had before, and she realised that Vane's wife had leaned on him heavily for support. Now that he was ill, she needed someone else's shoulder.

Vane was home by the time the funeral took place. He was wheeled into church in an old-fashioned bath chair for the service, and afterwards he sat silently in the drawing room at Vanbrough House, receiving the condolences of his friends and family but saying little. Emily had cried her tears for Simon the night she walked alone and sorted out her feelings, finding understanding and forgiveness for him and for her. She was conscious of a feeling of heavy sadness for the life that had been cut short – and for the father who had lost everything. Vane might not have been understanding as far as Simon's personal life was concerned but he was suffering now. She wished there was something she could say to comfort him but nothing could bring back his hopes and dreams.

Vane's daughter stayed for two days after the funeral. Emily found her pleasant enough, and infinitely more capable than Amelia. She was older than her stepmother, and completely wrapped up in her husband's life and work. She made all the right noises towards Emily and her father, but clearly didn't feel involved in the family's affairs.

After she had gone, Amelia confessed that she didn't care for Vanessa much. 'She didn't say anything when Vane married me, but I've always known she didn't approve. I think that is why she hardly visits her father these days.'

'Oh, surely not,' Emily said, though she had noticed some coolness between the two. 'She seemed quite upset over her brother and she was nice to me.'

'She can be as sweet as she likes, but you haven't seen the other side of her,' Amelia said with a wry grimace. 'Oh well, I don't suppose we shall see her again for months.'

If that was how Amelia felt it was just as well, Emily thought. She hadn't given much thought to the family – or the future, come to that – because her plans to leave with Terry would have to be delayed. She couldn't just walk out on Vane now; he wasn't well enough to start looking for someone to take over the convalescent home yet. Christmas had caught up with them, and the party for the men had to continue despite the shadow that hung over their own lives.

Emily was determined that they should have a Christmas tree with lights and small gifts for all their guests, and the party on Christmas Eve was already planned down to the last detail.

She spent the day checking everything, visiting the men, and talking to them and the relatives who had come to stay over the festive period. She spent longer with Corporal James Bell, who had no visitors, because the whole of his family had been killed during the Blitz.

Corporal Bell had lost both legs while on active service, but his family had been killed while they were eating their evening meal in their own house. Now he had no one and no prospect of being able to leave the home in the near future, unless someone would take him on. Despite that, he was cheerful and popular with the others, flirting with all the nurses and with Emily whenever she found time to sit with him.

That day he presented her with a small gift of a basket he had made during recreation classes, which he had somehow arranged to fill with flowers. The deep red chrysanthemums smelled fresh and exotic, and she was touched by his thoughtfulness.

'How lovely!' she said. 'This must have taken ages to make. I shall keep it in my office to remind me of you.'

'That's torn it,' he said, and grinned at her. 'I shall get double the enemas now, shan't I?'

'Oh, I don't know about that,' she said, laughing as he'd intended. 'I'll try to keep Nurse Baines from getting too ambitious with that side of things – for Christmas anyway.'

Emily walked back towards the house. She was wondering if there might be a letter or perhaps a card from Terry. She had written to him twice and sent a rather special card she had found in a local shop, but as yet he hadn't replied, which seemed a little odd. Of course he had probably been very busy, but he had promised to write to her, and to let her know how his search for a flat was going.

A pile of letters and cards was waiting for her in the hall. She picked them up, seeing several whose handwriting she recognised as belonging to people she knew. There were cards from Frances; Henry and Mary; Connor; and her friend Maura had put a letter inside with the latest pictures of her son.

Emily always enjoyed getting letters from Maura, who wrote every few months, and often sent photos of her little boy. The photos were never very clear but from what she could see Maura had a lovely child, and she seemed happy enough.

However, there was nothing from Terry, though right at the bottom of the pile she discovered a letter with a Cambridge postmark. Now who could that be from? Emily wondered about it as she took her post into the sitting room.

Vane had come down that afternoon. He was looking a little better, though he had declined to attend the party at the home.

'Is everything going well?' he asked. 'You've hardly had a moment to spare these past few days, Emily.'

'No, I have been busy, but I wanted it all to be right for this evening. It means so much to the men and their families.'

'Even more to those who haven't got any family.'

Vane sounded so unlike himself that Emily was struck. She felt anxious as she saw how grey he looked, wondering if he was close to having another attack. She put her cards and letters unopened on a little table and sat down in the chair near to him, feeling uneasy.

'How are you? Is there anything I can do for you?'

'I'm perfectly all right, don't fuss,' he said testily. 'Amelia fusses too much. I'm not about to die – even if I do look like the spectre at the feast.'

'Oh, not quite that bad,' Emily said, and smiled. 'Just a bit tired and feeling low, I expect.'

'What have I got to be cheerful about?'

'As much as Corporal Bell, I should think,' Emily said. 'At least you have Amelia and me to worry about you.'

'And for how long shall we have the pleasure of your company?'

'I don't know for certain,' Emily replied. 'I'm not thinking of leaving immediately. Once you are well again I might think about my own life. But if I do leave I shall arrange a replacement.'

'But you'll go,' he said. 'We can't expect you to stay now that Simon is dead.'

'Simon wasn't my main reason for staying,' Emily said. 'As it happens, I take my work seriously – and I am quite fond of you, Vane.'

'Humph,' he muttered. 'Can't see why. We've none of us been fair to you, Emily. Amelia told me you knew about Simon's little problem. Can't understand what got into the boy. Never been anything like that in our family before. I told him straight to stop messing about and do his duty by the family.'

'Well, that's all water under the bridge now, isn't it?' She smiled and picked up her post, taking it to her favourite chair by the window. She pored over the pictures of Maura's little boy, lingering over them as she wondered just who they reminded her of, then opened the rest of her cards. Opening the last of her letters, she realised that it was from her friend Carole Mortimer. It was ages since she'd heard from her. Carole had rung her a few times when she was working in Liverpool but this was the first time she had ever written to Emily. She began to read the first paragraphs, then as she realised what Carole was talking about, she stood up, gave a little gasp and fainted.

'Good grief,' Vane said as Amelia hurried to her side. 'What on earth has happened?'

'I think she fainted,' Amelia told him. 'Something in this letter...' She was patting Emily's face, opening the neck of her blouse. 'Are you all right, love? Was it bad news?'

Emily stirred, opening her eyes. For a moment she stared blankly at Amelia, wondering what on earth had happened to her and then, remembering, she felt the tears build inside her and begin to well over.

'He's dead,' she whispered. Her mouth felt dry, her lips rubbery as she tried to speak and found it almost impossible. 'Terry has been killed...'

13

Vane insisted that she go and rest on her bed for a while, and Amelia accompanied her, looking at her anxiously all the time. She wanted to send for the doctor but Emily begged her not to, and Amelia agreed reluctantly to let her have her way.

'Perhaps you've been overdoing things, Emily.'

'It was just the shock,' Emily said. Her throat felt tight and it was all she could do to keep from screaming at Amelia that she wanted to be alone. 'A friend of mine, a fireman, has been killed in a gas explosion...'

How simple and unemotional that sounded, as if she were speaking of a stranger, something that had happened to someone she hardly knew. Yet there was no way that she could tell Amelia that the news had torn her world apart.

'Yes, well, that is terrible, of course,' Amelia said. 'But you have been looking a bit peaky for a few days, Emily. If I were you I should make an appointment to see Dr Jones.'

'Honestly, I feel fine,' Emily said, though she was lying. Her heart felt as if it were being slowly torn in two and she was bleeding inside. She gave no sign of it, though her face was ashen and her eyes told their own story. 'It was just the shock. I shall rest for a while and then I'll get ready for the party this evening.'

'You aren't still going?'

'Yes, I am.' Emily raised her chin defiantly. This throbbing inside her head was almost more than she could bear, and her chest was so tight that she felt she might suffocate, but she had to keep going, because if she didn't... She would not be able to bear her grief. 'I can't let the men down – and I don't want anyone else to know about this if you don't mind. Would you leave me now, Amelia, please? You've been very kind but I would like to lie down and rest for a while.'

She needed to be alone to absorb her grief, to try and understand what had happened, to come to terms with what it meant, the death of her dreams.

Amelia nodded her understanding and went away, anxious to discuss her thoughts and suspicions with her husband. After she had gone, Emily decided not to lie down but went instead to sit in the chair by the window, taking out the letter from Carole once more.

Carole had had no idea that she was involved with Terry. Her letter had been a bald statement that her fiancé's brother had been killed in a gas explosion while attending a fire in the Docklands area of London and that she had attended his funeral. The news had come as such a shock that Emily had fainted, something she'd never done before in her life. She had been feeling well enough before that, Emily thought. It was Amelia's imagination that she was looking peaky. Tears trickled down her cheeks and she tasted their salt on her lips.

She stared at the letter in bewilderment. How could this

have happened? And so soon after she had left him, only a few days! Had he suffered? Carole's letter had told her nothing but the bare fact. She prayed he had not suffered, that his death had been quick, not slow and lingering.

It was so unfair, so cruel that Terry should die and that she should know nothing about it until after the funeral had already taken place. If Carole hadn't written to her she might not have heard for months, and she would have started to think that Terry had deserted her, that he hadn't really loved her.

But she knew that he had loved her very much indeed, there was no room in her mind for doubt. For a brief while they had been truly happy. At least she had that, Emily thought, fighting the wave of grief and despair that swept over her. She had been loved, truly loved. *But we had so little time!* The thought flashed into her mind: three days and nights, no more. Every nerve in her body was screaming in protest at the way happiness had been so cruelly snatched from her. She had done her duty in standing by Simon while she imagined he might need her, and then, when his confession had set her free, she had lost the man she truly loved.

Why? Why had it happened to Terry? Why must he be the one to die? She railed at a cruel fate and then remembered the night he had snatched that child from the burning house. He was brave and good and kind, and it made no kind of sense, no justice that he should die. But it was the kind of man he was, she realised. Terry would always have done his duty, gone that extra mile to help others, and Carole's letter said he had been trying to get an injured fireman out of the danger area when the gas mains exploded.

Emily stood up and went into the bathroom to wash her

face and get ready for the party that evening. She felt numb, her grief tearing at the curtain she'd dropped in place to keep it at bay. This wasn't like Alice refusing to accept Dan was dead, because she knew there was no hope of Terry coming back to her, but she couldn't let go now – her boys were relying on her for their Christmas party.

Amelia watched as Emily hosted the show that evening, introducing the various artists she had asked to perform for them, keeping up a light banter with the men and nurses, serving drinks and food, giving out the gifts she had bought and wrapped in pretty paper herself. Anyone who didn't know that she had received bad news would never guess that anything was wrong, but Amelia could see the shadow in her eyes, sense the pain she was suffering but refusing to admit.

However, Emily went through the motions and even made a little joke about Rose Baines being their own 'forces sweetheart'. She led the applause when Rose belted out Vera Lynn's popular songs and introduced the next act, but anyone who knew her must have sensed that something was wrong.

This friend must have meant a great deal to her, Amelia realised. Was he the friend Emily had been staying with that lost weekend, when Amelia had tried to find her and failed? There had been something about her when she came home that evening, a glow that came from inside her, and a look in her eyes. Was this man who had died her lover? Amelia had her suspicions, though she hadn't voiced them to Vane – but she had mentioned another idea that had been in her mind for a day or two now. It was something about the eyes, a certain look she had seen in other women, but it hadn't occurred to her that Emily might be pregnant until she fainted.

Of course she'd had a shock, but she hadn't fainted when Simon died or when she'd learned that Vane had had a heart attack, despite being very upset. This fireman had clearly meant a great deal to Emily, and it was possible, just possible, that she might be having his child, though perhaps she wasn't aware of it herself as yet.

* * *

Christmas passed in a haze for Emily. She hardly knew what she was doing as she handed out presents, smiled, talked and did all the things that were expected of her. A part of her was dying inside, her heart aching so much that she could scarcely bear it, and yet outwardly she gave no sign of her grief. Perhaps her manner was cooler than usual, a little remote, but in the general atmosphere of Christmas celebration it went unnoticed. Mrs Vane was a busy woman; she had things to do, and she couldn't be expected to join in all the practical jokes and games that the men and nurses got up to. They all respected her, liked her, but understood that she was busy and they mustn't intrude. Rose Baines asked her once if she was feeling unwell, but Emily smiled and said she was fine, and everyone else was too busy to notice.

Vane gave a small New Year's party at the house for his friends. He had asked Emily if she wanted to invite any of her family, but she had refused, knowing that they would all celebrate at home. She attended her father-in-law's party, making all the right noises, but feeling removed from the guests, as though seeing them from a distance. She was with them but apart, wrapped up in her private grief.

She worked longer hours at the home, doing more of the jobs that she had left to others previously, making certain that everything was as it ought to be. The nurses whispered that she was worse than any matron they had ever known, and that she would notice if a fly lighted on a window sill.

And then, in the middle of January, Emily was sick when she got out of bed in the morning. So sick that it left her feeling dizzy, and when she tried to dress she found herself unable to do so and had to crawl back into bed until the spell of nausea passed.

After a while she was able to get up again, and she began to feel much better. She ignored the sickness, dismissing it as her having eaten something that had disagreed with her, but then she was sick again the next morning, and the faintness was even worse. She decided to stay in bed for an hour or so, and she was still there when Amelia came up to ask what was wrong.

'You look pale,' she said as Emily gazed up at her from the pillows. 'Are you feeling unwell?'

'I was sick earlier and I felt faint. It will pass in a little while as it did yesterday, but I thought I would have a lie-in. Perhaps I've been doing too much, as you suggested.'

'Yes, I think you have been working too hard,' Amelia agreed. 'But have you considered that you might be pregnant, Emily?'

'Pregnant...' Emily stared at her. It was in her mind to deny it, but she suddenly realised that it was possible. She hadn't fallen for a child with Simon and so it hadn't occurred

to her to wonder; in fact, she had almost made up her mind
that she couldn't have a baby, and now the idea burst on her
like a bombshell. She pushed herself up against the pillows
to a sitting position, realising that the dizziness had passed. 'I
suppose I might be, Amelia. Yes, now I think about it, the
symptoms are just the same as Frances had...' Her eyes
opened in wonder as she began to understand what had
happened to her. She was having a baby – Terry's baby. She
was having Terry's baby! For the first time since she had read
Carole's letter, a flicker of warmth stirred inside her. Terry
wasn't completely lost to her after all. She was carrying his
child in her womb. 'Yes, I believe I might be, though I hadn't
realised – but what made you think of it?'

'I'm not sure,' Amelia said, and she sat on the edge of the
bed, smiling at her. 'You hadn't been looking well for a
while, and though that might just have been shock and
tiredness, I saw something in your face – something I've
noticed before. It's a look women get when they're
pregnant.'

'I hadn't even thought about it,' Emily admitted. 'But now
that I have – it occurs to me that I've missed my courses this
month. Why didn't I notice that before?'

'Because you've been desperately unhappy, haven't you?'
Amelia reached for her hand, holding it gently. 'Were you
very much in love with your fireman, Emily?'

'Terry?' Emily's voice was choked as she spoke his name.
'Terry Burgess. He was so brave, Amelia. I saw him rescue a
child from a house fire once, and... yes, I did love him very
much. I still do and it hurts terribly.'

'But now you will have his baby, won't you?'

'Yes, I shall have Terry's child.' Emily smiled at her as the
realisation finally burst inside her like a balloon of sunshine

breaking through the grey of clouds. 'Oh, Amelia, I'm going to have a baby!'

There was such a look of delighted disbelief on her face that Amelia laughed. 'Yes, my dearest Emily, you are going to be a mother. I think that is wonderful – just what we all needed to bring some light back into this house.'

'But what will Vane say?' Emily looked at her anxiously as she considered her father-in-law's reaction to the news. 'He wanted a grandson, an heir to the estate, so badly and I didn't give him one – and now I'm having someone else's baby. It's sure to upset him.'

'Don't you know how much Vane cares for you?' Amelia asked. 'He has been very worried about you these past few days, Emily. As indeed have I. We knew something was wrong but you seemed to retreat inside yourself and we couldn't ask, we couldn't pry.'

'It hurt too much to let it out,' Emily said, and she brushed at her face as the tears trickled down her cheeks and into her mouth. 'It still hurts terribly, Amelia. We only had three days together because I wouldn't leave Simon. I knew he didn't love me, not really, and I didn't love him – not in the way I loved Terry. I believe now that it was just a young girl's infatuation and if it hadn't been for the war I would never have married Simon.'

'It is sure to hurt,' Amelia said, looking sad. 'When you love someone it hurts to lose them. I loved someone once but he didn't love me. He married someone much prettier and I broke my heart over him, and then I met Vane. I didn't feel the same as I did about Richard, but I came to feel love for him, and I would hate to lose him. We are good friends. I think that was what Simon hoped to give you, the kind of friendship he knew existed between his father and me. You shouldn't feel bitter over what he did, because he couldn't help himself. I know he tried to resist Philip for a long time, but in the end his feelings were too strong. Many people think of what they had together as a bad thing, but for Simon it was real and honest. Can you understand that, Emily?'

'Yes, I have from the beginning,' she said. 'I saw them touching and I knew it was love. I might have been angry or disgusted if I hadn't seen the love between them, but I did and I understood that it was something they could not deny. We were going to get a divorce as soon as it could be decently done – that's why I went to Terry. We knew we had to wait to marry but...' She broke off on a sob. 'We wanted to be together.'

Amelia squeezed her hand. 'And now you have Terry's baby to look forward to – we all do. I am just so pleased and so excited, my dear. You can't imagine what a difference this will make to our lives. You will let us share your happiness, won't you?'

'But... Will Vane want me to stay here once he knows?'

'Do you have to tell him, Emily? Couldn't you let him believe it is Simon's child?'

Emily withdrew her hand from Amelia's. 'Surely you aren't suggesting that I should lie to him?'

'Would it be so very terrible? It would make him so happy – please think about it, Emily. Go to the doctor and make sure you are pregnant and not sickening for something, and think this through. Vane is a generous man. Nothing would be too good for your child, especially if it is a boy.'

'I don't think I can lie to him,' Emily said. 'I know you think it's kind to let him believe Simon and I were together somehow when he came home for a few days, but it isn't true. I like and respect Vane too much to deceive him.'

'Well, just think it over for a few days,' Amelia said. 'Think what it might mean for your child...'

Emily was silent as Amelia stood up and walked over to the door. What she had just suggested was terrible... Wasn't it? To deceive a man like that was cruel. If he found out one day... No, she couldn't do it, Emily decided. She would visit the doctor and make sure she was having a child, and then she would speak to her father-in-law and tell him the truth.

She decided to stay in bed until lunchtime, because if she had been doing too much the rest would do her good, and she wasn't going to take any chances. She wanted her baby – Terry's baby. She wanted it very much.

Frances was in the garden hanging out some washing when someone called her name and she turned to see her father-in-law standing just outside the kitchen door. She felt a slight reluctance as she walked back to greet him. She wasn't sure why she had begun to feel uneasy in his company of late, but there was something in the way he looked at her that made her uncomfortable.

'You shouldn't have to do this,' Sam Danby said, his eyes moving over her almost hungrily. Frances had put on a small amount of weight since the baby, which in his opinion only made her more appealing. 'Why don't you let me find you a woman to help you?'

'Millie comes in now and then,' Frances said. 'And I've heard about another girl who might want part-time work.' She had stubbornly clung to her independence, though Sam had been pressing her to go and live at the big house with him and her mother-in-law. 'Besides, I don't mind doing housework now that it is my own home.'

'Mind of your own, haven't you, Frances?' he murmured. 'I like that in a woman – and I like you. Marcus is a lucky dog. I wouldn't mind changing places with him.'

Frances swallowed hard. There was something in his tone, a look in his eyes that made her feel as if he were seeing her naked. She wished that Marcus would come home on leave – better still, that the war would end and he would be here for good. If she hadn't known that she had to be careful, she would have told Sam Danby exactly what she thought of him. But he was her husband's father, and he had been generous to them buying this house and giving them money to start off their marriage.

'I love Marcus,' she said, looking him in the eyes, challenging him. 'I wouldn't change him for anyone.'

'Young love,' Sam said, and laughed. 'Well, you'll soon get over that, my dear. When you've had enough of billing and cooing you may be looking for something different. I shall be around if you need me.' His inference was clear, chillingly so.

Frances didn't answer. She just stood staring after him as he walked away, a cold shiver trickling down her spine. Why did she always feel that there was something hidden about Sam? On the surface he was a genial, open sort of man who had done well for himself – but underneath she sensed something very different.

It didn't matter, Frances decided. Sam wouldn't try anything on unless she gave him the opportunity, and she would be very careful not to do that. Besides, the war couldn't go on for ever. Marcus would be coming home on leave soon and then surely his father would keep his distance.

Nothing terrible was going to happen to her. She dismissed the shadows that had seemed to come over her as she spoke with Sam. Emily always said she was lucky, and she always had been. Most things went her way. She didn't see why her luck should run out now. She had a lovely home, money to spend, a lovely child and a husband she adored. She couldn't see why anything would change. As long as Marcus survived the war and came home to her...

Alice had been up half the night with her son. He had a bad tummy upset and she had been nursing him as he cried almost non-stop. She knew his crying had woken her mother, because she'd heard sounds of stirring coming from upstairs. It looked as if she would have to think about finding herself a house of her own, and Jim had offered her his cottage again. He'd told her that he'd done it up a bit, and that she was welcome to have it for a few shillings a week.

'It is going begging, Alice,' he'd said. 'You could have it for nothing but I know you wouldn't accept it like that – so give me three and sixpence and it's yours for as long as you like.'

She knew that Jim hoped it wouldn't be long. He hadn't said anything much, because it was too soon. As yet there had been no confirmation that Dan was dead, and until then Jim wouldn't say what she knew was in his mind. But he was hoping that she would marry him one day, when she finally knew for certain that her husband was gone.

He couldn't be gone! Alice felt the protest rising inside

her. She refused to believe it, because it hurt too much. The pain didn't get better whatever people thought. If her lovely Dan was dead she would never stop grieving for him, and yet she knew that she would have to face up to it one day. It was hard to bring up a child alone. Her parents were good to her, her father would never see her starve, but she would have to learn to stand on her own two feet.

Danny was quieter now. He looked up at her, smiling, and her heart turned over. He was getting to be the image of his father, and she kissed his face, holding him to her, crooning softly. She was so lucky to have him, so lucky that she had had a little time with Dan before he left.

She glanced out of the window and saw that the post-girl had left her bike outside the gate; she was coming up the drive and she had something in her hand. It was a telegram.

Alice's heart turned over as the doorbell rang. She put Danny down in his carrycot and went to the door, feeling sick with apprehension. Her stomach was tying itself in knots and she could hardly speak as the girl handed her the small envelope.

'Perhaps it's good news,' the girl suggested, because she hated to be the one who brought the bad news to everyone.

Alice nodded but didn't say anything. She went back into the kitchen and sat down, staring at the telegram, not daring to open it. It was sure to be bad news and she didn't want to know.

'Did I hear the door?' Mrs Robinson asked as she came into the kitchen. She glanced at her daughter's ashen face and then at what she was holding. 'Oh, I see. Are you going to open it?'

Alice shook her head. She couldn't open it for the life of her. She felt sick and faint and her hands were shaking. She made no resistance as her mother took it from her, her eyes firmly shut as she heard the paper tear, her mouth dry with fear.

'Well, that's that then,' Mrs Robinson said, a note of satisfaction in her voice. 'At least we know now.'

Alice's eyes flew open, her chest tight with grief, and then she saw that her mother was smiling. How could she smile if it was bad news? Suddenly, she was desperate to know. 'What does it say? Is it about Dan?'

'He's a prisoner,' her mother said, and handed her the telegram. 'His name has just come through on the Red Cross lists apparently. They are going to write and tell you more about it.'

'Dan is a prisoner of war?' Alice stared at her mother, disbelief mingling with the joy. 'Oh, Mum... Oh, Mum...' she whispered as the tears poured down her cheeks. 'Oh, Mum, he isn't dead... He's alive!'

'That's what it says.' Mrs Robinson was grinning from ear to ear, as if it was her personal triumph, as if she'd always known he was alive. 'Well, he's in the best place, lass. All he has to do is sit tight and wait it out now. The war can't go on for ever, can it? He'll be home before you know it.'

'Oh, Mum...' Alice felt the relief and happiness washing through her like a great tidal wave. 'Dan isn't dead. He's coming home... He's coming home when the war is over.'

Mrs Robinson looked down at her grandson who was sleeping now, smiling, his little fist curled against his cheek. 'Ah, the little love,' she said. 'Won't your daddy be surprised when he sees you?'

Alice pulled a wry face. 'I'm sorry he woke you, Mum. I know it's early. I was thinking of telling Jim I would take his cottage, but now...'

'You'll do no such thing,' her mother said. 'Whatever next, Alice? You'll stay here with us where you belong, my girl. Your father will help Dan to get a house when he comes back. Save your money for then.'

'But I thought we might be disturbing you?'

'I'll put up with a lot more before I throw my daughter out,' Mrs Robinson said. 'Besides, he's such a love most of the time. I should miss him if he went. No, you stop here with us until Dan comes back. It's what your father wants. He would be most upset if you left us.'

'Oh, Mum,' Alice said, and hugged her. 'Oh, Mum, I do love you.' The tears trickled down her face. 'I'm so happy.'

'Well, I should think so too,' her mother said, and reached for her handkerchief, blowing her nose noisily. 'Well, this won't buy the baby a new dress, will it? I'll look after Danny this morning if you give your father a hand with the milking. He's got a bit of a chesty cough, and he won't ask, but he could do with some help.'

'Of course I'll help,' Alice said. 'I think Danny is over his tummy trouble now. I'll go and get changed then and leave him to you.'

'Yes, you do that,' Danny's grandmother said, and smiled her satisfaction as she bent over the cot. 'He'll be all right with his granny, won't you, my love?'

* * *

Connor saw Alice cycling down the road as he made his way to school. She smiled, stopped and beckoned to him, and something in her face made him run to her at once.

'It's Dan, isn't it?' he asked. 'You've heard from him, haven't you?'

'Not from Dan, though I may soon – but he's on the Red Cross lists, Connor. He's a prisoner in one of those camps in Germany. He's alive and will be coming home when the war is over.'

'That's great,' Connor said, and grinned at her. 'I knew he was too clever to get himself killed. Thanks for telling me, Alice.'

'I knew you would want to know,' Alice said, and she reached out to ruffle his thick dark hair. It was very like his brother's and he would have all the girls after him in a few years. 'When Dan comes home you can live with us, help in the garden and with his cars. You would like that, wouldn't you?'

'Yeah, smashing!' Connor gave a yell of triumph. 'You're all right, Alice. I'm glad our Dan married you.' And then he was off down the road yelling to her brother as he saw him at the school gate. 'Dan's all right. He's a prisoner of war…'

Alice smiled as she climbed back on her bike. Connor was happy, as Emily would be when she wrote to her. It was odd that she hadn't replied to her last letter with the pictures of Danny, but she would write again, just to make sure she'd got them. And she would go and see Frances that evening. Frances would pass the news on to the rest of her family. She was still on speaking terms with both Clay and Henry, who, the rumour went, did not speak to each other these days.

It was odd the way those two had fallen out, especially as Henry wasn't very well sometimes. He still hadn't got over his cough and his wife worried about him because he worked too hard. You would think that Clay would give his brother a hand on the farm now and then, but there was clearly a feud between them. Alice knew that Daniel had been worried about the farm when he was home; he had seemed to think that things were going badly wrong. Henry seemed to be managing to hang on for the moment, but he wasn't likely to tell his brother's wife or Frances if he was in trouble with money. Besides, times were hard all round. Henry would muddle through somehow and it would all come right – at least she hoped it would.

Alice shook her head. The farm wasn't something she could sort out. Even if Henry had got into debt again, the bank would surely wait until the war was over. Daniel would do that when he came home.

When he came home... The happiness bubbled up inside her again. *When Dan came home, when Dan came home.* The words formed into a marching tune inside her head. *When Dan comes marching home again, hurrah, hurrah.*

Daniel would be coming home when the war ended, and everything was all right again.

* * *

Emily walked in through the garden entrance. She was carrying a bunch of dark red chrysanthemums that she had bought in the village after leaving the doctor's surgery. She smiled as she took them into the flower room and found a suitable vase. Having arranged them in water, she carried them through to the front parlour. She had just finished placing them on a table by the window when she heard a sound behind her and turned to find Vane watching her, a speculative look in his eyes.

'You are back then, Emily?'

'Yes, I'm back.'

'Amelia said you had been to the doctor's?'

'Yes. He has given me some news – good news, I think.' She raised her head, her heart beating a little faster.

'I am glad to hear that, my dear. I was worried in case you were ill.' He looked so concerned for her that Emily's heart caught. How could she tell him that she was having another man's child?

'No, I'm very well. But I do have something to tell you – and I'm not sure how you will feel about it.'

Vane held up his hand. 'Before you say anything, let me tell you that I've been wanting to ask you if you will stay on here as Matron. I realise that you may not wish to live with us, though we would both love to have you here permanently, but it isn't a condition. I have a house in the village you could have if you wish – and of course there is the matter of Simon's legacy. He has a flat in London, which is yours, and some money...'

'I thank you for the offer,' Emily said as he hesitated. 'But I think you should hear what I have to say, Vane. You may not feel the same once you know the truth.' She drew a deep breath, her heart thumping. 'I am having a baby, but...' The words caught in her throat as she saw that Amelia had come in and was giving her a beseeching look across the room. She hesitated and then it was too late as she saw the expression of delight in his eyes.

'But of course, Emily. Amelia told me that you had hopes of giving us a grandchild. You must know that we could not be more delighted. It is the most wonderful news we could have, especially in the circumstances.'

Emily's resolution deserted her. How could she tell him now? She knew that she ought to speak out at once, because it was wrong to let him believe a lie – and yet she found that she could not destroy his last hope of an heir. She remembered wishing that she could do something to comfort him at the funeral, feeling the deep sense of loss that had overwhelmed him. Amelia had raised his hopes, and it would be too cruel to dash them now.

'You knew that Simon and I were planning to divorce?'

'Yes, I knew that it would happen in time,' Vane said, and frowned. 'He told me the day before he died. I did not approve of his relationship with that man, but I tried to understand – at the end, I really did try. He told me how well you had taken it and I knew that I could do no less. If you could accept their relationship then so must I, my dear.' He sighed heavily and shook his head.

'It couldn't have been easy for you,' Emily said. 'This house – your name and traditions – they mean so much to you.'

'Yes, my dear – and now you have given me everything I ever wanted. I shall be honest and tell you that although the money is mine to leave as I please, this house, the estate and the title would pass to a distant cousin if there was no heir.'

'I can't be certain of having a boy, Vane.' Emily's heart was racing and she could hardly look at him, because she felt so awful about deceiving him.

'No, of course not, my dear – but if your child should be a girl I am going to try and break the entail.'

'Can you do that?'

'Yes, if I pay enough,' Vane said. 'Don't look so worried, Emily. I have great hopes that your child will be a son.' He frowned slightly as he saw that she was still uncertain. 'Forgive me. I know you feel that I have been too dominant in this business of Simon's treatment...'

'No, I don't feel that way any longer. I resented it when you seemed to take over my life after Simon was wounded –

but I was confused, hurt, lost. I knew that something was wrong with our marriage, but I didn't understand. That has all gone now. I've forgiven Simon and I've learned to know you and to care for you. And I love my work here.'

'Then will you consider staying on? Either here or in your own house?'

'I should like to stay on,' Emily said, and smiled at him. She knew she would feel guilty when she was alone, because what she was doing was wicked. If her child was a son she would be party to a terrible lie and deception, but the die had been cast now, and she must learn to live with what she had done. 'And here in the house if you don't mind.'

'That would make Amelia very happy, and I should like it very much,' Vane said. 'We shall enjoy having you and the baby, Emily. However, if your life changes and you want to move on...'

'No, I don't think so,' Emily told him. 'I believe my life is here with you and our boys. I don't think I shall marry again. My work is enough for me, and of course I shall have my child.'

She had loved Terry very much, and at the moment there was a void inside her. She didn't think anyone else would ever fill that emptiness, and she owed it to this man to make a success of all that he was offering her.

'You shouldn't say that, Emily.' Vane shook his head at her. 'You are young and the world is full of people you haven't yet met, my dear. For the time being you will nest here with us and make our lives so much the richer, but one day you may spread your wings and fly away, and we shall applaud you when that happens.'

'Thank you,' Emily said, and her eyes felt wet with tears. 'You are truly kind.' She hesitated, then, 'There is something else I wanted to ask, Vane. I've just heard that my brother Daniel is a prisoner of war, and I wondered... You know so many people, and you have influence... Anything you could find out would be very welcome. Where he is, why it has been so long before they told us that he was a prisoner, that sort of thing.'

'Yes, of course. It will be no trouble at all. I shall be pleased to be of help to you. If your brother is on a Red Cross list they will know all about him. It may take a few weeks, but I'll see if I can gee them up a bit for you.'

'Thank you. I think I shall pop upstairs and lie down for an hour or so, and then this afternoon I shall go and see what is happening at the Dower House.'

Emily walked upstairs to her room. She had started to feel more tired than usual of late, but the doctor had told her it was quite natural for her to go through that stage.

'Just rest when you feel you need it,' he had said after examining her. 'The tiredness will probably pass in a few weeks and you'll feel full of energy.'

She felt a flicker of unease. Vane was being so kind and she felt so guilty – and yet was it so very wrong to give him what he believed was a wonderful gift? He had suffered because of what he saw as his son's unsuitable behaviour, and now that son was dead. Vane was still vulnerable after his illness and to have told him the truth might have destroyed him. Or was she just making excuses for herself?

Emily slipped off her shoes and lay down, pulling a light cover over her. She closed her eyes, thinking about the future. Her life was here now, but there was something she needed to do. Carole had told her that Terry was buried in London. She would go up to visit his grave very soon, lay some flowers and close a door on the past.

Vane had spoken of her finding someone new one day, but she thought that unlikely. She had known love and she had loved. From now on she would think of her work and her child. She had a good home, friends, and something to live and work for. What more could she ask for?

For a moment the memory of Terry's face as he first saw her that day at the railway station in London came into her mind and she recalled the thrill it had given her, the wonderful feelings she had experienced in his arms. Was it possible that she might feel that again one day? That she might love again?

A tiny seed of hope was working its way into her mind, though she thought it foolish. Some people looked for love all their lives and never found it. She had known real love; it was too much to expect it to come her way a second time. No, she must be content what with what she had, and that was surely enough.

The war could not last for ever, especially since the Americans had now mobilised against a common enemy. The Japanese had made a mistake bombing Pearl Harbor, but it might help shorten this terrible conflict. Sometimes the news was so bad that Vane shook his head over the newspaper and murmured of the unthinkable. But Emily could not believe that Germany would win. Surely something would happen to turn the tide their way? She refused to believe that so many of their brave men had given their lives for nothing. No, the war would be won and they would have peace again.

Outside, the sun had broken through the clouds and she could hear birds singing. Soon now it would be spring. Spring, when all was new and life began its cycle all over again.

Despite the ache in her heart, which never quite left her, Emily knew a resurgence of hope. Vane was right. She was young and the future was still there waiting for her.

Before she slept the thought came to her mind that for the rest of her life she would be living a lie, but she smothered the guilt. Perhaps sometimes it was kinder to tell a lie. Besides, it was done now and she hadn't the courage to break Vane's heart. After all, what harm could it do?

ABOUT THE AUTHOR

Rosie Clarke is a #1 bestselling saga writer whose books include Welcome to Harpers Emporium and The Mulberry Lane series. She has written over 100 novels under different pseudonyms and is a RNA Award winner. She lives in Cambridgeshire.

Sign up to Rosie Clarke's mailing list for news, competitions and updates on future books.

Visit Rosie's website: www.lindasole.co.uk

Follow Rosie on social media here:

 facebook.com/Rosie-clarke-119457351778432

 x.com/AnneHerries

 bookbub.com/authors/rosie-clarke

ALSO BY ROSIE CLARKE

Welcome to Harpers Emporium Series

The Shop Girls of Harpers

Love and Marriage at Harpers

Rainy Days for the Harpers Girls

Harpers Heroes

Wartime Blues for the Harpers Girls

Victory Bells For The Harpers Girls

Changing Times at Harpers

Heartbreak at Harpers

The Mulberry Lane Series

A Reunion at Mulberry Lane

Stormy Days On Mulberry Lane

A New Dawn Over Mulberry Lane

Life and Love at Mulberry Lane

Last Orders at Mulberry Lane

Blackberry Farm Series

War Clouds Over Blackberry Farm

Heartache at Blackberry Farm

Love and Duty at Blackberry Farm

The Trenwith Trilogy

Sarah's Choice

Louise's War

Rose's Fight

Dressmakers' Alley

Dangerous Times on Dressmakers' Alley

Dark Secrets on Dressmakers' Alley

The Family Feud Series

A Family at War

Standalone Novels

Nellie's Heartbreak

A Mother's Shame

A Sister's Destiny

Sixpence Stories

Introducing Sixpence Stories!

Discover page-turning historical novels from your favourite authors, meet new friends and be transported back in time.

Join our book club Facebook group

https://bit.ly/SixpenceGroup

Sign up to our newsletter

https://bit.ly/SixpenceNews

Boldwood

Boldwood Books is an award-winning fiction publishing company seeking out the best stories from around the world.

Find out more at www.boldwoodbooks.com

Join our reader community for brilliant books, competitions and offers!

Follow us
@BoldwoodBooks
@TheBoldBookClub

Sign up to our weekly deals newsletter

https://bit.ly/BoldwoodBNewsletter

Printed in Great Britain
by Amazon

53777012R00178